The Dogs Do Bark

Two women with a secret
and
the men who can destroy them.

D. M. Pinto

Copyright © 2023 by D M Pinto

All rights reserved.

No part of this publication may be reproduced, distributed, or transmitted in any form or by any means, including photocopying, recording, or other electronic or mechanical methods, without the prior written permission of the publisher.

This book is a work of fiction. References to real people, living or dead, actual locales, buildings and historical events are used solely to lend the fiction an appropriate and historical setting. All other names, characters, organisations, places and incidents portrayed in this book are either used fictitiously or are the product of the author's imagination. Any resemblance to actual persons, living or dead, is entirely coincidental.

First edition 2023

ISBN No: 979-8-3934-4928-5

When the truth is found to be lies, and all the joy within you dies,
don't you want somebody to love?
(Jefferson Airplane)

London 2016

Chapter 1

Two men square up for a fight. They've abandoned their cars with the doors open and engines running. Bobbing and weaving in business suits and ties, their shoes slipping on the wet road, they look comical. The pedestrians and smokers outside the shisha cafés shout insults from the pavement, and the drivers of the stationary cars, buses and taxis slump over their steering wheels and sound their horns, or turn up their music.

The police are on the way, Jen can hear their sirens rising above the chaos, and she crosses the road. A cabbie scowls at her. She waves at him, a sarcastic little wriggle of her fingers, then turns into the enclave of tree-lined streets known as the village. The armed police officer on the corner of the square glances at her and then looks away stifling a yawn.

Going from her world to that of the Laurences' is like crossing the border into another country. There are no scuffling men here, no shouted insults, no kebab shops or takeaways. The streets are peaceful, the houses a mixture of old and new, and the people sitting outside the cafés look affluent and complacent. Smart shops sell designer shoes and high fashion, the Patisserie offers exquisite pastries, too beautiful to eat, and the coffee merchant stocks thirty-four types of coffee beans. She doesn't care for the shoes or the clothes but she likes the coffee. If she wasn't late, she would stop to have an Americano and a pastry in one of the cafés.

Mrs Laurence is leaving the house when Jen arrives, her phone clamped to her ear in one hand, her briefcase in the other. 'I'm late, I've left a message on your phone,' she says, and she's off, walking fast. Jen lets herself into the house and goes downstairs to the basement. The kitchen smells of coffee and toast. Used cereal bowls and knives smeared with butter litter the table. The Laurences have been too busy leaving or receiving messages to put the milk back in the fridge, or the lid back on the marmalade jar. An ashtray with a lipstick-stained cigarette butt and Mr L's slimy cigar stub sits among the detritus, and the *Times* newspaper had fallen under a chair. She clears the table and empties the ashtray, holding her breath as she tips the contents into the pedal bin.

She fills the kettle and switches it on. While she waits for it to boil, she listens to her messages and watches women's high heels and men's shiny black Oxfords, Ugg boots and designer trainers swarm past the basement window. Their owners are escaping domestic life, leaving their homes and their children in the care of people like her. How would they cope if the nannies and au pairs, the housekeepers and chauffeurs, all decided to go on strike? Or, more radically, what if they locked their employers out of their homes?

It's a fantasy she indulges in whenever she feels that the Laurences are taking liberties. It would never happen. Police and security men walk the streets, some visible, some in plain clothes and as well dressed as the people they are paid to protect. That nice man studying the adverts in the estate agent's window, or the one talking to the coffee merchant outside his shop, might have a firearm tucked away where it wouldn't spoil the hang of his jacket. She makes her tea, retrieves the newspaper, and settles down at the table to read it. She has the house to herself, and this is her time.

*

Later, her work done, she leaves the house and the village and crosses back over the busy main road. If she hurries, she might have time for a shower and a cigarette before Angie gets home. Instead, she walks into an uproar. All four of the Brothers' dogs have escaped and are frolicking along the pavement. A woman hooks her fingers into her child's collar and drags him out of their path. The tourists and shoppers leap out of the way, stumbling into each other or lashing out hopelessly with shopping bags. The dogs ignore them; they're waiting for their masters.

The Brothers won't be far behind their dogs, and she takes shelter in the doorway of an empty shop. Daniel and Joseph Avery are dangerous. If they see her, they might make her their victim, bully her out of her rent money and the coat off her back. Or look through her and walk past her as if she didn't exist. You never knew with the Brothers; it could go either way.

She hears them before she sees them. Stomping along in big boots and wearing identical greasy jackets, they shoulder their way through the crowds and past her doorway. They wield their difference like a weapon; swagger and strut and throw hard stares at anyone foolish enough to make eye contact. Maggie trails along after them, leading Monalula by the wrist. She sees Jen and flashes a Vee sign at her.

Jen steps out of the doorway and bumps into a girl pushing an enormous baby buggy and she loses sight of the Brothers. When she sees them again, a man in a dirty blue suit is walking between them. He says something to Daniel and jabs his finger into his chest. Jen flinches – he can't know who he's messing with. The Brothers clamp him by the arms and continue walking, pulling him along with them. The man struggles, but the Brothers hold him fast. They're hard men, thick with fat and muscle, and he looks as if he hasn't eaten or slept for weeks. Craning his neck, he looks over his shoulder. He's looking at her and shouting something she can't hear.

The dogs are still causing mayhem. Noses to the ground, they're reading the canine messages on the pavement or cocking a leg to leave one of their own. Joseph whistles and they run to him, their squat muscular bodies scudding along the pavement like torpedoes, ready to pounce or chase. Their coats are glossy, their eyes are bright, and their collars are designer, but they would take chunks out of anyone who threatened their masters. The man in the blue suit stops struggling and watches the Brothers fix chain leads to the dogs' collars. He's given up the fight. Whatever he did to anger the Averys, she wishes him luck. The group of men and dogs walk under the flyover, and into one of the side streets leading to the canal.

School is out and teenagers from the local Academy swarm around her. Groups of boys huddle over their phones, ignoring the girls that sashay past them. Angie wanted a new phone, they'd argued about it last night. Remembering their raised voices and Angie's sarcasm drives any speculation about the man in the blue suit out of her mind, and she hurries along.

She'd hung up her coat and kicked off her shoes when she hears Angie's key in the lock. Preparing herself for battle, she goes to meet her. Stubborn and determined, her daughter can hold a grudge for weeks and her appetite for conflict is unlimited. Last night, though, she'd lost the argument. Jen couldn't buy her a new phone, or a laptop or a tablet, and certainly not an iPad. Angie follows her back to the kitchen and throws her book bag down.

'You're early, love.'

'I'm the only one in my class without a decent computer.'

Jen feels a pang of compassion for her clever, stubborn daughter; Angie is finding the transition from child to woman difficult and stands with her shoulders hunched and her back rounded. Jen wants to unwind her, to stretch her out vertebrae by vertebrae to her full glorious height. She'd told her to ignore the snide comments of the other girls. Told her that she'd gone through the same thing when she was her age. Told her she is beautiful. Angie had rolled her eyes and shrugged – what do I care? – but she'd turned away to hide her blush.

'If I had a laptop…' Jen didn't let her finish; she was too tired to engage.

'We've been through this. It's out of the question. I can't afford it.'

'You can afford alcohol and cigarettes, though.'

Angie flounces off, happy that she's had the last word, and slams her bedroom door shut. Her daughter knows how to make her feel guilty, but their argument has been less fierce than usual, and Jen relaxes. She arranges slices of ham on a plate, slides a tray of chips into the oven and dumps frozen peas into a pan of boiling water.

While she waits for the food to cook, she leans out of the window to smoke. Wine and cigarettes are expensive, but they're the only pleasures left to her. There's no money for nights out; and anyway, where would she go? She's too old-school for online dating or dating apps, and the one time she'd ventured into a bar she'd sat alone, staring into her glass. No one had glanced her way. It was humiliating. She was at her sexual peak and should have been wearing out old husbands or new lovers. Instead, too disillusioned for a relationship, and too wary for casual sex, she'd settled for drinking at home, the television and early nights. The oven timer pings: the food is ready and she adds an orange and a glass of water to the tray and takes it to Angie's room. Angie is at her desk and turns off her computer.

'Knock first, mum.'

'I did, you didn't hear me.'

'Put it on the chair, I'll have it later.'

'How was school?'

Jen hovers, hoping that Angie may confound her and tell her something about her day.

'It's just school, what do you expect.' She waits, radiating strained patience.

Jen doesn't have the energy for another argument, not tonight. Tonight, she wants to take off her bra, put on an old dressing gown, and watch something mind-numbing on the box. Back in the kitchen, she stares into the fridge: cheese, the remains of the ham, and half a bottle of white wine. It's six o'clock, officially her drinking time. She takes the bottle into the sitting room, turns on the TV, and falls asleep.

She wakes dry-mouthed and sweating. The television is mumbling away in the corner, Brexit, Brexit, blah blah, and she turns it off. There'll be a referendum in June. Call-me-Dave Cameron versus beer-and-boom Farage arguing the toss. In or out of Europe, she didn't care, she just wished they'd stop droning on, and get it over with. On her way to bed, she looks in on Angie. Even asleep she's guarded, her knees drawn up, her forearms crossed over her chest. The supper plate is on the floor, the orange untouched. The curtains are open, and she stares out at the street. Exhausted earlier, she's awake and restless now. The scene she'd witnessed that afternoon is troubling her. Conjuring up a mental picture of the Brothers and the man in the blue suit, she puts them back in the street and has them re-enact their drama like something from *Crimewatch*. The group of men pass her repeatedly; the Brothers mysterious and unknowable, the man desperate, his poor suit exposing his dirty bare ankles and bony wrists. She feels a flicker of recall: the echo of something she's lost. Then the men are gone, fading into the facade of the building opposite. Muttering something unintelligible, Angie kicks off her covers. Jen draws the duvet back over her daughter and pulls the curtains closed. Whoever the man is, whoever he thought she was, he meant nothing to her.

Chapter 2

The market traders were doing good business. Weekends were so busy that walking between the stalls slowed to a shuffle, but by midweek the locals could shop without being elbowed out of the way by outsiders and tourists. Jen sipped her coffee, then bit into her doughnut and felt the sugar and caffeine jitterbug through her veins. Music coming from a flat overlooking the street drifted over the murmuring of a group of men at the next table. Leaning back in her chair, she lit a cigarette and watched the action through half-closed eyes.

Her neighbours were queuing at the Halal butchers or the fishmongers and she watched a group of women sorting through a stall piled with shoes – find a pair that match and they're yours for a fiver. They were enjoying the search, chattering away in their language. One of them held up a single red stiletto, and they passed it around, cackling, then dug in for the other one. A woman in a tracksuit browsed the stall selling salwar kameez, before moving on to the one selling faux leather jackets.

Jen drained the last of her coffee, stubbed out her cigarette and left the café. Rail thin, and paler than pale, she towered over the other shoppers and attracted a lot of attention, not all of it appreciative. One of her boyfriends had called her Ugly Beautiful and Angie had told her that the boys on the estate call her Zombie Milk Shake.

'Their mothers are all into dyed hair and fake tans, so I wouldn't worry about it,' she'd said. 'Hayley's mum reckons you're striking, and the other mums are jealous.'

Ignoring the stares, Jen joined the crowd waiting for Mike to serve them. His stall was the best in the market, the fruit and veg always fresh and arranged with an artist's eye for colour. The stall next to Mike's was manned by his business partner, Hamid, and stocked the diva vegetables: aubergines and artichokes, chard and yellow spiky fruits that look like martial arts weapons, pomegranates halved to display the crimson seeds. The pungent scent of parsley, mint and coriander mingled with that of Turkish coffee from the café. Mike spotted her and left the browsers to make up their minds.

'What can I get you, darling?'

He weighed out her tomatoes and put them into a paper bag, along with some oranges.

'On the house. Sadie said to call her for a chat. Or come round. We haven't seen you for ages.'

Her shopping done, Jen made her way home. After the affluence of the village and the colour and energy of the market, the streets looked dirty and broken and the buildings dingy. Her flat was in a small private block bordering the estates. People were living above, below and on either side of her, people she'd ignored before moving into the area. Their world had been mysterious and frightening to her then. Their muffled conversations, their footsteps and their arguments had taunted her with the sense of other people's lives. Now, the half-heard conversations and laughter, the noisy arguments and music were a comforting background to her life.

She collected her mail and climbed the stairs to the third floor. The rooms in her boxy little flat were small but cosy and warm; she felt safe there. She was relieved to be home, and able to have a moment before Angie got back from school. If her daughter was trying to wear her down, she was succeeding. Angie would spend hours in her room and seemed preoccupied, brooding one moment and hyperactive the next. It wasn't unusual behaviour for a teenager, but she seemed more argumentative than usual and her demands more insistent. Sadie had suggested checking her Facebook page. Angie would be furious if she found out, but Jen told herself it was her duty.

Her room looked like the end of a busy day at Primark. Skimpy pants and virginal bras hung out of drawers and discarded outfits lay in heaps on the floor. The computer stood out, the blank screen a powerful presence, tempting her to pry. The desk and the shelves above it were tidy and ordered, and she rifled through the books hoping to find a clue to her daughter's inner life. There was an atlas along with the textbooks and young adult novels, and Angie had tacked postcards of Montmartre, a canal in Amsterdam, and one of Sumo wrestlers onto the pinboard above her desk.

Her girl must dream of travel and adventures, dreams she didn't share with her mother. All teenagers have dreams, and Angie's dreams were of the mystery of other worlds, and not the empty promise of fame or romance. Acknowledging her daughter's separateness made her cringe at the thought of being caught snooping. She riffled through the papers on her desk but left without tackling the blank hostility of the computer screen.

Angie slouched into the kitchen ready for battle as soon as she got home.

'I'm having my tea at Hayley's; I'll do my schoolwork there. Our computer's too slow.'

'It'll have to do, Angie, there's nothing wrong with it.'

'You have it then. Take it; put it in your room.'

She'd rolled the waistband of her skirt over to make it shorter, and her legs in black tights looked achingly long and childishly thin.

She stalked off. Jen followed her; she'd prepared her speech. She would ask her to stop harassing her and tell her she couldn't afford to keep up with Hayley or her other friends. Angie threw her blazer onto the floor and started to strip off the hated school uniform. Tie, shirt, and skirt joined the blazer. Jen folded her arms over her chest and ignored the challenge.

'Ask Gary to get me a laptop. He fancies you, doesn't he?'

It was an accusation, not a question. Angie liked Gary but saw him as a rival to the father she'd never known. When she was younger, she'd made up stories and drew pictures of him – stick figures at first, then romantic characters, cloaked and handsome, rescuing children from witches. Over the years, she'd shown interest again but accepted Jen's evasions. Jen thought she'd forgotten about him, but a few months ago, she'd asked what he'd looked like.

'You know what he looks like; I've told you.'

'Why don't you have any photos of him?'

'He hated having his photo taken.'

Angie had given her one of the looks she'd perfected to undermine her – a tilt of an eyebrow, a hint of a sneer – but didn't pursue it and hadn't talked about him since; absent fathers were common among her peers. She was wriggling into a pair of jeans. Her ribcage was narrow, the bones a shadow under the skin, the vertebrae of her spine a row of hard little knuckles. She zipped up the jeans and pulled on a T-shirt. It was Jen's; the Clash T-shirt Gary had bought her.

'Ask if you want to borrow something of mine, Angie, don't just take it.'

'You're too old for it, it looks better on me.' It was true, and all Jen's good intentions were lost.

'And you can stop pestering me for things you know I can't afford and tidy your room. I've been working all day.'

'Leave it, I didn't ask you to do it. I'll be at Hayley's.' Angie slammed out of the room, her skinny legs in skinny jeans, her Doc Martins unlaced.

Jen sat on the bed and stared at the floor between her feet. Her love for her child was tested daily. She wanted to rip the T-shirt off her back and lock her in the bedroom. Or give in and cry. Anger or tears. But she was too exhausted for either. She took it out on the clothes she stuffed into the laundry bag, punching them down, ready for a trip to the launderette.

*

The launderette was peaceful; there were no gossiping mums or noisy kids demanding attention. She could read in peace while waiting for her laundry. Liz was packing the service washes into bags and acknowledged her with a lift of her chin. Jen loaded the machine, opened her book, and retreated into Ruth Rendell's world of warped characters and hidden parts of London.

Later, her packing done, Liz looked over her shoulder at what she was reading. 'I've read that one. Set near here, Regent's Park. Someone murdering homeless people and impaling them on the railings. One of her best.'

Jen hadn't read about any murders yet, but she laughed at her friend's relish for the macabre. 'Talking about the homeless,' Liz went on, 'squatters have taken over a couple of the boats on the canal. Some of the kids are going down there to drink with them. Not Angie or her mates, older kids. All the same, you might want to keep an eye out.'

'It's not the Averys', is it?'

'No, they wouldn't drink with kids. They've got boats down there, though; they keep their dogs on one of them.'

A customer came in before Jen could question her. She waited until Liz had locked up and quizzed her as they walked home. Stooping to link arms with her friend, she shortened her stride; Liz walked at her own pace and wasn't to be hurried.

'Do you know what the Brothers are up to? They dragged a man into the market the other day.'

'I heard about that. Don't know much about it though. You should talk to Gary; he might know something.' Her attention was elsewhere. She pointed to a woman sitting on the kerb, her skirt up and her legs apart.

'Who are you looking at, Lizzie Fisher?' The woman tried to stand and almost fell into the road.

'Mrs Fisher to you. Get yourself home. You're a disgrace, showing your fanny to anyone passing.'

Jen laughed and hugged her friend's arm closer to her side; she would bet on Liz against an aggressive drunk any time. Liz Fisher had clout. All the same, she turned down her offer of a cup of tea; she wanted to get home and talk to Gary. He lived two floors above hers, and she climbed the stairs and rang his bell. She had to ring it twice before he answered the door. He stared at her blankly, then his face cleared, and he stood back to let her in.

'Come and have a look.' He led her into his study and pulled up a chair. 'I'm working on something in Paddington Basin.'

Images of glass and steel buildings filled his computer screen, and behind them, cranes reached greedy arms upwards. Jen didn't share his fascination with the Paddington site. Looking down on it from the flyover it looked soulless and austere, its earlier use as a dumping ground for wrecked cars shimmering under its new makeover.

'Liz said you might know what the Averys are up to. They captured a man on the street yesterday.'

'What did he look like?'

'Dirty, scruffy. Like a rough sleeper. Tall, skinny, longish black hair. He acted as if he knew me. I didn't want the Brothers to see me, so I didn't get too close.'

'I'll see what I can find out. I'll drop around later, Jen. We can talk then.'

He'd turned back to the screen before she'd left the room.

Angie was in bed and Jen was halfway through a bottle of wine when Gary turned up that night.

'No luck, Jen, no one could tell me anything.'

'It's OK; I don't suppose it's important.'

They hadn't spent time together for a while, and she'd expected him to stay, but he was restless; one glass of wine, a cigarette, and then he had somewhere to be, he said, there was someone he had to see. She heard him talking on the phone as he walked towards the stairs, heard him laugh and the landing door hiss shut behind him.

Chapter 3

Angie and Hayley rolled their eyes and scoffed when Jen asked them about the parties on the canal. Angie was especially scathing.

'Drinking with nasty old squatters? What do you think I am? And I don't drink.'

Hayley butted in. 'We know who goes down to the canal to drink, anyway, everyone does. They're losers.'

'Yeah, losers,' Angie echoed. 'Their parents don't care about them.' She shouldered her book bag and followed Hayley out.

Jen listened to the clatter of their heels as they raced along the landing. They were harsh, but their world was harsh. They passed kids as young as ten smoking weed and drinking by the canal and talked about the fights between the local boys and gangs from the estates as if they were episodes from a reality programme.

For all her sullenness Angie was an obedient child, but Jen decided to take Liz's advice and 'keep an eye out.' No teenager tells their parents everything. They live parallel lives and have their own language, a complicated social structure and street names. Even the adults whose job it was to work with them didn't know all they got up to. Angie and her friends kept out of trouble, but the danger of them being caught up in drugs or gangs, or being harassed on social media, hovered over them all the time. A walk by the canal in the fresh air would do her good. Shrugging on a fleece, she collected her keys and cigarettes and took a shortcut through the market and down to the canal.

The towpath was hard and crunchy underfoot. The boats were as tightly packed together as a terrace of workers' cottages, the decks busy with pots of plants and stacks of firewood. Someone was cooking bacon, the salty aroma overpowering the dank canal smell. A radio played, a kettle came to a boil with a shrill whistle, and someone laughed, the sound crystalline in the sharp air. There would be no squatters here, and she moved on.

Further along, the path was uneven and unkempt, and the boats squatted low in the water as if ashamed of their decline. The silence was oppressive; anyone here was either asleep or out of sight until she passed. Takeaway boxes and a rusty bike littered the deck of a boat nearest the bank, and she stooped to see through the window. The interior was squalid: the benches were covered in stained plastic, and the lino covering the floor was cracked and stained.

As she turned away a dog hurled itself at her shadow, barking hysterically. A solid body thumped against the glass and more dogs joined in, yammering and snapping as if they were fighting each other for the chance to tear her apart. They were the Brothers' dogs; she could make out their brindled coats and flat, snake-like skulls. Any moment someone could come out to see what had disturbed them. A cyclist was approaching, the silver stripes on his high-vis jacket flashing. She stood back to let him pass, her heart pumping and then followed him. Someone called out to her, and she almost lost her footing.

'Hello, darling.'

She risked a glance over her shoulder. A man sitting on the deck of a longboat smiled at her. She took a mental snapshot: dark, bare feet, a blue suit. His face was remarkable – vivid and intense, ravaged yet still beautiful.

'Hello, Jen.' Softly, this time, intimately. She pretended she hadn't heard. Although she was desperate to get away from the canal and the man on the boat, she forced herself to walk at a normal pace. Then risked another glance. The path behind her was deserted; he hadn't followed her, and she made it to the next exit and out onto the street.

Surrounded by people, she felt safe. Why should such a man know her name? She must have misheard. There couldn't be too many men wearing dirty blue suits; the man on the boat had to be the one taken by the Brothers. She'd had a good look at his face this time. She didn't recognise him, but the echo of his voice lingered, calling out to her from a distance, evoking a memory, fleeting, hardly recognised.

Hello, darling. Hello Jen. Four words, two fragments. They ran in her head like a line from an irritating song – an earworm that had burrowed deep into her brain. However much she repeated them, the memory eluded her; the more she strained to bring it to the surface, the more it retreated.

There had to be a simple explanation. Her world was a small one; she didn't venture far from her area; she didn't need to. If he hung out on the bench in the market, he might have noticed her passing on her way to and from work and asked someone who she was, someone who told him her name. She might have smiled at him, thinking he was one of the *Big Issue* sellers she saw outside the underground station. Idle and bored, his days empty, with no family or job to go to, he might have felt that her smile had forged a connection between them. It was something she might have done herself; she understood the need to construct an alternative to reality. It was nothing to worry about, she told herself and turned up the radio when she got home, hoping to drive out the insistent beat of those words. *Hello darling. Hello Jen.*

That night she dreamt she was falling, head down, her hands clutching at nothing, and woke with a jolt and a sense of foreboding. Her T-shirt was damp, and she peeled it off and lifted the hair away from the nape of her neck. Somewhere she had a dream diary, a hangover from a time when she'd read horoscopes, counted magpies and looked for signs that might signal a change in her life. Opening drawer after drawer she groped around until she found it buried under a pile of sports bras.

She put on a clean T-shirt and took the diary into the kitchen. Without knowing what she was looking for, she skimmed through the house dreams, sea dreams and dreams about searching for something or being lost. Dreams dense with unfathomable symbols. Falling signifies a loss of control. Then, a year ago, she'd recorded a dream about

Angie's father. He was standing at the end of a narrow corridor, beckoning to her.

She stared down at the page, then leant away from the words. She didn't want to believe it, but she had to face it. The knowledge that had flickered at the edge of her consciousness had worked its way to the surface: The man in the blue suit was Angie's father. Alex had worn bespoke suits and bought his shirts in Jermyn Street. He'd been vain, arrogant and reckless, without fear, his beauty so hypnotic that men, as well as women, broke themselves on his indifference. The man with the Brothers, the man who'd called out to her from the boat, was a victim; filthy, broken and frightened, but his voice hadn't changed.

'Mum?' Angie stood in the doorway. 'Is everything all right?'

Jen snapped the diary shut.

'It's OK. I couldn't sleep. Go back to bed, love. I'll make you a hot drink.'

'I had a bad dream,' Angie said. She was a little girl again; the sweet, loving child she'd been before deciding her mother was a fool.

'Come on, love, back to bed.'

Jen followed her daughter back to her room, carrying a mug of camomile tea. Angie's Bart Simpson T-shirt had slipped off one shoulder, and her legs were pale and vulnerable. She climbed back into bed, drank the tea and then lay down and pulled the duvet up to her chin. 'Leave the light on in the hall, Mum, and leave the door open.'

I'm infecting her with my fears, Jen thought. Gary would know if Alex was back, they'd been best friends when they were boys; they'd grown up together. She rang him the next day.

'It was Alex, Gary. I should know. I recognised the voice.'

'It's been a long time, Jen, over sixteen years. Why would he turn up now? It doesn't make sense.'

'What if he's come back for me, or Angie?'

'He left before she was born; he doesn't know she exists. Coming back wouldn't have anything to do with you or Angie. I'll talk to Mike tomorrow; they're related, cousins or something. He'll know if he's back. And remember, you have us now, he can't get to you.'

*

Two days later, there was a message on her phone from Gary. 'Don't panic, Jen. Alex *is* back but try not to worry. I'm going to be out of town, but Sadie will ring you later.'

Sadie didn't tell her much when she rang. 'It's better that you let Mike and Gary fill you in. Come for something to eat on Saturday. The girls are having a sleepover at Amina's house, we can talk.'

Four days to wait, Jen thought, agonised, four days for her to imagine Alex learning about Angie and seeking her out. By Friday, she was exhausted. She'd wrestled with the Laurences' high-tech hoover, dragging it up the four flights of stairs. Hot and tired, she opened a window to cool off. The afternoon light was golden and tender. A woman was taking washing off a spinner in the garden of the house next door. A small girl stood beside her holding a basket. The woman unpegged a row of small socks. Looking up at her, her voice clear and pure, the child spoke, and the woman laughed. She held out her hand to the child, and they walked into the house together.

Heartsick and envious, Jen laid her forehead against the window. There was a time when she and Angie had held hands, when they had laughed together and shone for each other. Each day had been an adventure. They had each other and were happy. Over the years, she'd watched each beloved version of her child slip away, to be replaced by another, equally precious. Each time, Angie had stood a little further away from her. Now she could lose her. Alex would find out, someone would tell him about her, and he would do to Angie what he'd done to her: claim her as his, and damage them both.

Chapter 4

Everything in Mike and Sadie's flat was big, bold and flamboyant. Overstuffed sofas faced each other on either side of a marble and gilt coffee table and shelves crammed with electronic equipment flanked the fireplace. A television the size of a small cinema screen was showing an old black and white film with the sound turned down.

Marooned on the sofa, and drowning in cushions and throws, Jen unwound her scarf and put it beside her. Mr Foo, Sadie's Pekinese, growled and popped his eyes at her from his basket. 'Shut up, Foo, you snotty little bugger,' Mike said. Sadie and Hayley loved Mr Foo. Mike barely tolerated him. He was puffing at a cigar while giving her a history of the estate; local history was his passion. Jen wanted to ask him to open a window but didn't like to interrupt.

A decade ago, the shelves were stacked with kids' toys and picture books, and a dolls' house had stood where the television was now. Mike had brought it home one day and set it up. Angie and Hayley had knelt in front of it, posing small figures in front of miniature furniture, immersed in their imaginary world, while she and Sadie watched them. They were young and strong then, the hard years of struggle behind them. Now they had to face a fresh challenge, and this time they were older and had more to lose.

Sadie came in from the kitchen carrying a tray of appetisers. 'All right, Jen? Did Mike offer you a drink?' She didn't wait for an answer. 'Get her a drink, love.' She arranged the plates on the table. Too many, and all before the main event; Jen could smell something roasting.

'Gary phoned,' Sadie said. 'He's on his way. He said to get started.'

Mike and Sadie bent their heads over heaped plates. They ate silently and with relish. They could have been siblings; she had thought they were when she met them for the first time. Both had ruddy complexions and thick gingery hair, both moved slowly and spoke with the rhythms and inflexions of their parents and grandparents, even great-grandparents: the Long family, like Liz's, had lived in the area since before the war.

The crudités and hummus were untouched. Sadie must have bought them for her. Dutifully, she dipped a celery stick into the hummus and took a sip of wine. Foo raised his head, staring at the door, and seconds later the doorbell rang. The little Peke scampered into the hall and the oven timer went off in the kitchen. Sadie left to deal with the oven, and Mike went to answer the door.

Gary strode in, crackling with energy, and bringing with him the buzz of the streets, of concrete and car exhausts, music heard through open windows, and a dozen conversations in as many languages shouted into phones at pavement cafés. Mike circled him like an anxious older brother, taking his jacket and ushering him onto the sofa next to her. Gary winked at her and smiled. Reassured for now at least, Jen relaxed.

They ate their lunch in the kitchen. Gary had spent the morning taking photos of the old warehouses and barges hidden away among the new buildings in the Paddington Basin. 'Remember this?' Gary showed Mike something on his camera. 'God, yes.' Sadie joined them. 'I used to sneak out of school to meet a boy there,' she said.

Paddington was an ongoing building site, the drilling and hammering part of the soundscape of the area. Knocking down the old and familiar, and building up the new, went on all the time, everywhere. She'd become immune to it, walking past gaping holes where shops and homes once stood without a thought. To Gary, Mike and Sadie, it was the demolition of their past.

Jen pushed her plate away; she wasn't interested in the photos, and she felt excluded by talk of their long-ago exploits. All three of them had gone to the school where the development was now. So had Alex. When were they going to acknowledge why they were here; when were they going to talk about him? She felt uncomfortable, bloated from too much food, and the drone of conversation was making her lethargic.

At last, Sadie cleared the dishes, Mike filled their glasses and they trooped into the sitting room and settled back on the sofas. 'Right, time to talk,' Mike said. 'I didn't trust myself to speak to Alex. It was better to let Gary meet him. You tell her, Gary.'

'Alex is working for the Brothers. He borrowed money from them to pay his gambling debts, and he can't pay them back. They've put him to work. He's living on one of their boats. They own him, Jen.'

They were wrong: no one owned Alex, not even the Avery brothers. He'd slip out of their grasp.

'Does he know about Angie? Did he ask about me?'

'He can't know about her; he didn't know you'd moved here until he saw you in the street. He won't bother you.'

Mike broke in. 'We talked about paying his debt to the Averys for your sake, Jen, but he'd see it as a weakness he could exploit. Let him pay his debt himself. We won't let any harm come to you. You and Angie are part of the family. Alex knows better than to mess with us.'

He stood up, towering over his wife and Gary. Jen saw the broad sloping shoulders and thick arms of a powerful man. The years might have softened him, but he could still snap Alex in two.

'I don't want to see him. I've put the word out. If he comes near me or mine, he'll leave in a sack.'

'He knows that Mike, I told him. He swore he'd stay away from you and Jen. He's destitute. I didn't recognise him at first; I would have walked past him in the street. He won't bother anyone, he's too ashamed.'

'So, what happens now?'

Jen wanted Mike and Gary to tell her that there would be no compromise. Tell her that Alex had to leave the area, to go back to wherever he'd come from.

'I'll keep an eye on him, and so will the guys in the market. Anything going on around here gets back to them. He's too scared to come near you but keep out of his way. Don't go down to the canal, and make sure Angie doesn't either. Just in case.'

In case Alex finds out he has a daughter, he meant, or Angie finds out the truth about her father. Every day would be fraught with danger from now on. Mike was yawning; it was time for her and Gary to leave. There was the usual flurry of hugs, thanks and compliments, of coats being fetched and shrugged on, but at last, they were on the street.

'Let's walk off all that food,' Gary said.

They walked towards Baker Street. Jen pushed her clenched fists deep into the pockets of her coat. Nothing had been resolved. Mike and Gary seemed to think they'd done enough to scare Alex, but she knew better. A party of French schoolkids blocked the pavements outside Madame Tussauds, and they had to separate. When she caught up with him again, he was staring at the pavement, preoccupied, his mouth hard.

They turned into Regent's Park. Crocuses and narcissi circled the bases of the trees. Another spring, another year. There was so little time for her to mend her relationship with Angie before the world claimed her. They found an unoccupied bench and sat down. Gary offered her a cigarette, and she took it. Her fingernails were bitten down to the quick.

'I could see you were panicking at lunch. Alex isn't going to ruin your life again, Jen. I won't let him.'

'I want him to go away. Can't Mike get rid of him?'

'How? He'd beat him up as soon as look at him, but he has a record. He could end up in prison again. It would destroy him and Sadie.'

'Why did he have to come back here? What use is he to the Brothers?'

'He's smart, Jen. The Brothers are shrewd, but Alex is clever, very clever. He's talented, a maths prodigy. It made him an outsider at school. Not that he cared. The Averys must be planning something that needs his brains.'

The Averys stalked the streets like warlords, their dogs by their side. They were lowlifes and bullies, but Gary was talking about them as if they were criminal masterminds.

'Couldn't he just escape?'

'He's got no money or ID, no shoes; they threw his shoes in the canal. All he has is that horrible suit. I don't think he wants to escape anyway; he owes money to people who make the Brothers look like Laurel and Hardy.' He stood up and held out his hand. 'Come on, I want to show you something.'

They picked up his car and he drove her into a grid of streets in the anonymous area somewhere between Maida Vale and Kilburn. There were no lights on behind the net curtains of the mean little houses, and no music played from basement flats. It was as if the occupants had hunkered down behind locked doors, waiting for a disaster to fall on them. Gary turned into a street identical to the ones they'd driven through and parked. He pointed out a house.

'The Averys own that one. It's where they were born.' The house looked unloved, the curtains pulled close, not a chink of light was visible, and the path was littered with rubbish, but it was still shelter.

'I thought they were homeless.'

'Not anymore; and anyway, not everyone wants to live like us. Street life suits some people. It suits the Brothers; they were living rough before they left school. They inherited money when their mother died and bought the house. They stay there sometimes. They own the ones on either side as well; they rent them out. There's more.'

'How do you know all this?'

'Their dad worked for Mike's dad, doing odd jobs in the market. He was an alcoholic. The Brothers hated him. He used to try it on with them until they got big enough to fight him off. Everyone around here knows; it's why there's a lot of sympathy for the Averys.' He started the car and talked as he drove. 'Their mum was never home; she ran a scrap yard over in Willesden, practically lived there. She made a fortune, but she didn't spend any of it on her sons, or the house.' He turned into a cobbled mews and drew up outside a row of garages and workshops with flats above them. 'All theirs. They have an interest in all sorts of things, but nothing that would affect you.'

Jen slumped down in her seat. The Brothers had fooled her. Or she'd been influenced by rumour, by the talk on the street. Daniel and Joseph Avery were more than they seemed. And now Alex belonged to them. Gary started the car and glanced at her. 'You OK?'

Despite herself, she felt conflicted. What had Alex got himself into? Theirs had been a relationship without intimacy, based on mutual need. They hadn't talked much and had never shared their stories as lovers do. Why hadn't she known he was a 'maths genius?' She'd made love to him and shared his bed, but she'd never asked about his past; Gary had revealed more about Alex in a few minutes than she had learned in a year. Older now and more experienced, she should try to understand him. Gambling was an addiction as damaging as drug abuse or alcoholism. Then she imagined him and Angie together. It must never happen. He didn't know he had a daughter, and she'd make sure he wouldn't find out. She owed him nothing.

Chapter 5

Mike had been with her when she'd discovered Alex had left. Someone banging on the door had woken her from a deep sleep. Insistent and demanding, it was an alarm signalling danger or disaster. She got out of bed and staggered to the door. Her relief at seeing Mike was so intense her legs gave way and she sagged against the door frame.

'Mike, for God's sake. What is it?'

'Where's Alex, Jen? He has the keys to the shop. The girl can't open up.'

Jen stared at him. All this racket for a set of keys. Mike looked embarrassed; they hardly knew each other. Alex referred to him as 'the phoney hard man' but was careful in his company as if he knew one uncensored word, one unguarded smirk, could be catastrophic. Conscious of her tangled hair and bare legs, she tugged her T-shirt over her thighs.

'What's wrong with your phone?' He noticed her dishevelled appearance. 'You all right? Have you two had a row?'

Alex didn't row. Alex would cajole and persuade, and if that didn't work, he would become cold and distant.

'He's away, playing poker. I'll get you the spare keys.'

She left Mike in the hall and went to look in the box where Alex kept his keys and petty cash. It was empty. She opened his wardrobe to look in the pockets of his suits. There were no suits – no suits, no shirts, no shoes. Just a row of empty hangers, and the lingering scent of his cologne. Mike found her staring into the empty cupboard.

'Jesus, girl, what's wrong? What is it?' He helped her sit down on the bed. 'You're as white as a sheet. What is it?'

She didn't have to tell him; he could see for himself. His legs gave way and the mattress sagged as he sat next to her.

'He's scarpered. I knew it. The little tosser has fucked off and left me in the shit.'

'What do you mean?'

'I mean he's buggered off. He hasn't been to the shop for days. The girl told me he borrowed her keys; she couldn't get in yesterday or this morning. Did he say anything to you?'

'He's been away a lot recently; I haven't seen much of him at all. He must have packed his things while I was out.'

'Do you know your phone's been cut off?' Jen reached for the phone on the bedside table and lifted the receiver and held it to her ear, clinging to it until Mike took it off her. 'Where do you think he is? Do you know where he might have gone?'

Jen turned away from him. It had been a while since she'd worked at the shop, a while since she'd been involved in Alex's life; she didn't ask where he'd stayed on the nights he didn't come home, and he didn't tell her.

'Jen? Look at me. Is he seeing another woman? Might he have gone to her?'

'I don't know. I don't think so.'

Mike looked disdainful; the women in his world knew where their men were, or thought they did.

Together, they turned out every drawer, every cupboard, every box in the flat, even the kitchen drawers and the cutlery box they had never used. Alex's passport, driving licence and the paperwork for the shop was missing. He'd been thorough; he'd left no trace. And he hadn't paid the rent on the flat for two months. Mike was organised and efficient, scanning the paperwork, deciding what might be important and discarding anything useless. When he'd finished, he stacked the papers up and brushed his palms together.

'That's it, then. I'll take this stuff home and have a good look at it.' He'd ignored her while they searched but looked concerned as he left.

'Will you be OK? Let me look through the paperwork and I'll get in touch. We'll talk it through, Sadie as well. Work out what to do next.'

Alone, reality hit her and she crawled back to bed and curled up under the duvet. She hadn't seen this coming. Alex had been morose and distant for a while, but she'd learned not to ask about the card games and his visits to the casinos or to question his mood. He'd tell her not to worry about it, and she'd ignore the nagging feeling that he was in some sort of trouble and went on enjoying the easy life, the smart flat, the cash thrown onto the table. That she hadn't loved him, had never loved him, had seen him as a way back into a world that had rejected her, shamed her. Not that it mattered to him: love wasn't what he wanted. He'd used her, but she'd colluded with him, put herself in his way and into his hands. The truth was hard to bear. It was late afternoon before she surfaced, a limp survivor, her sheets damp and tangled.

*

Alex had vanished, dived under the surface of their lives and disappeared. There was no word from him, no phone call or letter. Someone had told Mike he was in France, and someone else had said he was in America, on the poker tournament circuit. She harassed his friends until they stopped taking her calls. Mike took on the casinos and poker schools Alex had frequented until very polite, very big men in Crombie overcoats turned him away. He knew not to push his luck and backed off.

And then the biggest shock of all. She'd sat on the toilet staring at the test kit to confirm what she already knew. Dazed, she went into the bedroom. Made her bed. Put away her nightclothes, and laid out the clothes she would be wearing that day. All done without conscious effort. Dumping the kit into the wastepaper basket, she wondered why she wasn't frightened. Instead, she felt empty, a vacancy; a Mary kneeling, a woman waiting.

Alex meant nothing now; she couldn't waste her energy looking for him. That he had fathered this child meant nothing. She would wipe him out of her past and lock him out of her future. He was gone, good riddance; she could start again. Her child was waiting. A child, a daughter – she knew that already. She needed to be strong to do whatever had to be done. She would fight for her girl.

She sat on the edge of her bed and made plans. There was money, secreted away in an account Alex hadn't known about. It would see her through until she found a cheap place to live and a job. Any job would do if it paid enough to feed, clothe and house her, and let her stay healthy for the baby's sake. Her old boss at Cousins Fashions might take her back on, and if he couldn't he'd know someone who could. Her pregnancy wouldn't show for a while. She rang him.

He couldn't help. 'I use freelance models now; they're cheaper, but they're not as dependable; they all want to do catwalk or editorial. They act as if being a fit model is beneath them. We miss you, but times are hard.'

He cleared his throat, a nervous reaction she remembered from her days working with him. He was going to ask her about Alex. They hadn't been together long – less than a year. People got together and parted all the time, it wasn't unusual. However, it wasn't their relationship he was interested in.

'Alex owes me money, Jen. The shop's closed, and I can't get the stock back. I need to get hold of the guy he went into business with.'

She put him off and went to see Mike. He welcomed her in, led her into the sitting room, and made her comfortable on the sofa opposite his wife. He listened to what she had to say but didn't seem surprised.

'You did right to come to me first. I'll sort it.'

'Don't rush off,' Sadie said. 'Fancy a cup of tea?' She turned to her husband. 'Put the kettle on, love, then make yourself scarce.'

Sinking into the plush sofa, her back supported by a cushion, Jen relaxed. She could hear Mike rattling around in the kitchen. Sadie was pregnant and showing, and Jen longed to tell her she was too. She hadn't told anyone yet. Sadie ran shrewd eyes over her.

'How many months, love?'

Relief made her weak, and Jen let herself cry.

'It's the hormones.'

'Hormones my arse,' Sadie said, and Jen laughed. 'You can keep me company while Mike goes to the pub.'

Later, Mike had walked her home, tucking her arm in his. 'Not to worry, love,' he said as he left at her door. 'It'll be OK.

*

Neither he nor Sadie had ever asked her why she hadn't known how bad things were with the business, or with Alex's gambling. They'd embraced and supported her, turned away her stumbling attempts to explain herself, and even helped find her a flat near them.

'It's not your fault, don't blame yourself; you're just a kid. We were just as daft, and we're old enough to know better. Mike let Alex talk him into putting money into the shop. He feels responsible.'

'You're part of our family now.' Mike glanced at her. 'If you want, that is?' He was hesitant. 'We want to help. You can go to the social if you like, but I'd rather we look after you till you get on your feet; no one in our family goes on benefits.'

Sadie backed him up. 'You're not to worry; it'll be bad for the baby. Let Mike help. He's a proud man. He'll put it right.'

And he had. He'd kept the lease on the shop and converted it to a greengrocer's specialising in high-quality fruit and veg. When the flat above the shop became vacant, he bought it. He'd sold both the lease on the shop and flat at a profit two years later. She'd watched with admiration as he tore through the years, letting nothing get in his way. Alex wouldn't stand a chance against such a colossus. He'd turned disaster into an opportunity with relish, and used his anger as fuel; he welcomed the chance to prove himself. Now Alex's return had rekindled that anger, and by weird alchemy, Angie's interest in her father had peaked just as he'd reappeared. Her questions about him had become more accusing and confrontational.

'Why did he leave you? What did you do?'

'Why didn't you try to find him? Did you go to the police?'

Jen fielded her questions nervously, trying to reassure her daughter without giving too much away.

'It wasn't a case of who did what. And he wasn't missing. He just left. You don't go to the police, Angie, you know that. They wouldn't have been interested; anyway, they've got enough to worry about.'

'You drove him away. Why won't you talk about him?'

'Because I'm glad he left. He wasn't good enough for you.'

'So what does that make you?'

Jen always lost these battles. I should let her meet Alex, she thought. Let her see for herself that her father isn't the mythical cool dad, the good-looking, glamorous dad she imagined him to be, but the loser dad, homeless dad, the dad in thrall to a couple of thugs. She'd decided to write Alex out of her and Angie's life, thinking he was gone forever, and now she had to live with it. Sadie had told her it was a mistake. 'She'll start imagining all sorts, Jen. Tell her the truth,' she'd said. Now she was even more insistent.

'Just do it, Jen, in case Alex gets to know about her. Get it over with.'

'Tell her that her father was a liar and a cheat? That he betrayed us? He's a coward, and I'm glad he left. He would have been a terrible father.'

Mike agreed with her. 'It's your choice, Jen, but I don't want to hear his name.' His eyes had slid away from hers, and he hadn't looked at his wife. 'He's rubbish, love. Put him out with the trash.'

Sadie was shocked. Jen wasn't.

'I mean it, Sadie. Forget him. Anything that needs to be done will be done.'

Sadie started to speak, but he held up his hand. 'No, Sadie, let it be.'

Sadie didn't know the damage Alex could do. Mike did. Alex had hurt him, hurt his manhood and hurt his pocket. That Mike had turned a crisis into a triumph hadn't softened the blow to his pride, and Mike didn't forget an insult. 'Don't do anything daft, Mike.' Sadie was anxious, but Mike reassured her.

'Let the Avery brothers deal with Alex. If he tries to con them, he'll be sorry.'

Chapter 6

And then some relief; the Brothers and their cohorts had moved on, taking Alex with them. Gary had heard it from Mike, who'd heard it from his mates in the market.

'The Averys' have contacts in Leeds and Birmingham,' Gary told her, 'but they always come back.'

Hopefully, they would have ditched Alex by then, or he would have given them the slip. For now, she could stop looking over her shoulder and seeing him in every seedy loser. Financially, too, things were improving. She was covering for Liz at the launderette at weekends, and tonight she was helping at the Laurence's drinks party.

The black skirt and white shirt she needed were in a case on top of the wardrobe. She dragged a chair in from the sitting room and stood on it, got a grip on the handle and pulled it towards her. It fell, narrowly missing her head, and burst open, spilling out a heap of fabrics and colours.

Kneeling, she rummaged through the dresses and shirts, some as light as a breath, some dramatic and styled to arouse. She held a cashmere sweater to her face, and let a silk scarf run through her fingers like water. Laid tailored coats and fake-fur jackets on the bed, along with the handbags and high-heeled shoes that she would have worn with them. These were her Alex-era clothes, and she felt the past rush in; each garment told a story. He'd liked her to look smart and she'd put away her grungy combat trousers and trainers and let him pick out silk shirts and pencil skirts, trouser suits and narrow little dresses. They were beautiful, but she had never felt as if they belonged to her. It was as if she had raided another woman's wardrobe.

She held up a burgundy shirt, the first thing he'd bought her. He'd had a good eye; the style and the colour suited her. An ivory shift dress and matching coat caught her eye. She'd worn them at a fraught dinner with an American poker player and his wife in London for a tournament. Disturbed by the sense of danger she heard in the talk between Alex and the couple, she'd tried to engage the man's wife in conversation. The woman had met her efforts with a flat stare, as brutal a dismissal as a slap. Later, Alex drove her back to the flat in silence, his coldness an accusation. She'd failed him but she didn't know how. Later, he made it clear what he expected of her.

Impulsively, she stripped off her jeans and sweater, drew the silk-lined dress over her head and smoothed it over her hips. She slipped her bare feet into a pair of high-heeled shoes and shrugged on the jacket. The clothes fitted her; she was still as slender as a girl. The shoes felt alien; she couldn't imagine ever wearing them. They forced her feet into a ridiculous angle. She hobbled over to the full-length mirror. And there she was, her younger self. So young, so beautiful. So frightened, so vulnerable and uncertain.

She was overtaken by a wave of nostalgia and grief for the wasted years. For the choices she'd made and the chances she'd let slip away. Years of pent-up grief shook her, and she wept. Tears dripped unheeded from her chin and onto the dress. Who had she been then, and who was she now?

She was sitting on the bed in the coat and dress when Angie came home. The room was dark, and her hands and feet were icy; she'd been sitting there for over an hour.

'Mum, where are you, what's up?' Angie opened the door without waiting for an answer. 'Why are you sitting in the dark?' She switched on the light. 'Where did you get those clothes?'

Jen stood up, picked up her discarded jeans and T-shirt and clutched them to her chest, shielding herself against her daughter's ridicule.

'What are you wearing? You look like a drag queen.'

Despite the glib words, Angie sounded frightened. She looked at the heap of clothes on the bed. 'What's all this?' She held up a grey cashmere sweater, then a fake Astrakhan jacket.

'Where did you get this? I like it, can I have it?' She tried the jacket on and posed in front of the mirror. Jen watched, impressed by her daughter's switch from doubt and fear to youthful greed.

'It looks good on you; you can have it.' Jen turned away. Her daughter was too self-obsessed to notice her state.

'I get it,' Angie said. 'You wore these when you were young.' Still wearing the fake fur over her school uniform, she knelt by the suitcase. She held up a photo album and sat back on her heels. 'Are there any photos of me when I was a baby?'

'Let me see.'

Angie handed the album over and shifted her attention to a striped satin waistcoat. 'You must have looked like a right clown in this.'

'Take anything you want, and then let me get changed.' Jen put the album into a drawer and closed it quietly.

Angie had taken off the jacket and was holding a velvet camisole against herself, the album forgotten. 'I'll take this and the fur coat.' She posed in front of the mirror and draped the fur over her shoulders. She handed Jen her phone. 'Take a photo. Got any shades?'

Angie put the dark glasses on and posed like a star, head back and smiling, a parody of a celebrity. It might have been her when she was Angie's age but without the anxiety in her eyes and the tenseness of her mouth. Angie grabbed a narrow-brimmed trilby and jammed it on her head.

'These clothes are awesome. You must have been cool once. You should get yourself nice clothes and get me some while you're at it. You've let yourself go, Mum.'

'You look great, Angie. Now go, I've got to get ready.'

Jen packed the clothes away, put the suitcase at the back of the wardrobe and got ready for the party. Angie was spending the night at Hayley's, so she walked her there, listening to her chatter.

*

The house was dense with smoke and noise when she arrived. Mrs L thrust a tray of drinks into her hand and then left to socialise. Demure in the black skirt and white shirt, Jen threaded through the crowd, offering glasses of champagne to the overdressed men and women.

'Champagne, madam? Sir?' she murmured, acting the part. Revelling in her role-play, she went back to the kitchen, picked up another tray and turned into the throng.

The atmosphere was low-key, and the guests were still sober. Mr Laurence was deep in conversation with his first wife, a lawyer, their heads almost touching. Mrs Laurence was watching a woman with eyes that darted like spiteful fingers, touching one face and then moving on to the next. The people gathered around her looked uneasy. Jen offered the group drinks, and the dark-haired woman took one without taking her eyes off the man talking to her. She sipped her drink, watching him as if he were a specimen bought forward for her inspection. The poor man took a drink off Jen's tray, forgetting he was already holding one. The woman cut him off mid-sentence to start a conversation with a famous ex-model, leaving him holding the two glasses, his words falling into the space between them. He downed one of the drinks and handed Jen the empty glass without looking at her. Mrs L caught Jen's eye, her expression ironical, then came over and took the man by the hand, drew him away and introduced him to a woman standing alone.

*

Later, Jen walked home along the brightly lit main road. She dawdled along, passed the shops and the restaurants, checking out the windows of the pharmacies selling expensive cosmetics. Apple-scented tobacco and the hot smell of roasting meat hung in the air. Men sat at the tables outside the cafés, watching the street and smoking.

She walked under the flyover and waited to cross the road. Standing on the kerb, she felt the passage of the traffic that hurtled passed on her skin; the crossing felt risky, despite the crowds crossing with her. The atmosphere changed on the other side; the same road, but a different world. The fabric shop windows were bright and colourful, but the street lights were dim. The men and boys lounging outside the takeaways and off-licences watched her from under their hoods.

She hesitated before turning into the shortcut through the estates to her block. The narrow alley was part of the old street plan, the cobbles uneven and slippery with waste and urine and one she normally avoided, but she wanted to get home and take off her shoes; her feet were throbbing.

The party hadn't been a success; Mrs Laurence had told her to take the uneaten food home. She was garrulous, talking loudly to her husband, her tongue loosened by champagne.

'God, she's a bitch.'

Jen had thought she was talking about Mr L's former wife.

'She's missing the limelight, that's all.' Mr Laurence tipped the contents of an ashtray into a black bin bag. 'Missing being grovelled to, and all those freebies.'

So, not the former Mrs L then. It could be the ex-model or the disgraced politician's wife, or the much younger wife of a famous comedian. All the subjects of curiosity and gossip. Or the famous actress who had been the darling of the tabloids until she lost her looks. Jen had overheard these conversations between her employers before; they and their friends revelled in gossip. Even the Laurence boys gossiped, usually about their stepmother.

Something, a flicker of movement, the scrape of a shoe and a glimpse of a pale young face alerted her. Before she had a chance to react, a boy careered into her, winding her. She almost fell. A hand grabbed for the bag of food she was carrying and tugged hard. Jen hung on to it and screamed. He tugged harder. Her feet slid about on the cobbles, and her arm felt as if it would be torn out of her shoulder. A light went on in one of the flats overlooking the alley, and a window rattled up. He let go of the bag and she caught the tang of sweat and decay. He bared his teeth like a dog, then spat at her. He missed; his phlegm landed on the cobbles. Stunned, she watched him run away.

She hadn't had time to be frightened; it had been over in a second. She'd fought him off and won, and she felt euphoric, lifted out of her normal self as if by a charge of electricity. The night air was buoyant, adrenaline coursed through her veins and she ran the rest of the way home.

By the time she opened the door to her flat, shock had set in. She opened a bottle and poured herself a glass of wine, her hand shaking so much that she spilt most of it. She hadn't fought him off; the light going on and the window going up had driven him away. Had he been more determined, he might have beaten her up, and all for a Food Hall carrier bag full of party nibbles.

Boys that age don't like to lose, especially to a woman. There might be consequences. He might see her in the street and follow her. She should report it to the police. Sadie had been mugged a week ago; she'd let the kid have her bag, giving it up without a fight. The boy had waggled his tongue between forked fingers and laughed when she flinched. She rang her.

Sadie was pragmatic. 'There's been a spate of muggings lately, but if he didn't get anything, there's no point in reporting it. The kid who mugged me was a skinny white boy, half-starved and rat-faced. On drugs, I suppose. I'm twice his size, but he was too fast. Mike went out looking for him. He didn't find him, thank God; he would have given him a kicking, and got himself into trouble.'

Sadie must have been frightened, and letting the mugger get away without putting up a fight had been the sensible thing to do. But you wouldn't know how you'd react in a dangerous situation until it arose. Contrary to what anyone who knew them would expect, she'd put up a fight while Sadie had capitulated. Sadie wasn't a coward, and anything taken away from her could be replaced, but Jen felt that anything lost was gone for good.

Chapter 7

Unable to relax, she poured herself another glass of wine and took it into the bedroom. She remembered hiding the photo album earlier and took it out of the drawer. Climbing into bed, she leaned back against the pillows and settled the album on her lap. She hadn't looked at it for years. The photos were of a time when she'd been acting her life and not truly present in her days and nights. Looking back could be a mistake, but she wanted to see herself and Alex as they had been, and as her daughter would see them.

The first photo was of her and Alex sitting at a nightclub table, the cliché empty champagne bottle upended in an ice bucket in front of them. Her dress, one that Alex had bought for her, revealed her perfect shoulders and the delicate articulation of her collarbones. Alex was elegant in a well-cut suit. If Angie had seen the photo she would have known him as her father; they had the same bone structure, and skin tone, the same challenging gaze.

She turned the pages slowly and examined each picture. Here, she and Alex sitting outside Picasso's on King's Road. She was wearing her favourite fake fur, the one Angie had liked so much. Alex had turned away from the camera and was talking to a couple of girls. And here, walking hand in hand with him in Brighton. Then a series of snaps taken in Paris at the start of their relationship. In all the photographs, Alex was dominant. He shone out, his charisma leaving her a dim presence beside him.

Her younger self embarrassed her; she'd been too passive, too easily led, but she'd grown up fast. Living with him and hanging out with him and his friends in the casinos and clubs had toughened her up, forced her to become more assertive and to take back her light before he extinguished it completely.

The other photos were publicity shots of her time as a model. She wasn't much older than Angie when they were taken. She'd been spotted by a talent agent during the frenzy for young, louche-looking models, excited by her long, lean body and limbs, her pallor and her wide Jaggeresque mouth. She'd listened to the spiel and believed the compliments. She'd borrowed the money for her portfolio, but the photos hadn't flattered her. Too self-conscious and too insecure to manage the world she'd found herself in, she lacked the spark, the connection between her and the camera, and her walk was a parody of the aggressive stomp and belligerent stare needed for the catwalk. The photographers and agents who'd raved over her 'heroin chic' mystique and arresting looks, and who had told her she was fabulous, soon lost interest in her and moved on.

It still hurt to remember being scrutinised, judged and rejected. It had been a relief to admit defeat and take refuge with the Cousins. There she belonged as part of a team, a living mannequin, and her feedback was valued. She wondered how her life would have turned out if she hadn't left them to be with Alex. Her eyes were tired, and she shut the album and slid it under the bed.

*

She'd forgotten to set the alarm, woke late and had to rush to work. Mrs Laurence was at the kitchen table talking on her phone. She looked as if she hadn't slept; her skin was grey, and her hair unwashed. 'God, is that the time? I'll get out of your way.' She hardly glanced at Jen and continued talking on the phone as she left.

Mrs L rarely took time off from work. Whatever had kept her at home on a weekday was none of Jen's business. Or it could be. The Laurence's had been cutting back, little by little, in ways that wouldn't alert their neighbours. The cleaning agency, brought in to do the heavy work, had been reduced to an occasional blitz, and the organic vegetable boxes, the deliveries from the wine merchant, and take-outs from chic restaurants were all cancelled. But she was sure they couldn't do without her; she'd heard Mrs L's friends brag about how little they paid their 'wonderful little Polish woman', and seen the way Mrs L had turned her head away as if in disgust. They may not be 'mates', but her boss was a good employer.

As she reached up to a shelf, a pain in her shoulder reminded her of the battle with the street kid the night before. She paused in the act of putting away the loaf of bread and the jar of marmalade and remembered the kid's pale face and skeletal torso. He'd looked as if he was starving, but she refused to feel guilty; she would have let the little toe rag have the vol-au-vents and mini-tarts if he'd asked. Angie hadn't wanted them and so she'd thrown them away.

Mrs Laurence came back into the kitchen. 'Finish in here, Jen, then take the rest of the day off. I'm working from home today.' Trim and stylish in a tracksuit and canary yellow running shoes, her blond hair tied back, she was filling her water bottle at the sink and watching the street. 'If anyone comes to the door, don't answer it. Boys selling tea towels for a charity have been knocking on doors and pestering people. The police saw them off, but if they knock again, ignore them. Don't answer the door.'

*

A pale sun had broken through the clouds when Jen left the house. Intoxicated by the freshness of the breeze and the clarity of the light, she didn't want to go home. She cut through the back streets and went through the side gate into the park. The roar of traffic faded as she crossed the bridleway and walked deeper into the pale, thrusting greenery. People walked their dogs, and mothers pushed strollers, the flat light making them seem one-dimensional against the backdrop of lawns and shrubs. The promise of summer had tempted them to leave stuffy offices or overheated houses, and the Serpentine was crowded with hire boats and swimmers. Others queued outside the café. She wanted to be part of the holiday mood, and she decided to treat herself. She walked down the slope to the café and took her place in the queue.

The coffee and the cake cost more than she'd expected, and she fumbled in her purse to make up the difference. The couple waiting behind her huffed and shifted their feet. Before living with Alex, she would have been apologetic. Now, she refused to let them harass her. Let them wait, she thought, I'm not letting anyone spoil my day, and she stared back at them with the barely concealed contempt she'd learned from her daughter.

Carrying her tray carefully, she made her way to a table by the water. Her coffee was tepid, and her cake looked better than it tasted, but the view over the lake was uplifting. Light glittered and bounced off the water, swans dipped and glided, and gulls as sharp and pointed as arrows perched on a row of wooden pilings. Jen turned her face up to the sun. The murmur of conversation and the shouts and laughter of the swimmers and rowers washed over her. I wish every day were like this, she thought.

Gary told her she should get out more. 'You don't need money to go for a walk or take a bus ride to another part of London,' he'd said. 'Angie can look after herself. You should trust her.' But that was before Alex showed up.

The clatter of a tray falling, and muffled laughter alerted her, and she took up her coffee. A woman at a table near hers stood and pushed her chair away. She reached behind her head and adjusted the scrunchy holding her hair back as she walked towards the exit. Startled, Jen recognised her boss. So much for working at home. Like her, she'd been enticed by the freshness of the air and prolonged her run.

Jen finished her coffee and left the café. This afternoon was a gift and she wanted to keep it for herself, to stroll in the sun and make a full circuit of the lake. The undergrowth on the banks was dense and wild. An argument broke out among the ducks and geese, and they rose above the surface of the water, squawking and quacking, and with a flurry of wings and beaks and bright orange feet: something had disturbed them. She heard a raised voice and saw Mrs L standing in the middle of the path, shouting into her phone, unaware of the amused glances of the people passing. Jamming her phone back into her pocket, she launched off into a run, weaving effortlessly through the couples and families. The birds settled back on the water and glided side by side, serene and untroubled.

Someone had made her employer angry, and Jen felt uneasy. If the Laurences were having problems at home or work, it would affect her. She was still feeling anxious when she got back to the flat. Angie was home and she'd brought Hayley with her. Their voices and laughter reached her as she opened the door. She felt a rush of blood to her head; she'd forgotten about the photo album.

They'd found the case. It was open on the bed, and clothes littered the floor. The girls had dressed up: Angie wore a pencil skirt and the burgundy shirt, and Hayley bulged out of a floral cotton dress. They stared at her, and she stared back. No one spoke. Jen looked for the album, then remembered she'd hidden it under the bed. The girls looked at each other and then back at her. Hayley started to struggle out of the dress, tugging it over her head and muttering apologies. Jen picked out a dress, low cut and gathered under the bust.

'Here, try this on, Hayley; I think it would suit you.' She could feel Angie staring at her. Hayley slipped on the dress. The low neckline showed off her breasts, her best feature, and the dress hung from the gathering under the bodice, disguising her rounded belly and heavy thighs.

'Hays, that looks good on you,' Angie said.

Nothing fazed Hayley for long, and she did a twirl in front of the mirror.

'You can keep it if you like,' Jen told her. 'Now get changed and put the other clothes back in the case.' Jen panicked; she could see a corner of the photo album under the bed.

'Can I keep mine?'

Jen hesitated; Hayley looked like a teenager in her dress, but the skirt clung to Angie's hips and thighs and the top three buttons of the shirt were undone.

'When you're older.' Angie pouted but pulled on her jeans and T-shirt without arguing. Jen pushed the album further under the bed with her foot.

'Do your homework. I'll call you when tea's ready.'

'What's it like, being a model?' Hayley was struggling out of the dress, her voice muffled. 'Did you know anyone famous?'

'I didn't do it for long; it's not as glamorous as it seems. And no, I never met anyone famous.'

'Angie could be a model; she's got the looks.' Hayley wriggled out of the dress. 'I haven't. Anyway, I think models are lame.' She looked sideways at Jen. 'Not all of them.'

Having a mother who had been a model embarrassed Angie, but she'd told Hayley and sworn her to secrecy. Nothing stayed a secret in their world, and Angie hadn't blamed Hayley or been angry with her for gossiping. Jen did; Hayley could be spiteful. She waited until the girls were in Angie's room, then put the album in the case, and back on top of the wardrobe, out of sight and out of reach.

Chapter 8

Mrs L sent Jen a text the next day, reminding her not to answer the door. She was hoovering the stairs when the doorbell rang. Pre-warned, she looked through the spy hole. Instead of a teenager flogging tea towels, the man standing with his back to her was stout and greying, bald at the crown. He turned to ring the bell again; there was something wrong with his face. He waited, then pushed something through the letterbox and left. She ran up to the landing window. Peering from behind the curtain, she saw him cross the road and stare up at the house. His face was puckered and pinkish on one side. He looked too poor to be part of Mrs L's circle, his suit was creased and ill-fitting, his shoes down at the heel, the leather dull and cracked. Standing with his legs apart and his hands in his pockets, he seemed confident, even arrogant. People walked around him, but he seemed unaware of them. She watched him until he walked away, turned the corner and disappeared.

On her way down to the basement, she picked up the envelope he'd posted. It looked cheap and felt flimsy. It was addressed to Emily Laurence, the writing small and uneven. Emily was too girlish a name for her boss, reminiscent of poets or the Victorian novelists Angie was studying at school. She was an Amazon in designer suits, striding along in her Louboutin's or Jimmy Choos as if they were trainers. Jen turned the envelope over, but there was nothing written there, and she put it with the rest of the mail.

Before leaving the house, Jen made sure she turned on the alarm, checked the patio doors and windows and double-locked the front door; the man had made her nervous. On her way home, she called into the launderette to pick up her laundry. Liz was sitting near the open door, reading a newspaper. Groaning, she got to her feet, holding onto the back of the chair.

'What's up, Liz? Arthritis playing up?'

'I'll get your wash,' she said. 'I'll be OK in a minute.'

'You sit down. Let me get it.'

'It's the heat, love, too many driers going at once. Made me go all-overish.'

Jen made her a cup of tea, and they sat near the open door to catch the air. Liz was quiet, holding her mug close to her chest, and staring out at the street.

'It's not the same, is it, Jen?'

'What's not the same?'

'Here. Home. It's not the same.'

'But you love it here. All your friends are here.'

'There's only me and Elsie left now, and she's talking about going into a retirement home.'

'You'll still have me, and Mike and Sadie. And Gary thinks the world of you.'

'You're right. Take no notice of me. I didn't sleep well last night, I'm tired.'

Liz was prone to occasional bouts of gloom, but she looked drained and defeated, slumped in her chair as if she'd fallen into it. She was still distracted when Jen helped her pack the rest of the service washes. Her hands shook as she buttoned up her old grey coat, her eyes on the floor. Jen wanted to ask her what was wrong, but Liz would tell her in her own time. Her block was on the estate and newer than Jen's, built in the seventies, but pockmarked and grimy. At the entrance to her building, Liz clutched at Jen's arm.

'Walk up with me, will you? The lift's out, and I need a hand up the stairs.'

They took the stairs slowly. Outside her flat, Liz fumbled for her keys; she was breathless and uncoordinated. The climb had exhausted her. Mrs Asan, Liz's neighbour, was coming towards them from the other end of the corridor. She hurried forward when she saw them.

'Are you all right, Mrs Fisher? Oh, those dreadful boys, and now the lift.'

'Thank you, love. It was a bit of a shock, that's all. I'm all right now.' She was having trouble inserting the key into the lock. Jen held back from helping her. Liz unlocked the door at last. 'I'll talk to the council about the lift, get something done about it.'

Mrs Asan nodded. 'That would be a good thing, thank you. Let us hope.' She smiled at Jen, then hurried away. Liz opened the door and Jen followed her into the dark hallway.

'What boys? What's she talking about?'

'Come through to the kitchen.'

'What boys, Liz? What happened?'

Liz was filling the kettle at the sink, her back to her.

'I think they were the same ones that mugged Sadie and tried to mug you.'

'Who mugged you?'

'Give me a minute, Jen.' Liz ladled tea into the pot, reached into a cupboard and brought out cups and saucers; they rattled as she put them on the table. Although she was impatient, Jen waited, giving her friend time to steady herself. Liz filled the teapot and covered it with a knitted tea cosy. The routine of preparing tea for a friend had settled her; she was breathing normally, and her colour was better.

'Come on, Liz. What happened? What did Mrs Asan mean?'

'Two lads came into the launderette. They looked like beggars, filthy, their clothes falling off them. They thought I could open the machines and get the money out, but I can't.'

'When did this happen? Did they hurt you?'

'Yesterday. They pushed me. I fell against the dryer door. I'm bruised, that's all.' She drank her tea. 'They frightened me.' She put the cup down carefully. 'They called me all sorts of names, horrible names. They acted as if they hated me. The things they said. Sexual things. What they would do to me, make me do to them. They weren't normal, Jen. They were truly wicked.' She took a deep breath and looked straight at Jen.

'They took the washing out of the machines, threw it around and stamped on it. Pranced about with a poor woman's underwear. One of them shouted into my face, his spit all over me when I tried to stop him.' She was wringing her hands as she spoke. 'The other one ripped the top of my dress open. The buttons came off. They laughed at me, at my bra. One of them tried to pull it off, but I stopped him.'

Jen sat like a stone, fearful that any movement she made, any word she spoke, would cause her friend to break down.

'Mrs Asan saw me in the street afterwards. I told her I'd been mugged, but not about the rest. She'd heard about you and Sadie. It must be the same boys.'

Jen remembered her small show of defiance towards the boy who'd tried to mug her, her frightened call to Sadie. Gently, carefully, she questioned her friend, easing information out of her. The boys had taken her bag with her keys.

'I've got spares, Sal in the corner shop keeps them for me. I picked them up on my way home.'

Jen imagined her walking home, frightened that the boys might follow her. Sitting alone in her gloomy flat, listening for a sound, staring at the door.

'Did you call anyone? I would have come over, sat with you.'

But Liz wasn't listening. 'I let them get away with it. I'm a coward.'

Her proud, loyal friend, that strong vital woman was no coward, and she told her so. But Liz was lost, wringing her hands and close to tears.

'I better change the locks. They might find out where I live.'

'I'm phoning Mike, no argument. I'll just say you were robbed. He'll sort your keys out for you. I'll do it now. You can trust him.'

Jen rang him. Liz had recovered enough to suggest listening to the news on her radio while they waited and was steadier by the time Mike arrived, a locksmith in tow. Leaving the man to do his work, he sat next to Liz, his arm around her shoulders. She told him a sanitised version of what she'd told Jen – the boys had snatched her bag and run out;

she made light of it and left out the sexual abuse. Mike listened intently as she described the boys. The locksmith finished and gave Liz her new keys. She tried to pay him, taking money out of an old tea caddy.

'Put your money away, Liz,' Mike said.' It's sorted. You're not to worry; I know who the boys are; they've taken over one of the boats on the canal. We've caught them trying to nick stuff off the stalls. I'll get the men together and we'll chase them off. They won't bother you again.'

Jen didn't want to leave her, but Liz insisted that she went home.

'Elsie's coming over to stay with me. I'll be all right.'

They heard her lock the door behind them. Mike had been calm and rational while they were with Liz, but now he was all rage and energy.

'Little bastards are taking liberties. I'm glad Elsie's coming over. She needs someone with her. I'll speak to Lee and Hamid, and a few others in the market, and ask them to keep a lookout for the boys. I'd like to set Gog and Magog on them.'

Jen wished he would. Gog and Magog were the fiercest of the Brothers' dogs and Joseph's favourites.

'They're causing a lot of trouble. They'll hurt someone soon. Thank God they didn't hurt Liz.'

He stopped suddenly and grabbed at Jen's elbow. 'I think that's one of them.' The boy walking in front of them wore the tracksuit bottoms and vest or hoodie combo that was standard for boys around the estates, but his hoodie was dirty, one of the pockets torn and hanging. He must have heard them talking and looked over his shoulder.

'You want something?'

'You don't have anything I could use, son.'

'I'm not your son. Fuck off, old man.'

He was young but wizened, an older face superimposed on his young one. Mike ran his eyes over him, checking him out.

'Want a photo? Fucking paedo.'

Mike ignored the insult. He took a step towards him.

'Living on the canal, are you?'

The boy lurched back, almost stumbling. His body odour was rank. 'Not so tough now,' Jen said, but the boy ignored her.

They watched him pick his way along the pavement, as stealthy and sly as a feral cat. She imagined Liz cornered by him and others like him. How frightened she must have been, how humiliated, and how powerless.

'What did you mean, not so tough? Do you know him?'

'I think he's the boy who tried to mug me.' She hesitated; Mike needed to know what had happened to Liz, and what the boys had done. So she broke her promise.

'They didn't just steal her bag, Mike.'

Mike was apoplectic, incoherent with anger. Jen had to hold him back from rounding up his mates and looking for the boys there and then. Instead, she led him into her flat and let him rage.

'She was defenceless, a harmless old woman, with no one to stand up for her. I'm going to kill those little fuckers, believe me.'

She listened to his rant until he'd exhausted himself.

'We don't know for sure he's the one. Don't do anything now, you're too angry. You've sorted out the locksmith for her. She feels safer, and Elsie's with her. I'll let her rest tonight and see her tomorrow. She's not alone. She has us. Wash your face and go home.'

Watching from her window, she saw him come out of the building. He seemed disoriented, gazing about him as if he didn't know where he was. She sent Sadie a text, then lay down on the sofa and shut her eyes.

The clamour of the landline startled her, and she reared up in a panic. Angie. Was Angie home?

'Mum, it's for you. It's your boss,' Angie shouted. Jen shuffled into the hall and picked up the receiver.

'Jen. Is this an inconvenient time?'

Still half asleep, Jen mumbled a reply.

'Sorry to ring you at home. There was a hand-delivered envelope with the mail; did you see who left it? You didn't open the door, did you?'

'No, I didn't. You told me not to. An old man left it.' Jen was barely polite; she'd had enough drama for one day. Angie was listening. Jen put the phone down and smiled at her daughter. She was home. She was safe.

Later, Sadie phoned Jen to thank her for looking after Mike. 'He was in a state when he got home. Liz was his mum's best friend; he's known her all his life.'

'I was worried he'd do something stupid.'

'Little bastards. Whoever they are, they're causing trouble around the area. They're out of control. I don't blame Liz for not going to the police, but something needs to be done about them.'

'They terrorised her.'

'I'm glad you and Mike were there for her. He's taking the guys down to the canal in the morning. He said to meet him at Liz's tomorrow night, around seven o'clock.'

Chapter 9

Over the years, Jen had gotten accustomed to the dreariness of Liz's home, but she'd never understood it. It didn't reflect her character. It was gloomy, and the kitchen smelt of cheap meat and overcooked vegetables. Everything was clean but bleak. There was no comfort, no effort to make the place homely, yet Liz herself was positive and proactive; the go-to woman, the woman who knew the ropes, knew how to work the system. Mike had put Jen in touch with her when she needed advice about her landlord.

'Talk to Liz Fisher,' he'd said. 'She gets things done.'

She'd arranged to meet her and had watched her make her way across the courtyard of her building, weaving through the children playing. A posse of women stopped her, and Liz listened to what they had to say. They seemed angry but listened when she spoke. The group broke up eventually, and Liz picked up the shopping bag at her feet. One of the women shouted something in her language and a teenage boy loped over and took it from her and walked her to the gate. A smaller child hung onto her arm, and she bent to talk to him. She stopped to exchange words with the women watching their children, then made her way to where Jen waited.

The shopping bag was full of books she was taking to the second-hand bookshop, and they'd bonded over a love of reading. By the time Liz had guided her through the endless evaluation of contracts and writing letters, they had become the best of friends. It hurt Jen to see her brought so low by boys little more than children.

Mike arrived, puffing and grumbling about the broken lift.

'I was right; I knew I'd seen that little sod before. He and another one have taken over a boat near where the Averys keep their dogs. I'll talk to my mate at Paddington nick, but I don't expect the police can do anything. There was no sign of a break-in, and they're older than I thought they were. We told them to stay clear of the launderette or they'd get a kicking.'

He gave Liz a mobile. 'Use this if you need me. My number's on speed dial. I've had a word with Sal in the corner shop. He'll keep an eye on things. They won't bother you again. I must get back. Sadie sends her love. Come for lunch on Sunday, Elsie as well. We're having a bit of a get-together.'

Liz saw them out. Mike waited until they were out of earshot.

'No wonder she was scared. There were three of us, and we are all big blokes, but those kids shocked us. They look as if they'd lived underground all their lives; they're as white as maggots, and their clothes were filthy. They stood on the deck of the boat and cursed us. I thought Hamid would faint. He winces if anyone says bloody. Lee said they were like the skeletons in one of the video games he plays. We laughed about it later, but they gave us the horrors.'

Jen recalled the boy who'd tried to mug her baring his teeth and spitting. She was glad to reach the safety of her building. Angie was sprawled out on the sofa, reading something on her phone. Jen poured herself a glass of wine.

'Do you know anything about the boys squatting on the canal? The young ones.'

'Creepy white boys? Yeah.'

'What about them? Come on, Angie, it's important.'

'I told you. Creepy white boys. That's it, that's what everyone calls them. All anyone knows. Why?'

'They've been causing a lot of trouble.'

'Duh.'

She was the idiot again, Angie the streetwise know-it-all.

'Go to bed, Angie.'

'Stay away from them, Mum. They're scary. They even scare the Somali boys. What's this Hayley told me about a party?

*

Sadie was in her element, darting about, passing plates, pouring drinks and making sure everyone was happy. Mike turned the music up, and Gary pulled Elsie up to dance. A burlesque dancer in one of her earlier lives, she showed off her moves, using a feather boa as a prop. Jen took Elsie's seat next to Liz. She looked exhausted, the skin around her eyes puckered and dark.

A cheer went up; Elsie had hooked the boa around Gary's waist and was bending back, her hennaed hair brushing her waist, her spine a beautiful arc, her limbs elongated and her feet curved like crescent moons.

'Bendy little thing.' Liz was proud of her friend's acrobatics. 'She's a beauty, or used to be.' She rubbed her hands together as if she were washing them, pulling at the fingers. 'We used to walk to school together. Look at us now.'

Flushed with success, Elsie joined them, and Jen gave up her chair and left to circulate. Gary handed her a drink. 'You look sad. What's Liz been telling you?'

'The mugging affected her, she's not herself. I'm worried about her.'

'Liz will be OK. Look at her, strong and steady. She'll cope. A mugging's not going to defeat her.'

He didn't know; all he knew, all anyone knew, was that muggers had stolen her bag.

'Don't worry about Liz now, Jen. When are we going to talk?'

Angie, Hayley and Hamid's two boys were sitting in a circle in the corner of the room, out of the way of the adults, heads down over their phones. Angie looked up, and Jen panicked.

'Not now, not here. Sorry, Gary. There's too much going on right now.'

She was dreading the conversation. They'd had it before. He was patient, but she couldn't put him off much longer. Using Angie as an excuse was cowardly. She watched him talking to Liz, making her laugh. He was a good man. She would be devastated if she lost his friendship and his support. He deserved better.

*

Jen set out the glasses and opened a bottle of wine, plumped up the cushions and turned all the lights off bar one. It looked as if she'd set the scene for seduction rather than a serious talk about their future. The bell sounded, three short bursts, their signal. It was too late now to regret her decision, and it was ridiculous to be so nervous. She ground out her cigarette in the pristine ashtray and threw the cushions around, and considered taking the bottle of wine and the glasses back to the kitchen. The bell rang again. Three rings. She glanced in the mirror before she answered the door; she was wearing an old pair of jeans and hadn't brushed her hair.

Gary had dressed up; he was wearing his best suit and a shirt instead of a T-shirt. He was holding a book, turning it repeatedly in his hands. He handed it to her. 'It's something I did a few years ago. I thought you'd like it.'

His gifts flattered her: anthologies of poetry or short stories, and art or photography books. She hadn't known he'd published one himself. Grateful for the distraction, she bent her head over the book and a photo of a shop on Praed Street, the rows of heads wearing hysterically unrealistic wigs in the window. It had been unique, and famous in its way. She'd forgotten it until now; it was as if it had never existed. The photos of the little shops and cafés, the small businesses depicted in the book were gone now, replaced by others almost identical; a never-ending cycle.

Gary was sitting close to her, his thigh touching hers, and her blood quickened; she'd missed him. She examined his sharp profile, the jutting cheekbones and strong jaw, the black curls brushing his collar. He was from the same traveller stock as Alex.

'I need to know where I stand. I want more than friendship, Jen.'

She'd sent him away. He'd been getting too close, seeing too much. He was a good man. He had a good life; he worked for himself and was successful and talented, interested in his world, and cared for her. She knew about his marriage at eighteen, the divorce at twenty, and the long relationship with a girl who'd left him when he wouldn't commit to marriage.

She knew him; he thought he knew her. Longing to be as honest as he had been, she'd tried to be as open, sure he would understand, but the words stayed lodged in her throat. She missed him. If she lost him, she'd regret it all her life. She had to break through the barriers she'd put up. After all the angst, her mind settled in an instant, and she held out her hand.

He followed her to the bedroom, carrying the bottle and the glasses. They undressed with their backs to each other, then dived under the covers, breathless with wanting. Jen was clumsy and awkward, but glad they had made it that far. It had been a long time. They needed to discover each other again. But their bodies had a memory, they knew each other and the signals they'd used, the words or sounds, the touches that told them when to hold back or when to quicken, were still there. Later, they sat back against the headboard, smoking, and talking in whispers.

'Do you think Angie heard? The walls are so thin. I don't want her to know about us yet. She's showing more interest in her father. It could get awkward.'

'I think you underestimate her. Tell her the truth about him.'

'What if she wants to meet him? He might try to use her. I can't trust him. He used me as bait.'

She'd known why Alex paid for the clothes he wanted her to wear, why he paid for the hairdressers and beauty treatments, and the expensive spa membership. 'You just have to look gorgeous. Smile, flirt a little, tempt them,' he'd said, 'you don't have to go through with it,' and she'd smiled and flirted, all the while resenting him. How weak she'd been.

'He could use Angie. Parade her around to tempt the punters.'

Her daughter, her luminous, bright child, dangled like a promise in front of the eyes of men who risked all on the turn of a card. Men in love with losing.

'What punters? Who'd trust him, in his state'?

Gary pulled her down beside him and held her, but she was reluctant to be soothed and freed herself, she needed her anger.

'I wasn't much older than Angie when I met him. Don't let him come back here. Make him disappear.'

'I won't let him hurt you or Angie. Neither will Mike.'

He underestimated Alex. And so she told him what he needed to know, said the words that had functioned as a straitjacket in all she did. The words that had stayed locked away for too long. She spared him nothing, or herself; stripped away any ambiguity and laid herself bare. He put his hand over her mouth.

'I know,' he said. 'I've known for a while. He told me, said it was "some girl". Years ago, just before he disappeared. I'd seen you together.'

'Why didn't you say?'

'I was waiting for you to tell me.'

He'd known. As a rejected lover, as a valued friend, he'd known yet said nothing. He turned his back to her, reaching for his cigarettes. The curve of his back was as taut as a bow primed for the arrow. Yes, you understand, she thought, and the relief was enormous. She reached for the ashtray on her side of the bed, consciously mirroring him. They turned back together, leaned against the headboard and talked; only made promises they knew they could keep. They made love again, this time without urgency, and talked some more.

It was getting light when she saw him out. They could hear the traffic building up on Marylebone Road. She watched him walk away, her arms crossed against the clean chill of the morning. It was OK, they were OK. Her doubts would fall away in time.

Chapter 10

Jen's umbrella was a tangle of broken spokes and wet fabric. It was useless against the rain. Maggie called out to her from under a shop awning.

'Oi, Jen. Got a cigarette?'

Jen joined her and they huddled together. Maggie stored the cigarette away in a tin. Her hands were red and looked sore. Jen dumped her brolly into the nearest bin and pulled her coat over her head. 'I'm going to make a run for it. Fancy a cup of tea?'

They ran, Maggie scowling and making Vee signs at the cars that sprayed dirty water on their legs. The nearest café was popular with the students and staff from the nearby college, but they found a table for two next to an old-fashioned radiator. Maggie pulled her chair closer and hunched over it, warming her hands. Her clothes clung to her meagre torso and her hair was thin and stuck to her cheeks and skull like string. The whites of her eyes were the colour of curdled milk, and spider veins scuttled over her cheeks.

Maggie lived hard. There was a time when Jen had found herself with nowhere to live and no money, the streets her only choice. It wasn't something she talked about, certainly not to Maggie. She'd heard her rant about the kids who thought a fortnight of sleeping rough gave them entry into her world. Maggie wasn't homeless, she informed anyone who listened; the streets were her home. Offered a flat, she'd lived in it for a while, then came back to the streets and the company of her fellow vagrants. She'd felt too isolated and missed the camaraderie of the drifting group of outsiders. Hardcore, tough, and unsentimental about her life, she had no illusions. 'I'll probably die out here,' she'd said, 'but I don't like rooms. Rooms frighten me.'

What about winter on the streets, Jen thought, didn't winter frighten her? The frozen pavements, the icy rain, the punishing wind? And the abuse? Jen had watched drunks urinate on sleeping street people and had heard the insults: 'Get a fucking job. Wanker. Tosser. Dirty bastard.' Seen the phlegm hawked up and spat onto threadbare blankets. And worse. The beatings and the burnings, the rapes and the violent sexual abuse. Maggie was tough, but no one was that tough. She was tucking into the sausage roll Jen had bought her, putting it down between bites and patting her lips with a paper napkin before taking a sip of tea. Her grubby fingers and black-rimmed nails left smudges on the thick white china. Dulled by dirt and lack of sleep, brutalised by alcohol and dehumanised by years of sleeping in shop doorways, yet she sat with her back straight and held her cup daintily. It was hard not to pity her, safer not to show it.

'I did a course with that lot,' she said, nodding towards four women at a table near theirs. 'Computers for beginners. I was rubbish, they gave up on me.'

All four of them? Did they pass her between them like a displaced refugee? Had she been part of a government initiative – give her a skill, get her off benefits and the streets? Good luck with that, Jen thought. Maggie grinned at her; one of her front teeth was missing.

'How the fuck was I supposed to get a job? Or a computer?' She shrugged off the government's tricks. 'I don't need any of that rubbish anyway.' Jen had never heard Maggie swear before, and she looked baffled and hurt rather than angry.

'You still seeing Gary? I went to school with him, he's fit.'

'What was he like at school?'

'Teacher's pet, clever. Nice with it. Passed all his exams. Not like me.' She picked up her sausage roll, took a tiny bite and chewed thoughtfully, her eyes fixed in concentration.

'Did you know his mate, Alex?'

'Yeah. He's with the Brothers now. How the mighty have fallen. He ended up in the hospital not long ago. No one had seen him for years. Got beaten up. Badly. Serve him right.'

This was news; she needed to know more but had to be careful. Notoriously short-tempered when sober, Maggie could turn in a second.

'Really? What had he done?'

Maggie ignored her and continued eating. Jen waited, fixated on the working of her jaws. Someone must have told her to chew each mouthful a hundred times. She wanted to bombard her with questions and shake the answers out of her. Maggie swallowed at last and took a sip of tea.

'Don't know. Someone found him in the street and took him to St Mary's.'

'How do you know it was him?

'One of the market guys told me. The fish guy. Lenny. His mate works at the hospital. He recognised him.'

'When was that?'

'Last year. I don't know. October, November. It was dark early.' She was impatient and stared threateningly at the college lecturers, who were pretending not to eavesdrop.

'Did you tell Gary?'

'Nah. Didn't see him. Got nicked for begging and went over to Notting Hill. Anyway, Gary wouldn't care. He hates Alex. He might have been the one who beat him up, he'd done it before.'

Gary had never mentioned a fight. Maggie was staring at the crumbs on her plate.

'Can you remember anything else?'

'I don't know. What's with the interrogation?' She flung herself back in her chair, knocking the table, sending cups and plates skidding. The college women were staring.

'What are you looking at?' Maggie was revving up. The women dropped their eyes, fiddled with their statement scarves, or lifted cups to lips. Jen tried to distract her.

'Do you want another cup of tea, Mags?'

'It's Maggie to you. And yes, I would like another cup of tea. And another sausage roll, thank you.' She threw a hard stare at the women, who all shrank a little. 'Remember me? You had me for computing.'

Jen bought Maggie her tea and sausage roll and left her intimidating the IT tutors, and went to talk to Gary.

He was in his studio. He put aside what he was working on and switched on his computer. 'I've got a photo of her. Maggie had a crush on Alex and followed him around everywhere until he told her to get lost. He was brutal.'

He opened a folder and trawled through it. 'Here we are. Good-looking kid and clever with it.'

Jen leant in closer. Maggie at the same age as Angie, and as beautiful, looked back at the camera, her expression a combination of innocence and cynicism.

'The family moved away. Maggie reappeared years ago.'

Poor Maggie, her teenage love rejected. Jen knew how brutal Alex could be. It was no wonder she was bitter.

'I don't know what happened to her, why she ended up living rough. The family was OK.' Gary closed the file. 'She's not dependable, Jen, she can't remember what she did last night, let alone months ago. So, someone beat Alex up. It goes with the territory. I beat him up myself once.'

Jen didn't ask him why; she wasn't ready to find out.

'Our best bet is Lenny. He's a friend, and he knows Alex from the old days.'

*

The market was quiet; people wandered around, but no one was buying. Gary introduced her to Lenny. He was cleaning fish; half a dozen fish heads stared gloomily up at the sky from a barrel next to him. He cut off the head of an enormous cod, flipped it into the barrel, and then wiped his hands on a bloody tea towel. Silvery scales clung to his fingers and onto the dark hairs on his forearms.

'Yeah, I remember. My mate's a porter at the hospital; he saw someone bring him in.' He washed his arms and hands, took a flat fish out of a box and slapped it onto a chopping board. 'He told the doctors he didn't know who beat him up, but he told my mate it was a couple of bouncers from the casino. They'd taken his winnings and his Rolex watch. But you know Alex; you can't believe a word he says.' He made an incision at the tail end of the fish and tore the dark skin off with a ripping sound that made Jen flinch. 'Discharged himself. Got dressed and walked out in his bloody suit and torn shirt. Lovely suit, my mate said. Always liked good clothes, did Alex.' He wielded the supple knife delicately, cutting along the backbone of the fish and sliding the blade under the translucent flesh. He washed and wrapped the fillets and handed the parcel to Jen with a bow.

'Nice to meet you, Jen. Good piece of fish, that; Dover sole. Grill it and squeeze a bit of lemon over it. Lovely.'

They thanked him and walked home in silence, thinking over what Lenny had told them.

'He may have been mugged, it's possible,' Gary said at last, 'but it could be something to do with the money he owes.'

Alex had fallen onto a hard place; beaten and in thrall to the Brothers. If Jen saw him now and if she could bear to talk to him, she'd ask him how it felt to be alone, with no home, his only friends a pair of Paddington thugs. Pity was the ultimate revenge.

Later that night Gary made a performance of serving the fish, issuing orders in French as he brought the dishes to the table.

'Asseyez-vous, s'il vous plaît Madame, Mademoiselle.'

Angie stared down at her plate.

'What's the green stuff on the fish?'

'Parsley. A herb. Try it.'

She and Angie rarely ate together, and never with Gary. Angie took a small bite; herbs made her suspicious. She hadn't seemed surprised to see him in the kitchen, and they had watched him show off his cooking skills. The fish was delicious, subtle and delicate.

'Do you like it?'

'Yeah. Can we have it again, Mum?'

'Yes. Why not,' Jen said, although she wondered how much Dover sole cost. She'd watched Gary prepare and cook it. It was simple and quick, and so was the watercress salad he'd put together; she should be able to manage it.

'Aren't you two having wine, seeing as we've gone all French?' Angie had polished off the fish and was helping herself to the salad.

'I'm cutting down, and Gary's working later.'

'Not staying the night then, Gary.'

'Er, no. Not tonight.' Gary rolled his eyes at Jen. She turned away, her cheeks flaming.

'Well, don't mind me. What's this?' Angie dangled a stem of watercress in front of Gary.

The phone rang, and Jen escaped into the hall to answer it.

'Is Angie there?' Sadie sounded irritated, and Jen could hear Hayley in the background shouting at her mother. 'Have you checked her Facebook page?'

'Not for a while. Why?'

'Well, you should. And tell her to take the photos down. Hayley wants to talk to her.'

Jen hurried back to the kitchen. Porn. Grooming. Trolls. The evils of the internet. Gary looked up. 'What's the matter, Jen? Who was that?'

'Sadie's cross and Hayley's in hysterics. She wants to talk to you, Angie. About the photos on Facebook. What photos?'

'They're just photos of us dressed up.' Angie sounded surprised. 'I put them up last night, after school.'

'Go and talk to Hayley, then come back and show me.'

They could hear snatches of Angie's conversation and Hayley's garbled voice; she was still shouting.

'It can't be that bad if they had their clothes on,' Gary said.

'Are you serious? Don't joke, Gary.'

'It's OK, she can delete them.'

Angie came back and flung herself into a chair.

'Some posts said Hayley's fat. She thinks it's my fault.'

'Come on, Angie, let's have a look.'

'It's nothing, Mum.'

'All the same.'

'I'll make some coffee,' Gary said. 'Call me if you need some help.'

Dragging her feet, Angie followed Jen into her room and watched her clear a chair of discarded clothes and draw it up to the desk. 'Hayley knew I was going to do it, we talked about it.'

Angie brought up her page. And there she was, wearing the fake astrakhan jacket her mother had worn for breakfast in Chelsea, looking bold and sassy and all of twenty, smiling a celebrity smile. Then a series of photos of Angie and Hayley modelling 'my mum's cool clothes'. Clothes that were chosen for their allure, in poses they'd copied from girls and women who flaunted their availability.

They read the comments in silence. Most were complimentary, but there were some rude remarks and a few suggestions about what they would do to Angie and Angie's cool mum, even the fat one.

'Need any help?' Gary stood in the doorway, carrying two mugs. He came and stood beside Angie.

'The fashions in the nineties were cool. The photos are great. Do you know how to delete them?'

Jen left Gary and Angie to delete the photos and rang Sadie.

'Silly little buggers.' Sadie sounded placated. 'It's nothing to worry about, totally innocent. Poor Hayley – "the fat one". She's threatening to go on a diet. It's not a bad idea, me and Mike as well.

Chapter 11

Mrs Laurence had a visitor. Jen heard the bell, then a voice on the intercom. Mrs L answered the door and led her visitor into the drawing room. It was the second time this month that she'd taken time off work, and Jen was curious.

The dishwasher finished its cycle, and in the silence, Jen heard a man shouting, then a ragged tattoo of footsteps. There was a muffled thump. Someone or something had fallen. Then another shout; Mrs L this time.

Don't get involved, Jen told herself. Pretend you haven't heard anything. Then imagined her boss bleeding or unconscious. She couldn't ignore it. She climbed the stairs up to the hall and hovered outside the door. Before she had time to knock or call it was flung open and a man pushed past, his stink enveloping her. He slammed the front door so hard the fanlight above it shook. Taking a deep breath, she stepped into the room. Mrs L stood at the window, half hidden behind the curtain. One of the occasional tables lay on its side, a lamp beside it, the silk shade bent out of shape.

'Is everything all right?'

'My visitor knocked over the table. Nothing to worry about.'

Jen righted the table and put the lamp back. The shade was beyond repair. Mrs L sank onto a chair against the wall, her face drawn, her eyes cast down. Jen hesitated.

'It's all right, Jen.'

Jen went back down to the kitchen. If Mrs Laurence wanted to pretend nothing was wrong, she would too. Noise from the street filtered through the open window over the sink, and she reached up to shut it. Someone was standing on the pavement, the dun-coloured and down-at-heel shoes directly in her eye line. She'd seen those shoes before, and the creased and shapeless trousers. She heard the soft thud as the feet climbed the steps to the front door. The bell rang and then stopped. She relaxed, but then another ring tore around the house. It stopped for a second then started again, relentless and demanding. Unable to bear the noise any longer, she ran up the stairs and opened the door to the drawing room. Mrs Laurence was still in the chair, her eyes shut and her hands over her ears like a frightened little girl.

'He'll go. Leave it.' But he didn't go; he held his finger on the bell. They were helpless, unable to escape, held there by its threat. It stopped at last and, in the silence, Jen heard Mrs Laurence's harsh breath.

'Didn't you hear me? I said go.'

She left Mrs Laurence as she'd found her, cringing, her eyes screwed shut. Whoever the man was, he'd sent a message of intent.

The silence in the basement felt sinister after the clamour of the bell. Outside in the street, a car door slammed, and a woman laughed, breaking the unnatural quiet. Jen filled a glass with water and drank it. She told herself nothing truly awful had happened. Violent arguments occurred in the drawing rooms of houses like the Laurences', or rented flats, or the bedrooms of suburban homes. No one knew what went on behind closed doors. But she was hurt; her boss had never spoken to her so sharply.

An hour later, Mrs Laurence came into the kitchen. Dressed for work, a coat over her arm and carrying her briefcase.

'Jen, can we talk? Maybe you could make some coffee.'

Jen made the coffee and then sat at the table, facing her boss. They'd never had coffee together; it felt awkward. Jen heard herself swallow. Mrs Laurence's hand shook as she lowered the cup back to the saucer. Jen glanced at her boss and caught her eye. They were each searching the other's body language, looking for clues to what was going on behind the false calm. The atmosphere was fraught with suspicion. Mrs L broke the silence.

'I'm sorry you had to witness that. It was an accident; my friend is very clumsy.'

Jen stared at her in disbelief. Did the woman think she was stupid?

'If I'm going to be in the house alone, I need to know he's not going to come back. He scares me.'

Mrs Laurence put down her cup. 'Christ, I'm so sorry.' She was wailing like a child, the sound as shocking as glass shattering. 'I don't know what to do.'

Embarrassed, Jen drew back and the wailing stopped, cut short. She pushed a packet of tissues across the table. Mrs Laurence wiped the mucus and tears off her face and dropped the soiled tissue on the floor.

'He's my father,' she said. 'He's my father, but I fucking hate him.'

Her accent had changed from a middle-class drawl to the mishmash accent spoken on the estates. 'I haven't seen him for years; I thought he was dead. I fucking hate him. He wants to drag me down.'

'Well, don't let him.' Jen answered her woman-to-woman. As she would to a friend. Mrs Laurence recoiled and the glance she threw at her was poisonous. She pushed the packet of tissues back across the table.

'You're right.' She drained her coffee and took her cup to the sink. Holding it under the tap she rinsed it repeatedly and then placed it on the draining board. 'I'll replace the lampshade, or get it repaired.'

'What about…'

Mrs Laurence interrupted her. 'I'll deal with it. There are always police around. I might have a word with them.' She looked at Jen briefly, her lips thinned, her expression cold then turned away without speaking and left the kitchen. The front door closed, and Jen heard her pause before she continued down the steps.

Ill at ease, Jen went up to the ground floor and locked the door from the inside, then went back to the basement. The basement had always felt familiar and comforting but now she felt threatened by the dull shine of stainless steel and granite, the relentless tick of the kitchen clock, and the hum of the refrigerator. She'd grown used to her boss's aloofness, but their relationship would change now. Mrs Laurence had let Jen see who she truly was, who she'd been before she married Mr L. Jen would have to be on her guard.

"He's my father, but I fucking hate him." It was something that a rebellious teen might say, not meaning it, or only meaning it at that moment. Jen said the words aloud, hearing the full import of them in the quiet kitchen. Mrs Laurence had meant every word; she hated her father, and her father was a dangerous man. Jen remembered his violence, the toppled table, the slam of the front door. The arrogance of his posture as he stared up at the house. Whatever had gone on between him and his daughter in the past, he expected to get what he'd come for, and wouldn't give up until he had it.

Jen knew the distress of being stalked, the helplessness and the guilt. She'd been stalked by someone she'd slept with a few times and then avoided. Younger than her, lovesick and hoping for sanctuary in her bed and at her table, he refused to believe she didn't want to see him and followed her in the street, rang her bell at night, waking her and her daughter and demanding to be let in. He veered from making threats to pleading. She'd refused to acknowledge him. He'd followed her to the Laurence house one day and rang the bell. Jen had listened to Mrs L deal with his blustering. She had pointed out the armed policeman on the corner, the cluster of police hovering outside the ex-politician's house. He'd left, humbled and frightened and totally out of his depth.

Mrs L had flipped her hand contemptuously when Jen tried to explain and apologise. 'Not interested,' she'd said. 'Just don't bring your problems to my house again.'

Jen was grateful for her help, but her refusal to listen to her explanation humiliated her. The boy – she couldn't remember his name – had given up; she'd never seen him again. Mrs L had scared him off, but her father was older and tougher.

What was it to her, Jen told herself. What went on in this house, with these people, was none of her business. Before she left the kitchen, she kicked the soiled tissue under the chair.

*

Jen made a coffee and sat at the wooden table in her kitchen. She moved aside the unopened mail and out-of-date newspapers and lit a cigarette. The arrival of Mrs L's father had forced her to think about her own, something she had refused to do for years. Like Mrs L's father, he'd been a bully, but his rage was cold, his cruelty subtle. She and her mother had tiptoed around him. There were rules: No talking at the table. No visitors. The radio and television turned off after the ten o'clock news. And the cleaning. The walls and the floors, the windowsills and the skirting boards, the light fixtures, and even the cords that dangled from the ceilings. The inside and outside of all cupboards, everything to be scoured and scrubbed until all warmth was washed away. Start at the top of the house, work your way down to the bottom and start again. A never-ending deep clean. The walls and surfaces were to be kept clear; books and photos and pictures were useless clutter. She'd hated him, hated the weekly inspection, but had put his training to effective use; she'd learned how to clean like a professional.

But there was nothing she could learn from his cruelty or his rules. The bathroom door was to be kept open, whether it was her or her mother in the bath or on the toilet. Even if he was out. 'How would he know,' she'd asked her mother. 'If he's not here, how would he know?'

Her mother said nothing or did nothing when he disciplined her. He'd loved that word. Discipline. The whiplash sound of it. Jen's mattress was taken to the shed if she disobeyed; another word he savoured. The door locked. A bucket as her toilet. He rarely touched her, but when he did it was always the same. 'Roll up your sleeve,' he would say, and he would pinch and twist the flesh of her upper arm and stare into her face until her legs gave way and she cried out.

His fingers were long and bony, like pincers. She remembered the fear she'd felt when he looked at her, and the hatred. How humiliated, pinned down and helpless.

His death when she was twelve was sudden, and she'd been sent away to stay with an aunt. When she returned, all signs of him had been swept away, even the shed. A bare patch of earth was all that remained. However hard she tried, Jen couldn't remember his face or the sound of his voice, but she remembered the smell of oil on his hands and his overalls on the back of the shed door. The light glinting off his glasses.

'He didn't suffer,' her mother had said. 'The order of the funeral is on the desk if you want to keep it, but don't make a fuss.'

Jen didn't grieve for him. She didn't know how he had died, and her mother refused to talk about it. Life had gone on as if he'd never existed. His death should have freed her mother, but she behaved as if he were still following her as she wielded the bleach and the polish. Jen refused to help; she'd seen how other families lived, and she was old enough and big enough to defy her mother. She'd been glad her father was dead; she'd fantasised about killing him herself. Her fantasies had scared her. Surely, she'd thought, a child shouldn't want to kill her father.

Angie's closest friends were lucky, they had good fathers. Mike adored Hayley and spoiled her, Hamid loved and respected his sons and they looked up to him. Amina's father put all his dreams in her hands and worked two jobs to send her to a private school. All were good role models: they loved their children and showed it. Before Gary, Mike had been the only significant man in Angie's life, and the memory of her throwing her arms around his legs and looking up at him, Hayley pushing her off – *'my daddy'* – still hurt her. Her child's silent bewilderment, her cowardly efforts to divert her, still hurt as much now as it had then. And later, pre-teen and angry because Jen had forbidden her to get a tattoo. 'My dad left because he hated you. You're horrible.' And she, tired and stressed, snapped back.

'He doesn't know you exist, and if he did, he wouldn't care.'

Telling the truth and regretting it before the words had settled. Too late, the damage had been done, the wound inflicted. Angie, her mouth trembling, her small hands clenched into fists.

'I hate you.'

She'd turned away, refusing to comfort or explain. Burning with resentment, she'd erased Alex from their lives. Sadie had tried to persuade her to talk about him, but she'd refused, too blinded by fear to see clearly. Angie might not talk about her father anymore, but she must think about him. She would confront her mother about him one day. She'd better be ready.

The slam of the flat door, the thump of Doc Martens, and a book bag hitting the floor alerted her, and Jen put out her cigarette. Angie was home, and something had upset her. She had been affectionate lately, sharing moments with her, feeding her little snippets of information. It had been like before adolescence, and Angie's struggle to untie the bond between them.

'They come back to you,' someone had told her. 'Let them get through this stage, and they come back,' and Jen hoped it was true. Still, she knew her daughter; any misplaced word or attitude might ruin their fragile truce. She knocked on Angie's door.

'You all right, love? Not worried about your exams?'

This was a touchy subject. Angie was studying every night and seemed confident, but snapped if Jen brought it up.

'I'm not worried. I'm on top of it. Stop going on about it. Don't keep asking me.'

'Can I come in?

'No. Can't I just get changed in peace?'

Jen resorted to bribery.

'I wanted to talk to you about your birthday.'

'I don't care about my birthday.'

'Well, I do.'

'You always get it wrong, anyway. The phone you bought me last year was crap. Forget it.'

'OK, let's talk about that. I don't know what you like, you don't tell me.'

The door sprang open, and Angie grabbed at her hands and pulled her into the room.

'I didn't mean it. I'm sorry.' She flung herself face down on her bed. 'I'm sorry, sorry, sorry.'

'It's OK, Angie. It doesn't matter about the phone. I thought you liked it.'

'It's not that, not really. Hayley tells everyone you can't afford to buy me a good one. She hates me.'

Jen struggled to find the right words.

'Of course, she doesn't hate you. You've been friends for years.'

'She said the photos I put on Facebook made her look fat and I chose them on purpose.'

'You took the photos down. They weren't there for long.'

'Everyone saw them.'

'But you both looked beautiful.'

'Hayley is fat. I kept telling her, but she just wobbled her belly at me. She said she didn't care. Now it's my fault.'

'It'll blow over. You and Hayley are like sisters.'

'Not anymore.' She sat up and scrubbed at her eyes with a tissue. 'We're so over. What's for tea? Not pizza again I hope.

Jen hurt for her. She and Hayley were both stubborn and if it were to be the end of their friendship, Jen wondered how the dynamics among their group would change. She'd seen the shifting alliances, the jostling for popularity, the betrayals and meanness of the girls when they were younger. Angie and her friends seemed to have settled and found their place among the various groups. Not the cool kids or the nerds, but somewhere in-between, friends with common interests. If Hayley continued to blame Angie for her fat-shaming, it would change, people would take sides and form cliques, and both of them would be hurt.

Angie needed her support. She might not know that she did, and might not accept it when she offered it, but Jen would keep her eyes and ears alert to any bullying or unpleasantness. And she would talk to Sadie about checking her Facebook activity.

Chapter 12

Mrs L would be in the hall or lingering in the basement when Jen arrived for work. It was as though she couldn't leave without seeing her first and took pleasure in pointing out a smear on a polished surface or a thumbprint on a glass. There was an unspoken threat in everything she said. Today she was waiting by the front door, pretending to check her appearance in the hall mirror. Making a point of looking at her watch, she shook her head, then looked at Jen, her eyes hard in her narrow little face.

'You'd better get on, then, hadn't you?'

She opened the door to leave, pausing to look back. In the rush of light from the street, Jen saw the weak chin and the spiteful mouth; a mean girl who'd fought her way out of a sink estate to take her place in a world she aspired to and who was fighting still.

Jen wasn't intimidated; she'd seen through the immaculate veneer, the features enhanced by the subtle application of makeup, and the malnourished frame adorned with clothes that cost more than Jen earned in a month. All the same, she admired her boss's chutzpah. Being married to an attractive and successful man while holding down a prestigious job would take a keen mind, a will of steel, and skill in bed.

By the time Jen had checked and put away the weekly grocery delivery, hoovered the bedrooms and cleaned the bathrooms she was exhausted, but sure that Mrs L could have no cause to complain. Before she left, she shut all the windows and double-locked the door to the patio. Pausing on the doorstep, she peered up the street. The tables outside the cafés were occupied, and two women sauntered past, loaded with bags from the shops on Oxford Street. A policeman stood on the corner of the square and two others seemed to be patrolling. Security was high in the area.

Once she'd hurried to work, eager to be there; now she hurried away. She'd loved the house, and her job, but knew it was time for her to move on. Her only other significant job was with the Cousins, showing off clothes she couldn't afford, to buyers whose customers were twice her size. Clothes hung well on her lanky frame, and she knew how to show them off, and how to look after them. She could put her knowledge to use. There were stalls in the antique market that specialised in vintage clothes. She would talk to one of the traders and get ideas from them. Eager to make a start, she made her way to the market. Lenny was at his stall and beckoned her over.

'You and Gary were asking about Alex, yeah? He's been seen around. I thought you'd want to know.'

She felt her heart come untethered from its moorings and drop.

'When was this?'

'Last week sometime, by the canal.' Lenny wiped his hands on his apron. 'Are you OK? Sit down. You look poorly.' He pulled out a chair and spread a clean tea towel over the seat. 'Do you want me to get someone to take you home? I can ring Gary; I've got his number.'

'I was dizzy. I'm all right now.'

She stood up, but it was too soon; she felt as if she was drowning, gasping for air. She took a deep breath and the noise of the market flooded back. Fish. She could smell fish. Lenny's face was a blur, a child's scribble. A couple were waiting for service. It gave her time to collect herself.

'Give me a minute, Lenny. You get on, you've got customers.'

Alex had never been out of her thoughts, but the threat he represented had become abstract. Now it was real, immediate. She waited until Lenny finished serving the last customer. He shrugged off her thanks.

'You sure you don't want someone to walk you home?'

'I'll be fine. Low blood sugar. I missed my breakfast.'

'Alex was looking good, Jen. Him and the Averys were loved up, pally, laughing and chatting like mates.'

She could see his lips moving, he was still talking, but she couldn't hear him anymore. Her head felt empty and light, floating above her. The smell of fish was overpowering, and she broke away leaving him in mid-sentence; she had to get away, get home, get back to her flat and shut the door, lock it. Some of the stalls were already selling off their remaining stock, and she dodged people carrying boxes or bags of vegetables and fruit. Someone nudged her, a corner of the box they were carrying grazing her hip, and she sped up, kicking out at broken cardboard boxes and rubbish, anything between her and home and safety. Home, she had to get home, she'd be safe there.

She turned into her street and bent to relieve the stitch in her side, fighting for breath. Someone took her hands and called her name.

'Jen, it's all right, love, breathe with me. That's right, breathe in, breathe out, slowly, slowly.'

She knew that voice; Elsie was breathing with her, breathing for her.

The stuttering thump of her heart gradually slowed. Elsie let go of her hands, and Liz took her arm. They led her to her flat. Elsie dabbed a cold flannel over her face, and Liz bumbled about making tea. Their voices sounded muffled, and then it was as if someone had turned the sound up and now they were shouting. The room came into focus. She reached for the cup Liz handed her.

'That's better, love.' Liz rattled biscuits onto a plate. 'Get your strength back.'

'I thought I was suffocating. Thank you, Elsie. You were brilliant.'

Preening, Elsie launched into a story about her time as a burlesque dancer. 'I used to have terrible stage fright,' she said. The flat door banged open, cutting her off in mid-anecdote. Angie was already talking by the time she burst through the kitchen door.

'I've made up my mind. Miss Hanson said I could get into a good university if I work hard in sixth form next year and get the grades I need.' She stopped, brought up short by the appearance of the two old women. 'Hello, Mrs Fisher.' She glanced at Elsie; her expression uncertain. Flamboyant, her hair hennaed a glaring red to match her scarlet lips, Elsie was an unlikely companion to Liz – a flamingo beside a pigeon. She'd taken over, drawn Angie's attention away from her, and Jen was grateful. She staggered when she stood up. Talk about school and university would have to wait.

'What's wrong, mum?

'I've got a headache; I need to lie down. There's bread and cheese, and salad in the fridge. Sorry, love, it will have to do.'

'I'll make you some Welsh rarebit, Angie,' Elsie said. 'Got any mustard?'

Jen left them and crawled into bed. The sheets were cool, and she pulled them up over her shoulders. She could hear the voices from the kitchen, heard Angie laughing, and Liz or Elsie clattering dishes. The sounds were comforting, and her muscles relaxed, the tenseness draining away. Her nails were digging into her palms, leaving little crescent moons of pain. She let her hands open, a finger at a time, letting go of her fear. Her breathing slowed and she slept.

She woke with a start. A dirty yellow light seeped through the curtains. It must be evening, and she was safe, in her bed. And then she remembered. Alex. Alex was back, and she'd run through the streets in a panic.

Her legs felt weak, but she got out of bed and crept down the passage, one hand against the wall to steady herself. The smell of fear rose from her damp clothes and the sweat on her skin and in her hair. For once the water in the shower was hot enough and she stood under its flow and scrubbed her skin until it was sore, shampooed her hair, turned her face up and let the water run into her eyes, her ears, and her mouth.

Cleansed, in fresh clothes and with a renewed sense of purpose, she went to check on Angie. The panic she had felt earlier has been like a storm in her head. Now she was calm. Forget Alex; what mattered was her daughter's future. Angie wanted to go to university. She glanced into the kitchen on her way to her room. Three cups and three plates were draining in the rack. Elsie and Liz had kept her company and cooked for her, and eaten with her. She knocked on her door, wondering how to explain her behaviour to her daughter.

'You OK, Mum? Is your headache better?' Her eyes were on her screen; Angie was doing her homework.

'Much better. How was the Welsh rarebit?'

'I didn't know one of your mates used to be a stripper.'

'Don't let Elsie hear you call her that. She was a burlesque dancer.'

'Whatever. The cheese on toast was great. I like your friends. They were telling me about the war. They've only just left.' She turned back to the screen. 'Can we talk later? I've got to finish this essay.'

Her daughter had taken one of those quantum leaps into maturity that young people make, but Jen felt inadequate, not up to the job of guiding her through the next stage of her life. Angie had put her headphones on and was scanning the screen. Jen looked over her shoulder at the document she was reading: Modern World History. She was making notes in a book on her lap. Jen knew what she could do to help her, so she phoned Gary. He had friends who could 'source' things, and maybe save her some money.

But he was doubtful.

'A new computer and a laptop? Are you sure?'

'Of course, I'm sure. I've got money put aside.'

'I'll see what I can do. But Jen...'

'Yeah, I know. Alex is back.'

'You don't sound too bothered.'

'That's because I won't let him come near her. He's not going to mess up our lives. I'm going to find out where he is and what he's up to. I'll talk to the Averys if I have to.'

'You'd have to be careful. Wait for me. I'll pick up food on my way over. We can talk about it.'

She laid the table in the kitchen, opened a bottle of wine and poured herself a glass while she waited for him. It was time she took control. Time for her and her daughter to surge ahead, to step out into the world, confident and fully armed. Striding around the kitchen, she started to make plans. Decorate the flat for a start. Angie's room first. She wasn't going to end up like Liz, her home stuck in the past. Lenny had said Alex was looking good; he and the Averys must have pulled off a scam. He must have money. Angie would get a degree and would follow her dreams. Learn what she was capable of and not be afraid. Alex would pay for it, pay for everything. He had to pay.

The bell rang; three short rings. Gary. Exhilarated, she rushed to the door and led him back to the kitchen, pulling him by the hand, talking, telling him what she was going to do.

'What are you on, Jen? You're hyper, slow down.'

'Alex should pay up; he should put something towards his daughter's future.'

'You're going to tell him about her, then? He might want to meet her. You OK with that?'

He was opening the cartons of food and taking plates out of the cupboard.

'Gary, stop that. Listen.'

'I can listen and do this. You need to eat something.'

He wasn't listening. She took a plate out of his hand and threw it against the wall; watched it cut through the air and heard it shatter. Watched the shards of china slide against the skirting board. She had to clear it up, but she couldn't move. Gary lifted her, carried her to the bedroom and laid her on the bed. He took off her shoes and pulled the covers over her, lay down beside her and let her cry until, drained and exhausted, she slept.

When she woke she could smell fresh coffee and heard the radio and the murmur of voices and laughter from the kitchen. Last night she'd made a fool of herself; thrown a plate at Gary and talked rubbish. Pulling her dressing gown around her, she shuffled across the hall and stepped into the kitchen. Angie and Gary looked up, their faces welcoming. The coffee smelled wonderful.

'Are you better now, Mum? Gary said your headache came back.'

Gary poured her a cup of coffee and then went back to discussing a television programme he and Angie liked. It was just another weekday morning. She listened to them talking; they were equals. Angie left for school, and she and Gary were alone.

'Did Angie hear me last night?'

'Her door was shut. I checked. She was listening to music. You slept well. Do you feel better?'

'I made a fool of myself…'

Gary interrupted her. 'You've been under a lot of stress. Liz told me about your panic attack; she was worried about you.'

Overcome, Jen folded her arms on the table and put her head down. The attacks had been so sudden. One moment she was making plans, the next she was whirling out of control. Gary shook her shoulder, and she sat up and took the coffee he handed her.

'It's a lovely day, we could take some time off, and go for a walk.'

'Mrs L is being difficult. She might sack me.'

'Call her, tell her you're not well. She seemed all right before the trouble with her dad. You said she was decent. She must be as stressed out as you are, more probably, but you've got enough to deal with.'

*

They walked up to the summit of Primrose Hill. Unfit and panting, but grimly determined, Jen trudged on, one foot stubbornly in front of the other. Gary strolled beside her, pretending not to notice her struggles.

She'd brought Angie up here often when she was little. Sometimes they'd walked up the slope backwards or looked at their feet and counted the steps, not lifting their heads until they reached the top.

'I had a look at Angie's set-up; she could do with a new computer. I'll sort one out for her birthday,' Gary said. 'My shout. And talking to the Averys isn't sensible. The Brothers have their own morality. And they're not comfortable around women.'

He was being tactful; it was a terrible idea.

'I don't know what I was thinking. Anyway, they give me the creeps.'

At the top of the hill, they collapsed onto one of the benches facing the view. Families picnicked on the slopes, passing around sandwiches and paper cups of juice, and tourists clustered around the information board. The London skyline glittered in the distance; old London spread out at the feet of the modern buildings that stood among the cranes like visiting aliens. Gary unpacked their lunch: chicken and crisp cos lettuce in wholemeal bread, a salad of cherry tomatoes and olives, and white wine in plastic beakers. They ate in silence, gazing out over the tops of trees towards the zoo and the zigzag outline of the aviary. There were no threatening fathers here, no beggar crime lords, no creepy white boys. No Mrs L, with her lists and complaints, and her desire to intimidate and control.

'This is my favourite place. It's on a sacred hill. We'll come up here one night, bring Angie. See London lit up.'

'She used to love it here.'

They both had until Angie lost interest in exploring the parks and canals, and her own days were taken up with keeping house for another family, her nights with a bottle of wine and the television.

'Too busy, maybe.'

Too hungover, she thought. Too lazy, too depressed. Too scared. Too tired.

'It's not easy, bringing up a kid on your own. You've done a grand job. My dad brought me up himself. My mum did a runner. He was a good man, my dad. He did his best, but he had to work shifts, and he left me to look after myself. Trusted me. We muddled along and got through. And it taught me to be self-sufficient.'

'Like me and Angie, then.'

'You do more than muddle through. You arrange your life around her. She's a credit to you.'

'You turned out ok, your dad must have been a good father.'

'He was. I loved him, but I didn't show it, something I'll regret all my life. He died just after my divorce.'

Jen thought of her father, his reticence, her mother's coldness towards him, and their coldness towards her. Gary's memories of his father were sad and regretful, but loving. He poured the last of the wine, and they settled into a contemplative silence, shoulders and hips touching.

Chapter 13

June was a momentous month. The Brexit referendum came and went. The UK would be leaving the European Union. Jen didn't care one way or the other. Liz had nagged her about voting, she had said she would and then forgot. Gary had voted but kept his opinions to himself. The highlights of the build-up to the vote for Angie and her friends had been Bob Geldof and Nigel Farage shouting at each other from boats on the Thames. She could hear their laughter from the kitchen.

Angie was happy with her new laptop, a birthday present from her and Gary, and she needed it; she'd had an exam every day and revised every evening.

Angie and Gary were comfortable together. He treated her like an adult, and she respected him. They'd settled into a routine; Gary spent the night with them unless he was working, and they all ate the evening meal together in the kitchen. At first, Angie refused to join them for meals at the table and took her plate into her room. Now she stayed with them and sometimes sat at the table to do her homework while Gary cooked.

Although she never talked about Hayley unless prompted, Jen knew she missed her. They had taken different paths, Angie working for her future, Hayley revelling in the moment. Angie spent more time with Amina now; they studied together and matched each other in their ambition and determination, but Jen knew Angie missed Hayley's irreverence and her daring.

Sadie grumbled about her daughter constantly. 'Her hair is purple, and she's taken up with a bunch of Goths or Emos, or whatever they're called. She's dyed all her T-shirts black and wears fishnet tights with her Docs. She's infatuated with a boy. Mike is beside himself.'

'She's not interested in uni,' Angie had told Jen. 'The kids she hangs out with are all right, but they take themselves too seriously. And she's got a boyfriend. Adam this, Adam that.' She'd curled her lip. 'They do everything together. Saddos.'

Jen glanced at the clock; Angie should have been home an hour ago; she was always home on time. If she was going to be late, she rang to let Jen know. Scrabbling around in her bag for her phone, she fought off the images that haunted her; Alex and Angie together, Alex poisoning her daughter's mind, telling her...Was this it? Now, when she was beginning to see a future for them both? Always fearful for her daughter, Alex's presence had turned imagined disasters into possibilities. About to text her, she heard Angie's key in the lock.

'Why are you so late?' Jen threw the phone onto the table. Angie flinched. Her cheeks were flushed; she looked as if she'd been running.

'There was a fight on the canal. It was horrible; grown men beating up kids. They kicked them and dragged them by their hair. It's not right, Mum.'

'What kids? Are you hurt?'

'Gary was there. He tried to stop it. He's right behind me.'

They heard his steps in the hall. He went straight to the sink and poured himself a glass of water. There was a dark mark under his eye.

'It's OK, it's nothing,' he said.'

'Sit down and slow down, the pair of you. You first, Angie. What were you doing on the canal?'

'We were just hanging out. Me and Hayley and Adam.'

'They were with the boys on one of the boats, the weird ones,' Gary said, and Angie shot him an agonised look. He ignored her. 'They're squatting on one of the Averys' boats. They threw stones at the Brothers' dogs.'

'The dogs were barking at them. They were scared.' Angie was surly, but her voice trembled.

'The dogs were nowhere near the boys. Magog was hit.'

'Where were you when all this was going on, Angela?'

'On the towpath, but Mum...'

'Who else was there?'

'Some kids from school, and the losers that hang around the canal: Maggie, Fat Pam, that man with one eye. Some others, I don't know their names. And a skinny man. He didn't do anything, he was laughing.'

Gary signalled something with his eyes and gave an almost unnoticeable nod of his head. Alex. Her worst fear: Alex and Angie in the same space.

'Look, it's over,' Gary said. 'The Brothers had calmed down by the time I left, and the boys were back on the boat. Who are they, anyway?'

'They're the ones making all the trouble. They mugged Sadie and tried to mug me. They attacked Liz.'

Angie shook her head. 'They wouldn't do that.' But she sounded doubtful. 'They wouldn't hurt an old lady.'

'Does Mike know Hayley's going down to the canal? He'll go mad if he finds out she's mixed up with what goes on there.'

'She's not mixed up in anything and neither am I. Why do you always think the worst?' She stomped out of the kitchen. 'I don't want dinner,' she shouted. 'Leave me alone.' Her door slammed shut.

'Well, that went well,' Gary said.

Angie came back into the kitchen. 'Don't tell Mike, mum.'

'I will if Hayley doesn't. And you were told not to go down to the canal, it's not safe. Now you know why. We'll talk about it later. Do your homework.'

Angie opened her mouth as if she were going to object but thought better of it. Gary waited until he heard her door close.

'I tried to persuade her to leave. To be fair, she kept out of the way. Hayley and Adam got involved, shouting at the Brothers.'

'Alex must have seen her.'

'He doesn't know who she is. And he was watching the Averys give the kids a battering. Angie was right, it was brutal.'

'She shouldn't have been there.'

'It's where the kids go now. As far as Alex is concerned, she's just another teenager.'

He was toying with a packet of cigarettes, turning it in his hands; he was hiding something.

'Did you know she went down there?'

'I was looking for Adam; his dad's a mate, and he asked me to keep an eye out for him. He's worried about him. I was surprised to see Angie with them.' The bruise on his cheek was turning violet. Tomorrow it would be purple. She wrapped ice cubes in a tea towel and held them to his cheek.

'Who hit you?'

'It was someone's elbow. A couple of the alkies got involved, and some of the older kids, including Adam. It was chaos, out of control. I'm glad Alex had the sense to lock the dogs up.'

Jen thought about pouring herself a drink, then changed her mind. 'I'm going to talk to Angie.'

Angie was face down on her bed, still dressed in her school uniform. She'd been crying.

'Is this about Hayley?'

'She doesn't care about me anymore. All she cares about is Adam.' She sat up. Strands of hair were sticking to her wet cheeks and Jen brushed them away.

'Is that why you went down to the canal? Because you want to be with Hayley?'

'Everyone goes there after school. I've only been a couple of times. Amina won't go with me. Her dad would ground her.'

'What about the boys on the boat? How do you know them?'

'I told you. The creepy white boys, remember? I don't *know* them; I know *about* them. I'm sorry for them. They've got nothing. No parents, no money, nowhere to live.'

'What about social services? Why don't they get help?'

'How should I know?'

'They're not your problem, or Hayley's. Mike and Sadie are going to be furious.'

'Is that all you care about? Mike and Sadie?

'I care about you. I want the best for you. Don't mess up your chances of a decent life.'

'I've got a decent life, Mum. That's the point. Not everyone has; the boys haven't.'

Angie was a good person, she cared about the boys, but they didn't deserve her compassion. They were wicked, and Jen would never forgive them for what they had done to Liz. Angie should know the truth. And so, she told her about the verbal sexual abuse, about the threats, but not that they'd stripped her to the waist. Angie listened, her face pale.

'Poor Mrs Fisher. Oh, poor lady. How could they?'

'I'm trusting you, Angie. Don't repeat what I've just told you. Liz would be mortified. Mike knows what those boys did. He'll go crazy when he finds out Hayley's involved with them. He will find out, news gets around. Don't go down to the canal and keep away from the boys. They're dangerous. You said so yourself. Get changed,' she told her. 'We'll eat later.'

She wanted a glass of wine, to disappear into the warm glow of mild inebriation, but Gary beckoned her over before she had a chance to open the fridge.

'Come and look at this.' He handed her his camera. 'I took these a few days ago. Adam's dad asked me to find out what I could about the canal boys. He's worried about their influence on Adam.'

The boys were sitting on the deck of the boat, as ragged and as filthy as Victorian street kids.

'I watched them for a while. There's something about them, the way they're so close. They look alike. I think they're brothers. I'll put it on the computer. Come up to mine tonight, and we'll have a proper look.'

Later that night, they shared a bottle of wine and studied the photos on Gary's widescreen monitor. He pointed out something he'd missed before; an old tin bath on the deck of the boat, piled with stones and rubble: ammunition, ready for invaders.

'It's them against the world.'

Jen didn't answer; she was studying the oldest boy. He reminded her of the foxes she'd seen lurking by the bins; he had the same close-set eyes and narrow skull, the same wary expression. But the boy wasn't an urban fox or a feral cat, he was a child, not much older than Angie, half-starved and desperate. Jen stifled any sympathy she might have had. He was the boy she and Mike had met on the street. The one who'd mugged Sadie, and who'd tried to mug her. More than that, and worst of all, he had humiliated Liz. Liz, who had never harmed anyone, had so little and yet was content.

'They're in a desperate state,' Gary said. 'The Brothers gave them a terrible beating.'

'Good. They deserve everything they get. I wish the dogs had got them. I wish Gog and Magog had torn them to pieces.'

'That's a bit strong, Jen.'

She'd betrayed Liz twice already, so she betrayed her for the third time. She could trust Gary. He listened without comment and was silent after she'd finished speaking. He roused himself at last.

'The Brothers will throw them off their boat, but there's bound to be trouble.'

Chapter 14

Jen had always felt safe in the Laurence's house but now she worried that Mrs L's father would show up when she was alone. His ruined face haunted her dreams. Gary had named him Mr Pink, after a character in a film she'd watched through splayed fingers. He joked about him but understood her fears and tried to reassure her.

Mrs L wouldn't have the same level of support from her husband. Theirs was not an equal partnership; he had the air of entitlement that came from a solidly middle-class background – minor public school, a university degree – and an established place in the world; she had the white knuckles and tense mouth of the second wife and social climber. No wonder she looked haggard. They hadn't been married long, just six years. Gossip had decided she was a marriage breaker and a gold-digger. That she had a career of her own didn't count. She was young and beautiful; she didn't kowtow to anyone and that made her suspect in their eyes.

The atmosphere in the house was tense. The Laurences were in trouble, financial or marital, or both. She'd noticed the sudden silence when she walked into the newsagents and the barista's covert glances in the coffee shop. Every morning there were more empty bottles clustered around the waste bin and the ashtray overflowed with cigarettes ends and cigar stubs. Her boss had been abrupt when Jen told her she would be taking time off. 'Make sure you get everything done when you get back,' she'd said, and Jen hadn't seen her since. She didn't know what was more unnerving; facing up to Mrs L's malice or worrying about why she was ignoring her.

Climbing the stairs to the boys' bedrooms, she noticed that the oak bannisters were sticky to the touch and the landing and the stairs needed hoovering. Small signs of neglect were everywhere. Once she would have taken pleasure in the warmth and shine of the wood. Impressed with the beautiful house, the tasteful décor, the modern kitchen and the bathrooms, she'd imagined sleeping in the master bedroom, keeping her clothes in the walk-in wardrobe, and entertaining guests in the formal dining room. Now all she noticed was that the bannister needed polishing.

The boys' bedrooms were a mess of clothes and plates of cold pizza, half-empty cups and glasses. Their jeans, T-shirts, sports clothes and underwear all came from high street stores. The Laurences were thrifty as far as the boys were concerned, although they spent a lot on their own clothes. Clothes were an important part of their image and looking after them was a vital part of her job. Not for the first time, she thanked the Cousins. Gifted teachers, they had trained her well, taught her how clothes worked and how to recognise and judge the construction of the garments she modelled. Under their tutelage, she discovered that she had a talent for hand sewing and fine work. When needed, she stood in for Mrs Cousins in the office and helped Mr Cousins entertain the buyers. Her skill set was wide and varied; she *had* been a professional, and a valued member of the Cousins' business; she must stop underestimating herself. There would be the right job for her, she just had to think more creatively. It was time she started looking around at what was out there.

She heard Mrs Laurence leave the kitchen. She was going for her run. Standing back from the window, Jen saw her emerge onto the pavement and set off towards the market. It was a change from her normal routine; she usually ran in the park. She ran with a long stride and perfect cadence, effortless and graceful; she was at her best when moving. Seeing her run was a pleasure akin to that of watching an elite athlete or a dancer and she watched her until she turned the corner.

Back in the basement, Jen sorted out the boys' laundry, loaded up the washing machine and started on the ironing. Spreading a shirt out on the board, she checked it for missing buttons or frayed cuffs. Ironing usually soothed her, but today she was agitated. She couldn't put off deciding what to do about Alex any longer. Gary had promised he'd speak to him, but he wasn't on the boat. Nor were the Brothers or their dogs. He'd had better luck with Mike, letting him know about Hayley's participation in the fight on the canal. Apart from that, nothing had changed.

The front door slammed; Mrs L was back. Instead of going up to her bedroom, she was on her way down to the basement. Jen shook out the shirt she'd ironed and examined it. Satisfied, she hung it on the clothes horse to air then picked up the iron and tested its heat. Mrs Laurence was at the door watching her, but Jen didn't look up.

'Jen, I'd like to ask you something.'

Ask, not tell. So not a harangue about her taking time off, or a complaint about her work. A puff of steam escaped from the iron as she stood it on its edge. 'OK, fire away.'

She wanted to know about the rough sleepers. She'd seen them outside the café in the market and wanted to know if there was a hostel or a centre they used. For one wonderful moment, Jen thought about introducing her to Maggie.

'Try asking at the library, or look at the council website,' she said instead, then shook out another shirt and thumped the iron down. Mrs Laurence turned away. By the time all the shirts were hanging on the clotheshorse, she'd left for work. Why would her boss be searching for someone among the homeless? It couldn't be more out of character.

'I think she's looking for her dad,' she told Gary later. 'He scares me and he scares Mrs L. If he's still around I need to know.'

*

The next day was bright and fresh, and a light wind blew through the landing window. Jen pretended to fuss with the curtain. Gary was sitting outside the café opposite, wearing a tracksuit and bright orange trainers. They looked like orthopaedic shoes at the end of his long skinny legs; he'd bought them so he could follow Mrs L on her run.

'I need to get fit anyway. I'll follow her, see where she goes. See if she finds who she's looking for.'

He came home complaining about his knees.

'She went to the market, and the hostel in Paddington Green, but she didn't go in. If she was looking for someone, she wasn't trying very hard. Why didn't you tell me she was training for the Olympics? I could keep up in the streets, but she shot off like a bloody greyhound as soon as we got to the park. My knees won't take it, Jen.'

It didn't matter; Mrs L was hungover and bad-tempered every morning but hadn't mentioned the rough sleepers or the hostels again. She resumed her normal routine: a run in the park, a shower and then off to work. Gary's expensive new trainers were left in the hall, for Jen and Angie to trip over.

Jen discussed leaving her job with Gary as he pottered about in her kitchen. Playing devil's advocate, he listed the benefits of staying where she was against the uncertainties of striking out in a new direction. 'It's an excellent job, and you were happy there until the father showed up. But now you're stressed out and unhappy. Maybe it's time to move on.'

She agreed. Apathy had kept her where she was and there was no place for apathy in her life now. Leaving the familiarity of her job terrified her, but she needed to think about her future. She knew the direction she wanted to take; something to do with clothes was vague, but it was a start, and she revisited her plans to have a look around the antique market.

Held in an old art deco building, the market was crammed with stalls. Several of them sold vintage fashion, and she browsed the rails in one of them. The quality of the clothes was fantastic, and so were the prices. A floral thirties dress cost £250, but it was pristine, the colours were as sharp and the material as crisp as when it was made.

'Won't fit you, darling, slender as you are. Waists were tiny then.' The woman sitting at the back of the stall was watching her. Jen summoned her courage and asked her if she needed any help.

The woman put down the piece of lace she was repairing. 'Go up to the café and bring me down a tea, and we'll have a chat.'

She didn't have a job for her; she dealt with theatrical and television companies or serious collectors, but she was generous with her advice. 'You've got a lot of experience; it should stand you in good stead. You could try for a job in the theatre. An internship. That's how I started, helping with the costumes. Anyway, love, keep in touch. I might need help in the future or know someone who does. I'm Iris.' She handed Jen a card with the name of her business – Vintage Fashion – and her details. Jen tucked it away carefully; Iris could be a useful contact.

Her phone rang as she was on her way home. By the time she'd fished it out of her bag, it had gone to voicemail. Gary wanted her to come to his flat: it was nothing to worry about, but she needed to see something. Intrigued but apprehensive, she abandoned her plans for struggling with the internet.

Gary opened the door before she rang the bell; he'd been looking out for her.

'What's so urgent?'

'While I was following your boss, I managed to get some shots of her on my camera.' He took her over to his computer. 'They're not brilliant, I didn't want to get too close, but look at this.'

He brought up a photo of Mrs Laurence. Without make-up and with her hair pulled back, her features stood out sharply, the bones prominent. 'Don't say anything yet.' He closed it and brought up another: the boys he'd photographed on the boat.

'I noticed the likeness straight away, and I merged the two photos. What do you think? Here, look now.'

On the screen were photos of the boys and Mrs Laurence side by side. The likeness was unmistakable.

'I need a drink.' While Gary opened a bottle, she examined the photo. The boys were a younger, less nourished version of her boss: the same bone structure, the same features.

'They must be related.'

'Do you think she might have been looking for them? There's more. Wait for it; it gets better.'

He brought up another photo. Now, two smaller boys sat alongside the older ones. He'd inserted a shot of Mrs Laurence standing beside the smallest boy. They looked ghostly, bleached by the light and almost transparent. Jen felt the hairs on the back of her neck stir.

'I don't know when the little ones showed up. They're related. It's a bloody family.'

The boys' closed and secretive expressions and Mrs L's obvious unhappiness reminded her of the photos she'd seen in old *True Crime* magazines. Her fingers ached from clenching her fists.

'They frighten me.'

'What are you frightened of? Those boys are victims. So is Mrs Laurence. That woman is suffering; look at her; you can see it in her face. The boys, too. They're more to be pitied than blamed.'

Chapter 15

Word on the street was that the canal boys were brothers. Gary dug deeper and quizzed Mike and Hayley and the men in the market: Their mother had died, an older sister left home, and their father had disappeared. The two older boys went into care and the younger ones were fostered out. The older boys, the ones that had caused so much trouble, distanced themselves from social services as soon as they were able.

'They've kept a low profile since the fight with the Averys,' he told Jen, 'and since the little kids showed up.'

Mystery surrounded the little ones. Gary suspected they had run away from their foster homes. It was a sad and sordid story, and one Jen had heard too many times.

'The other kids see them as outlaws, they protect them, idealise them. There are all sorts of rumours about them, especially the oldest one. Rebellious kids like Hayley and Adam see them as heroic.'

Gary seemed to have forgotten what they had done to Liz.

'The boys aren't our business. What about Alex, Gary?'

'Alex isn't trying to hold his family together, and he's not as visible as they are. He's not visible on the canal anyway. Not since the fight.'

'Could he have gone away again? Can't you find out?'

'And then what? Will you have a panic attack every time there's news of him? What's the worst that can happen if he finds out about Angie? I don't think Alex cares. If anything, he might worry you'll sue him for child support.'

But it was what Angie would think about her father that worried Jen. Would she see him as a heroic figure, rejected by her callous mother? Or romanticise him as she had when she was little? Jen still had one of the drawings she'd done then: a family, a mother and a father with two kids and a dog. She'd scribbled over the face of the father figure. Her poor little girl didn't know how lucky she was; an absent father was better than one like Alex.

And so it went on; thought chased anguished thought, ideas were examined and rejected, lurid scenarios imagined. Gary thought she was frightened to act.

'You're letting him hold you back, Jen. Face up to it; tell him and tell Angie and deal with the outcome; you'll survive, and you're not alone. You have me, and Mike and Sadie, to back you up.'

But it was her life that would change. Hers and Angie's. Gary and Mike and Sadie wouldn't be affected, but their life would be changed forever.

'My life is with you: what happens to you happens to me. And Mike might do something that would put him back in prison if he thought Alex would hurt you or Angie.'

'But we don't know where he is. We need to find him.'

'I'll get Mike onto it,' Gary said. 'He hears all the gossip on the market.'

*

They met Mike in his local. The pub was crowded and noisy, and they pulled their chairs closer to the table. Eager to share what he knew, Mike put his glass down and drew a notebook out of his pocket. He put on his spectacles and consulted his notes. Gary was grinning; Mike was acting like a fictional version of a private investigator.

'OK. The Brothers and Alex made some money up north. They were running a gambling scam in the casinos there. I trust the guy who told me. Kevin. He's an ex-squaddie, down on his luck, but he doesn't drink or get high. He looks after the dogs when the Brothers are away. The scam was Alex's idea and the Brothers put up the cash. Kevin said they were clever; they didn't go after a big win, not enough to draw attention to themselves, and moved around from city to city. They made enough for Alex to pay back his debts. I don't know where he is now, but the Averys are holed up in one of their properties.'

He sat back and chugged his beer as if the speech had made him thirsty. He watched them, his small brown eyes peering over the rim of the glass and waited for their reaction.

'Holed up?' Gary asked. 'Are they in hiding?'

'I don't think so.' Mike consulted his notebook again. 'They're in a flat in Praed Street. Alex might be with them. I'll give you the address. They're thinking about carrying out the same con in another part of the country. They're talking about the West Country. Plymouth.'

Closing her eyes, Jen laid her head against the back of her chair. The fruit machine hooted and burbled, coins clattered, and a woman screamed at her good luck. You made your own luck, or you put coins in a machine and took a chance. The stone in the pit of Jen's stomach lodged deeper; the bird trapped in her ribcage flew up to her throat. She breathed in slowly and breathed out. Concentrated on the feel of Gary's cool fingers on the back of her neck, the drone of Mike and Gary talking.

Her eyes opened and she sat up and slammed both palms on the table. Mike lurched back in his chair. Gary didn't move. A couple at the bar swung their stools around and settled down to witness a scene.

'Why would Alex stay with the Averys now he's paid off his debt? With money in his pocket, he won't need the Brothers. They can't take his shoes away, keep him on one of their boats or in one of their scruffy houses.'

'He likes to think big, he's greedy, and if he needs the Brothers to bankroll his next scam, he'll hang around.'

'I can't wait for that. I'll move, take Angie away.'

'Why should you? You're overreacting.'

The man at the bar sniggered and nudged his woman. Mike gave them the hard man's stare, fixed and implacable, and they turned back to their drinks and saucer of nuts.

'It's not about me. It's about Angie. Can you imagine what it would do to her if Alex claimed her? Mike, you have a daughter, you understand.' Beside her, Gary stirred; she must have hurt him, but she'd explain later.

'And she and her boyfriend are giving me grief. Gary's right, moving would be overreacting, and what good would it do? You'd have to leave everything you know. They might go away again soon. Plymouth, remember? And what about Angie's school? University?'

Everything he said shamed her. She would be running away. And she hadn't meant it. Moving had been an empty threat, born out of despair. She glanced at Gary. He was looking down at his hands. He and Mike were supportive, but it was down to her; they couldn't act for her. She had to talk to Angie before Alex found her, or she found him. She couldn't live like this any longer, not able to move ahead or make plans. But where to start, what to do? If she confronted Alex, her anger and bitterness might cause her to say or do something that would destroy any sensible outcome.

'Don't rush into anything, Jen. You and Gary talk it over. I'm with you, remember.'

Mike left them then, reminding Jen to call Sadie, and she and Gary walked home through the crowds. They'd stayed on after Mike left and moved into the restaurant for a meal. It could have been the effect of the bottle of wine they'd shared, but she felt calmer. Gary would never let anything bad happen to her or her daughter. She'd told him how much she trusted him, hoping to make up for hurting him earlier, and they both trusted Mike. They would find a way to end the uncertainty. She would plan and take advice before acting. Beside her, Gary faltered and missed his step, and she steadied him. But he hadn't tripped; he was staring across the road.

'That's the kid from the canal. Who's he talking to? I hope it's not what I think it is. He can't be that desperate.'

The boy's hood shadowed his face, but Jen recognised his skinny torso and limbs and the way he stood with his weight over the balls of his feet, ready to make a quick getaway. The man had his back to them. He turned under the light and walked away, but Jen had seen his face. The boy stayed where he was.

'Thank God, he turned him down. Predators see kids like him and think they're theirs for the taking.'

'It's not that, Gary. Not in the way you mean. That was Mrs Laurence's father.'

Gary was staring after him. 'Mr Pink? I didn't see his face.'

Jen was watching the boy. Whatever Mrs L's dad had said to him had punctured his bravado. He wiped his nose on his sleeve, and Jen caught the shine of tears on his face.

'Poor kid,' Gary said, and for the first time Jen saw the boy as he did, a desperate teenager who wandered the streets, on the lookout for any way to survive.

'They've got nothing. No parents, no money, nowhere to live,' Angie had said. Gary and Angie were compassionate by nature; she was learning from them, but it wasn't easy. They watched Mr Pink turn down a side street that led towards the Basin.

'Follow him, Gary. Find out where he goes. I won't come with you, he'll recognise me.'

Jen watched him go. He was soon lost among the crowds. The boy started to walk away, his head down, his hands thrust deep into his pockets. Whatever had frightened or hurt him must now be driving him on; he was purposeful, walking fast, going somewhere. She hurried after him. She might learn something.

Chapter 16

He turned into Paddington Station and she almost lost him among the crowds. When she caught sight of him, he was standing outside one of the concessions, and the other boy in the photo had joined him. Jen placed herself where she could watch them. Both were thin and dirty, and their unhappiness and resentment created an almost visible barrier around them. They exchanged words. Whatever he heard angered the younger boy, and he kicked out at a nearby newsstand. The older boy put his hand on his shoulder, and he calmed down.

They left the station by the Praed Street exit and took off, walking fast. They ducked into a shop doorway, and she risked a glance as she walked past. The younger boy was emptying his pockets and handing coins to his brother. They seemed oblivious to their surroundings. Staring into the window of a pharmacy, she waited until they appeared again. They passed behind her and into a fast-food outlet selling chicken and hamburgers. Peering around the signs offering two-for-one burgers, she watched as they counted out their money. The assistant scowled and checked the coins twice before handing over the carrier bags by his fingertips, ostentatiously avoiding contact. Even here, where the customers were poor or drunk, the boys were treated with contempt.

Clutching their greasy bags, the boys took off again, and Jen followed them. Their scuttling walk and the way they kept close to the buildings looked as if they hoped the brickwork would absorb their skinny selves. A police car sped past, the siren whoop-whooping urgently. For a moment she imagined turning the boys in for the muggings. Imagined them locked in separate cells in the 'central London location' that usually held terrorists and bombers. But the police wouldn't take any action without proof, and the boys had two hungry kids waiting for them to bring them something to eat.

She followed them until they turned down to the canal. The boat they were squatting on would be almost uninhabitable, damp and cold. They were suffering from hunger and a lack of love and shelter. It was no wonder they were hostile to the world of adults; they had no family to rely on, social services had forgotten them, and their peers either sneered or mythologised them. They lived outside any normal parameters and had to fend for themselves. It was a tough world for young people, and they had it tougher than most. But grudging admiration for them wasn't the same as sympathy. She knew she could never trust them, even as she pitied them.

'They were taking the food back to the boat,' she told Gary later. 'I'm surprised the Averys haven't made them leave. The younger boy must have been begging; they paid for it in loose change. They look half-starved.'

'If they're related to Mrs L, they may be related to Mr Pink,' Gary said. 'I saw him go into a pub and order a pint. His name is Ted Mason. I know the bartender; he told me he started drinking there months ago, and he gets chatty when he's had a few.

On her way to bed, Jen checked on Angie. Her room was chaotic, clothes everywhere, but she was asleep under a thick duvet, a half-empty mug of tea and the remains of a sandwich were on the floor by the bed. She was safe and warm; she had a home, and people who loved her, unlike the canal boys. She imagined them huddled over the food, eating it with fingers stiff from the cold and damp. But they weren't her problem; neither was Ted Mason or Mrs L; Alex was. While he was around, she couldn't relax; things can change, and disaster can come suddenly. She had to act before it was taken out of her hands.

*

A gang of skaters had taken over the courtyard outside Sadie's building and were sitting on the wall, their skateboards at their feet. They wore expensive jeans and looked self-assured and well cared for. Their cheeks were smooth, and their hair shone. Not so the boys squatting on the canal; their cheeks were pitted and sunken and their shoulder blades were as sharp as knives, their fingers as dirty as the coins they counted. One of the boys noticed her looking at them. 'She's scoping us out,' he said, 'she must be up for it.' Another grabbed his crotch and jerked his hips. 'Come here and bend over. I'll do you.'

She turned on them, her rage hot and sudden, and said unforgivable things about their sex, their looks, their parents. They were delighted, and threw the insults back at her, tenfold.

'Old bag, skank, suck my dick.'

She was glad when she entered the building and could no longer hear them or feel their eyes on her. Sadie answered the door in her robe, a towel wrapped around her head.

'Is this an inconvenient time?'

'I was about to phone you. Want a glass of wine? Hayley's here, with Adam.'

Jen was surprised; Mike disliked Adam.

'I'm keeping him close. He's too involved with the squatters on the canal. His parents are desperate. We can't follow them everywhere, but I don't believe in respecting Hayley's privacy now. I'd be daft not to keep a close eye on what's going on. My house, my rules and she knows it, and so does he.'

They heard Mike come in. He popped his head around the door. 'Hayley home?'

'In her room, with Adam. Check on them, Mike.'

Mike left, and they heard him knock at Hayley's door. 'He's brilliant with her. Teenage girls need a good male influence in their lives.'

It was a way in.

'I need your advice, Sadie, yours and Mike's.'

'Is this about Alex? Mike told me he was around again.'

'I've got to talk to Angie about him. I should have done it years ago. I've screwed up.'

'You made mistakes, get over it. You were a kid yourself when you had Angie. It's not easy to bring up a child alone.'

'I had you and Mike.'

'Not the same, love. Mike and I had each other, and I still had my mum when I had Hayley. You weren't much older than Angie is now. You did right by her, but it must have been hard. You must have been lonely.'

Jen watched Sadie towel her hair dry and hang the towel over the back of the chair. Yes, it had been hard. Mike and Sadie were her friends, but it was just her and Angie when she closed her front door at night. Wine and TV were no replacement for human warmth, for someone beside you when you woke from a nightmare. The years of loneliness until she'd allowed Gary back into her life were all too recent.

'I need to know how to approach her. I need to know the right words to use. I need advice. We've never sat down and talked about him in any depth, and she's stopped asking about him; I don't know how she feels.'

'Don't put it off. She'll have rights. Whatever you do, keep social services out of it.'

Young women armed with degrees and theories snooping into her life; a nightmare scenario, one she hadn't thought of. She hadn't thought about Angie's 'rights' either, not in the way they meant. She'd thought about her needs. Alex might have rights. He might see his daughter as someone who could provide the love or security missing in his life, and demand access. Or he might use her as he'd used her mother. But he had too much to hide; hopefully, he wouldn't risk coming to the attention of the authorities.

'Trust her. She would never choose him over you if that's what you're scared of. Forget the past; if you knew what I got up to before I met Mike, your hair would turn white. And what about my husband, the ex-con? Sort things out with Angie.'

Of course, she was scared Angie would choose him, and she was frightened about how she would appear to her daughter, past conversations lodged forever in her memory.

'You drove him away. Why won't you talk about him?'

'Because I'm glad he left. He wasn't good enough for you.'

'So what does that make you?'

Angie's scorn had silenced her and struck her mother through the heart.

'I need to know how to approach her. Rehearse strategies.' It was a word she'd heard on the radio or read in the newspapers. It felt foreign to her, and she felt false using it, but she needed to learn the language, to adopt the attitude.

They took their wine into the study, and Sadie logged on to her computer. She knew her way around the internet: Mumsnet and Net mums, parental advice sites, sites for legal advice, for fathers, teenagers. She gave Jen a lesson on how to use a search engine efficiently and made her promise to think about her way forward. 'Do it, Jen. Stop putting it off.'

The skaters were still sitting on the wall when she left, their heads bent over their phones. She ignored them. She'd come to a decision – she would tell Angie about her father, but not yet. She needed time to prepare and to do her research. To know all the possible outcomes. And she needed to find out what Alex was up to and what his plans were.

Chapter 17

Mrs L was leaving the house as Jen arrived the next day. 'We won't be going away this year. I've decided to go ahead with the deep clean. There's a parcel, take it to the post...' She enunciated each word carefully and walked away as if along a tightrope. She was acting like a sober version of herself. It was a mediocre performance, hammy and pitiful. Jen wondered if she was still searching for her father or the boys.

People wearing overalls took over the house. Although she only saw them once a year, she knew their names and that their lives were hard and precarious. Some of them stopped to chat with her. Sofia helped her lay out the tea and coffee cups for the workers.

'Remember Abel?' she asked her.

Jen nodded. 'The tall, shy boy?'

'Well, he's not with us now. He's back in his own country. He didn't want to stay here anymore. Poof, he's gone. Maybe we all go. Who knows?'

Jen left her and her team to their work and retreated into the utility room. As she mended seams and broken zips, she felt hopeful. A fresh start, a new beginning was a good thing and nothing to fear. The pile of clothes to be mended gradually diminished, those back to their best piled up beside her. Next, she climbed up to the top floor where the boys slept. She needed to go through their cupboards and sort out anything they had grown out of. A year ago, they had been awkward, blushing and shuffling, their voices rising and falling comically. Nourished by healthy food and exercise, muscular from playing rugby, they acted as if the world belonged to them. Older now and bolder, they made sexual comments about women in her hearing, daring her to respond. In revenge, she'd emptied their stash of grass into the toilet and flushed it away.

Their wardrobes were stuffed with clothes, and she put aside anything that looked too small for them and packed them into a sports bag. In the kitchen, she looked for tins of food that had slipped to the back of the cupboard or been stowed away on a high shelf. Sardines, ham, beans – healthy food that didn't need cooking and better than the diet of grease and gristle the canal boys lived on. An old-style can opener, one with a short, curved blade, sharp enough to stab through metal, caught her eye. There was a corkscrew secreted in the handle and something for opening bottles. It was rusty, and she cleaned it before dropping it into the bag. Tins of food were no good if there was nothing to open them with.

The workers had left for the day, leaving her to lock up. On her way out, she remembered the parcel. Tucking it under her arm and slinging the sports bag over her shoulder, she left the house and headed towards Praed Street and the post office.

The cost of the postage used up what little money she had, but her fridge was full, and there was most of the bottle of wine left from the night before. She put the receipt into her purse. Mrs L would reimburse her, she was scrupulous about that sort of thing.

She escaped into the street. The late afternoon sun lit the soot-dimmed facades of the buildings, but Praed Street would always be depressing. The hospital and a major railway station within yards of each other added to the air of transience; the people going about their business looked apprehensive and harassed. A footstep, the clink of a chain and a panting breath alarmed her, and she turned, ready to defend herself.

Close behind her, too close, were Joseph Avery and his brother, Daniel. Their dogs strained at their leads. For years she'd avoided the Averys, ducking away when she saw them in the street and had never made eye contact. Now she could see the blackheads on Joseph's nose, the stubble on Daniel's chin, the broken veins on their cheeks. Her mind stalled, and she stared at them stupidly. Joseph tugged his dog's lead. His hands were broad and clean, his fingernails clipped, and she caught the glint of a heavy watch on his wrist. They were watching her, the contempt in their close-set eyes unnerving.

'Didn't mean to scare you, love. You're Alex's girl, aren't you.' Daniel grinned at her, but Joseph remained unsmiling, his eyes gunmetal cold over the hard ridge of his cheekbones.

'I'm not his girl.' Her voice shook, and she took a breath and steadied herself. They weren't the Krays or the Richardson's, those legendary old-time villains, and not bad-boy estate gangsters; they were street-level hustlers who knew how to invest their money.

'I'm not his girl, but I need to speak to him. Can you tell me where he is? I've heard he hangs out with you.'

'We don't hang out with anyone.'

The dogs were waiting, pressing against their masters' legs and quivering with devotion. One of them sniffed at her feet and she wanted to scream.

'Give her a stroke, love, she likes you.' Daniel was the peacemaker; his smile was conciliatory. Even the dog was grinning. She could see the black leathery inner lips of her mouth, the sharp point of a yellow tooth.

'Come on, Daniel. Stop flirting with Alex's girl. Sorry. Gary's girl.'

They knew about her and wanted her to know that they did. The crowds broke around them, giving the men and the dogs a wide berth. Joseph frightened her, but she was determined not to be intimidated. She bent to stroke one of the dogs.

'Which is Gog, and which is Magog?'

'Hear that, Goggy, Moggy? You're famous. Old Milk Shake here knows who you are. Those two are Gussy and Flossy.'

Joseph shook the lead he was holding, rattling the chain. 'Let's go, Daniel.'

'I need to speak to Alex. If you see him, can you tell him?'

Joseph was already walking away. Daniel joined his brother. They stalked up Praed Street, the dogs leading the way.

The Averys knew too much about her, but she'd stood up to them, she'd stroked their dogs. Gog and Magog, named for mythical pagan giants, defenders of London, infantilised to Goggy and Moggy. Up close, they looked friendly and like any beloved pet. Their coats shone, and their eyes were bright and eager. Everyone knew that the Brothers were soft on their dogs, but not that they treated them like babies. There would be no swinging at the ends of leads to strengthen their jaws for Moggy and Goggy, no running on treadmills for Flossy and Gussy.

Exhilarated by the encounter, she hurried home. The Brothers' clothes were dirty, their matching suede jackets greasy and their jeans stiff and shiny with wear, but their hands were clean, their teeth and nails well cared for. And they didn't smell, unlike Maggie, whose odour came before her and lingered after. And Joseph was wearing a watch. Homeless people didn't usually have watches, not for long.

But they weren't homeless, she reminded herself; they were property owners and landlords. She had seen them up close and stripped of their mystique. Even the dogs were not as frightening as their reputation. She'd heard their bark, but she had never heard of them attacking anyone. The Averys were less than their reputation threatened. Or more than. You never knew with the Brothers.

Back home, she threw the sports bag onto the kitchen table and waited for Gary. He'd been against her talking to the Averys. Asking them about Alex was risky, but the words were out of her mouth before she'd had time to censor herself.

Gary surprised her.

'It might be the breakthrough we need. They might get in touch.'

'There's something else.' She emptied the sports bag and showed him what she'd taken from the house. 'I thought the kids could do with some decent clothes.'

'Change of heart, Jen?' He held a black parka up against himself. 'Wouldn't mind this myself. Won't she miss them?'

'I'll say I took them to the charity shop. She owes them something; I'm sure she's related to them. Even if she isn't, her stepkids' closets are full of clothes they've grown out of.'

Together, they sorted through the clothes and emptied the pockets. Gary held up a packet of Rizla cigarette papers. 'What do posh public schoolboys need these for?'

'Same as you. Not our business. What about this? Could it hurt someone?' She showed him the tin opener.

'Probably, but they might already have a knife. They're easy to get hold of.'

As well as the cigarette papers, they found money; pound coins from the pockets of jeans and anoraks, and a ten-pound note stuffed in the pocket of a denim shirt. A bonus for the boys, and they put the money back where they found it.

Adam had told Gary that the boys wouldn't accept charity. But what was begging but a plea for charity? Charity paid for their food from the chicken shack. But who knew what justifications they made to keep their self-respect? She'd made enough excuses for herself in the past; she was in no position to judge anyone else. They decided to leave the bag on the deck of the boat and hope that need would override pride. Watching from the street, she saw Gary tote the bag along the towpath, saw him hesitate and then throw it onto the deck of the boat. He waited for a moment, then joined her.

They were on their way home when they saw the boys heading towards the steps down to the towpath. The two younger boys were smaller versions of their older brothers, their faces pale and pinched, and if anything thinner than their siblings. The sharpness of their bones was visible through their joggers and T-shirts. They all carried takeout bags from Burger Heaven. Their pores must exude grease, living as they did on cheap takeaways. She imagined them finding the bag of clothes, trying them on, arguing over them. Or tossing them out, to lie muddied and abandoned on the towpath.

The boys were a mystery, almost spiritual in their desire for self-sufficiency and isolation. Even the feral kids who had the run of the estates kept their distance from them. They were taking on a mythical status. The market traders, less easily spooked, made jokes about the older boy, but Lee knocked on wood when he was mentioned. They hadn't seen him wipe his nose on the back of his hand and rub the tears from his face like a five-year-old.

Chapter 18

The example set by Sofia and her friends motivated Jen. They'd risked leaving their countries in the hope of a better life; now they may have to leave it all behind, and yet most of them seemed determined to fight on.

She had the old computer in her room and she fired it up and reeled through pages of job descriptions, training courses and degrees. Unable to copy a document, she steeled herself to ask Angie to show her how.

Angie was at her desk and positioned herself between Jen and the screen.

'Mum, do a course. Stop asking me.' Jen caught a glimpse of her Facebook page, but Angie closed it down before she was able to register it. She picked up a book from the desk and pretended to examine the cover.

'Everything OK, Angie? You're not worried about anything, are you? I hardly see you these days.'

'I'm OK, Mum. Don't fuss.'

Before she left the room, Jen glanced back. Angie was watching her, her face as blank as a dish, but her shoulders were, curved in towards her centre protectively. Angie was hiding something. Questioning her wouldn't work; she would just roll her eyes – as if, whatever – and give nothing away.

Now Jen wished she'd followed through with her decision to check her online presence. The adolescent Angie had grown into a confident girl with her eyes on the future. It was a balancing act; respect her privacy but insist that Angie was more open with her. Sadie made a point of monitoring Hayley's movements, but Jen was sure she didn't know as much about her daughter as she thought. No parent did. Angie was settled now, she had a goal – university, a career, and she wanted to travel. If she suspected Jen didn't trust her, it would undermine their relationship. But there were dangers out there. She pictured the boys outside Sadie's house, the way they'd grouped around their phones, sniggering, and heard again the vicious words they'd thrown at her.

She went back to her research but stopped when Gary came in. He leaned on the back of her chair to see what she was reading. They read in silence until Gary pointed something out to her: suggestions about an internship or voluntary work at a theatre or film company. 'I can ask around. I know some of the people at the Tricycle.'

'Mum?' Angie had crept into the room while he was talking. 'Can you come and have a look at my Facebook? It's not much, but I don't know what to do.'

Gary's smile faded. Jen felt sick. She touched Gary's shoulder to reassure him and steady herself before she followed Angela back to her room.

'I don't know what to do.' Angie was vibrating with tension.

Jen knew. Semi-literate technically but psychic where her daughter was concerned, she knew.

'Mum…'

'Now.'

Angie hesitated; 'I'm sorry mum, I kept these,' she said then turned on her Facebook page. And there it was: a photo of her wearing her mother's clothes, the clothes she'd worn while she was with Alex, the clothes he'd chosen for her. 'Me in my mum's clothes.'

The messages, three in total, seemed innocuous at first reading. He called himself Retro Boy.

'You look good, Retro Girl.'

'Clothes are great. Mum must have been hot. Does she have a name?'

And then the last message, the least of them, simple and brief, but the most menacing, hinting at intimacy.

'Hello, darling.'

'That one came just now.'

Jen tamped down the fear and kept her voice steady.

'Unfriend him, or whatever it is you do. Who is it?'

'I don't know. I thought he was OK at first. I wanted to know why he asked about you. I don't like it; it's weird. Can we let Gary see them?'

Gary had followed her into Angie's room, carrying two mugs of coffee. He handed one to Jen and sipped his while scrolling through the messages. 'Retro Boy sounds more like Retro Man. Don't bother replying. Just unfriend him, Angie, and block him.' He was casual and Angie visibly relaxed; her shoulders dropped, and her colour returned.

Jen took her cue from Gary and remained calm.

'Let us know if he gets in touch again. Finish now, it's late.'

As soon as she and Gary were alone, she let her fear surface.

'Why is he asking about me? It must be someone from my past. She looks like me, especially when dressed in my clothes.'

'It could be, and it could just be someone messing with her head, trying to manipulate her. It's what they do, these people.'

They were both pretending; she knew who it was and was too frightened to face it and he was protecting her.

'It's not him, Jen.'

'It is. Hello, darling?' And she was back by the canal, the early morning light, the dank air, the shock of his greeting. 'He wants me to know. It's a message.'

Gary picked up his keys from the table and slipped them into his pocket. 'I'm going to find him. I'll talk to the Brothers; they'll know where he is.'

His face was flushed, the lines on either side of his mouth deeper, his jaw set. She wanted to hold him by the sleeve, stop him from leaving, take his keys out of his pocket and hide them away. If Alex or the Brothers hurt him, it would be her fault.

'Let me come with you.'

But he was determined to go alone. 'You'll complicate things.'

She heard him walk along the landing and the thud of the landing door closing. He was a gentle man, not quick to anger, but he'd fought Alex once, he might fight him again. The two most important people in her life were threatened, because of her weakness.

'Where's Gary going?' Angie was standing in the doorway. In her PJs, and her face scrubbed clean, she looked young and vulnerable and sounded subdued.

'Up to his flat, he's working.' The lie came easily; she wanted to distract her, to create an atmosphere of normality. 'Come and have a look at this.' Jen logged back on to the job descriptions she'd been reading. 'Tell me what you think.'

'Are you leaving the Laurences'?' Angie was biting her nails, something she'd never done before. Jen pulled her hand away from her mouth.

'Not for a while.'

'Hey, this sounds great. Wardrobe Supervisor? I've never heard of it. You should do it, Mum. You could work in films or on TV. How cool is that.'

'I'll need to do a course.'

'We could study together. I'll help you.' She yawned, stretched, and then bent to kiss Jen's cheek. 'Do a computer course, at least. Night, Mum. Love you.'

Her daughter seemed to have recovered from her shock. Jen turned on the television and watched the news, hoping to distract herself, but she couldn't concentrate. She gave up and went to bed. She was trying to read when Gary returned. He looked tired but unharmed.

'Did you find him? What did he say?'

'I didn't see Alex, but I found the Averys' hanging out in Praed Street. Alex is staying in one of their flats. They agreed to set up a meeting for you and him tomorrow afternoon.'

He undressed and crept into bed beside her.

'I think I should come with you.'

'Not a good idea. There's too much history between you and Alex.'

' You never told me why you beat him up. What did he do?'

Gary looked surprised. 'He stole my camera. My first. I'd saved up for it. We got over it, but I couldn't trust him after that.' He put his cold feet under her legs, warming them. 'How's Angie? Is she OK?

*

Mike was against meeting Alex, Sadie was for it; their argument raged back and forth. Jen and Gary were reduced to spectators. Worn down by Sadie's patient reasoning, Mike gave in, as long as he could be nearby. 'Just in case.'

'There's no need. He's not violent.'

'Desperate men can change, Jen.'

Jen was suspicious of Mike's motives. But let them gang up, she thought, they may be right. She was exhausted, sleep-deprived and stressed. She'd been moving towards a dramatic finale, albeit reluctantly, and now it was close: a meeting with a man she barely recognised. Their affair had been short, yet the threat he represented had hung over her life for years.

She mustn't falter, she must look him in the eye and let him know who she was now, and see for herself who he was. The years might have taught him something, as they had taught her, but she doubted it. She'd seen him humiliated, dragged along the street, his feet barely touching the ground; but he was an addict, and addicts learn to cope with humiliation and abuse. To ignore it or to reshape it into something they can live with. However often he'd lost in the casinos or at cards, he believed the next game would be the one that would bankroll the next enterprise. Night after night she'd listened as he outlined his plans for a business venture or a scam, all dependent on the next big win.

He was riding the euphoria of a successful gamble when they met; he was high on success and flush with money; she was bored and resentful. Their infatuation had struck them simultaneously; she was as much a danger to him as he was to her. They had brought something destructive out in each other, a six-month-long psychosis followed by months of revulsion. Wounded by past rejection and failure she hadn't recognised the shadow that lay behind his glamour. As it was, she was hypnotised by him, a willing victim. He was an opportunist and had used her inexperience to mould and exploit her. But she'd also seen an opportunity and grabbed at it. And that was her responsibility.

Chapter 19

Reg Cousins had pointed out the men to her. The younger man was dark and striking, his suit a miracle of tailoring. He looked as if he could be an actor or someone she'd seen on television or in *Vogue* or *GQ*, advertising expensive watches or luxury cologne. His colleague was homely, and as broad across the shoulders as a boxer. Reg hung the clothes she was to show on the rail: outdoor wear first, day and evening wear to follow. He turned her face towards the light. 'Nice but do something dramatic with your hair.'

Jen shrugged on a long black coat, well cut and sharply tailored, then pulled on knee-length black boots. She'd drawn her hair into a high ponytail, kept her skin pale and her eyes understated. Lily, the head tailor and her mentor had frowned – too subtle – but nodded approval when Jen painted her big mouth and full lips scarlet. The effect was dramatic and suggestive. Lily straightened the shoulders of the coat and tugged at the sleeves. Satisfied, she gave Jen a little push. 'Go on, girl, do your best. We need their business.'

Lengthening her spine and throwing her shoulders back, Jen stepped into the showroom. Modelling is acting, and she channelled the fifties society models she'd seen in old copies of *Vogue*: haughty, cold and untouchable. Mr Cousins hovered over the men, paying court, eager to close the deal. He glared at her and mimicked a smile, but he was wrong; she wanted to create a drama, a small piece of theatre for the man in the beautiful suit. The man was relaxed, his long legs crossed, his fingers linked and resting on his thighs. His colleague was stolid and watchful, a minder to a prince.

After the black coat the camelhair, left open to show an aubergine silk blouse, tucked into black trousers. The man watched her, while his colleague took notes. Occasionally they would lean toward each other and confer. Then her favourite, and a bestseller, the trouser suit. Her legs were long and slender in pinstripe wool, and the boxy oversize jacket slipped off her shoulder, showing a glimpse of a low-cut chemise. Next, Lily helped her into the narrow slip dress, pale and subtle and as revealing as nightwear.

Pausing at the door to the showroom, she held her pose for a little longer. She wanted him to see her, not the dress. He met her gaze, challenging her. She walked, and the cool satin on her thighs felt like a breath. Turned once, twice, and the brush of her ponytail against the bare skin of her back made her shiver.

The showroom door swung closed behind her, and she stumbled into the bathroom. Had her pose been seductive or ridiculous? Had she just made a fool of herself? She rested her forehead on the mirror and the dampness of her skin misted the glass. Lily knocked on the door. 'Hurry up, they want you in there.'

Jen wiped off most of the makeup and splashed water onto her face. Pulling on her leggings and tying the laces of her trainers brought her back to herself, and she walked into the showroom.

The men turned to watch her and she smiled, although her lips trembled. Reg introduced the two men to her. Alex had bought up the lease of a shop in fashionable St John's Wood High Street, and there was talk of a second shop in Finchley. Mike, his colleague, was a silent partner. Alex congratulated her on her presentation and asked her questions about the clothes, then turned away. Mike ignored her. She listened while Reg plied the men with information and statistics; he was hoping for a substantial order. The men continued to talk business and left her to hover on the edge of the group, holding an empty glass. Humiliated, she made an excuse to leave. Alex smiled, shook her hand, but hardly glanced at her.

Could she have been mistaken? He had seemed more interested in her than the clothes. Lily had seen how confused she was.

'Didn't take much notice of you, did he?'

Her words were harsh, but Jen knew she wasn't malicious. She shrugged, but her friend wasn't fooled.

'I know a chancer when I see one,' she said. 'He's a slick character, that one.' She was examining the dress, checking that it was still pristine. 'I saw the way he was watching you. You weren't mistaken. He'll try it on. He'll find a way to ask you out.' She hung the dress on a hanger. 'If he does, say no. Reg doesn't like his staff fraternising with the customers anyway.'

She didn't care what Lily said. Lily was old, at least forty. She was jealous. So what if he was playing her; if he asked her out, she would go. And who she dated had nothing to do with Reg. She'd forgotten how secure she'd felt in his employ. 'No hanky panky here, darling,' he'd said. 'Not from the customers, and not from my girls,' and she'd felt safe and valued. But that was then, and now safety had become boring. She wanted him to look at her again, she wanted to look at him. To see him. Her longing would slam into her without warning, leaving her bent over and panting, and kept her turning restlessly in her bed at night. She had to find a way to have him.

*

Later that week he was back. Jen was standing in her underwear while Lily and her assistant fitted a dress to her body. Peering through the frosted glass of the workshop window, she watched Reg usher him into his office. Lily unpinned the dress and handed it back to the tailor. 'It needs to come in a touch at the shoulder,' she said, and they moved over to the sewing machines.

Jen dressed, repaired her make-up and brushed out her hair. Reg had arranged to have lunch with a buyer later, so his meeting with Alex wouldn't take long. The door to the office opened and the two men walked out. Reg always walked his customers to the lift. They must have made a deal; they were shaking hands and smiling. There were businesses on every floor, people coming and going all the time and the lift was slow. If she was quick, she would catch Alex on his way out.

She left the workroom and hurried down the back stairs and into the street. She was there, at the front of the building, pretending to be on her way in when he pushed his way through the revolving door. He didn't seem surprised to see her.

'I was hoping to meet you again,' he said and took her arm. 'Fancy some lunch?'

He'd booked a table at a restaurant on Charlotte Street. They didn't talk on the way to the restaurant, didn't touch, and their glances towards each other were loaded with risk. The waiter led them to a table for two and seated them, toadying to Alex, fussing over him, but barely noticed her, seating her without looking at her.

Over lunch, they talked about his new venture. He loved clothes, he told her and loved fashion. He'd thought about opening a men's clothing shop, but his partner had persuaded him that there was more money in women's fashion. She fixed her gaze on his hands, on his mouth, and thought of dark rooms and heat and damp, rumpled sheets.

He leaned over to wipe a fleck of cream from her lip. 'He doesn't know much about clothes, but he does know about business. We're looking for someone to run the shop, someone who understands what women like. Would you be interested?'

Of course she was interested. She was tired of being a hanger for the clothes she modelled, tired of the overweight old men she showed them to. Tired of the way their hands stayed just a second too long in the small of her back, and how they always, always, looked at her breasts. 'Yes,' she said. 'Yes. I'm interested.'

He'd laughed and written down his number on the napkin. The woman at the table next to theirs had picked up her glass to drink and stared at Alex over the rim, ignoring her companion.

*

She left the job she loved and the people who tutored and supported her. Left security and kindness for glamour and uncertainty. Refused to be moved by Reg's disappointment in her, or by Lily's barely concealed scorn. Left behind her damp room in Bayswater and the landlord who looked like a serial killer in bedroom slippers for a flat in St John's Wood and her place by his side and in his bed. The job selling clothes to wealthy housewives didn't last long; business was slow, and she was bored.

'You're wasted in the shop anyway. You can help me entertain my clients. Chat to the wives, that sort of thing.'

By day, he coached her: how to dress, how to wear her hair, how to talk to the men he introduced her to. In bed, he laughed at her clumsiness, her inexperience. He led her, and taught her the things she needed to know; she was greedy, for him, and for sex. Their battles lasted through the night and left them both wrung out and hateful. She wasn't sure if she wanted him or needed to conquer him but knew she would never love him. She watched his hands as he dealt the cards, his mouth as he lied, and her desire became cold and determined. Saw how he listened and sipped his drink, while others gulped at theirs. Women and men drew close to him, and she watched him turn them away. Sitting beside him, seeing the spiteful glances towards her made her feel powerful.

Their obsession with each other had taken a dark turn. 'Do it for me,' he'd said. 'It will help me, and I'll make sure it's safe.'

'Do what?' she asked, although she knew; she wanted to pin him down, to force him to put what he wanted into words. He did. There could be no misunderstanding, and she agreed to do what he asked. 'You don't need to sleep with them. But if you do…' and he'd shrugged. 'It's up to you.'

He'd woken something in her and she wanted to see how far she would go, wanted to know how it felt: sex with strangers, without strings, sex for the sake of it. On my terms, she told herself, even though he chose the men. At the very least, a West End show, a meal in a nice restaurant. It was up to her if she wanted to take it further. Her choice.

The first time was easy. No show, but dinner at a fashionable restaurant, and a drink at the hotel bar before he led her to his room. Money hadn't been part of the deal; Alex hadn't mentioned it, and she hadn't asked, but it had been there, a thick roll of it on the bedside table. She'd seen it as she undressed, and it thrilled her. It was there later when she stepped away from the bed and the man lying there. The man, swarthy and inscrutable, picked up the cigar that he'd left to smoulder in the ashtray and watched her dress.

She didn't look at the money, but it was in her peripheral vision as she watched him sit on the bed to put on his shoes. Without a glance at it, he shrugged on his coat, gave her a peck on the cheek and left. She heard the lift doors shut. She waited, standing by the bed. Five minutes. Ten. He wasn't coming back. The money was hers. She snatched it up and sat on the bed to count it. Whatever arrangement Alex had made with the man, this was her money, and she was determined to keep it. The next day, she opened a bank account.

It happened again, weeks later. This time the man handed it to her, wordlessly. And then again, and again, and the thrill was gone, and it became just a transaction, money for sex. Until one night, reaching for her clothes, she caught the scent of cigarette smoke, a glimpse of grey shantung, the sleeve of a jacket. She thought she'd imagined it until she found the nub of a spent cigarette on the windowsill. Camel. Alex's brand. 'I thought you realised, Jen,' he'd said when she challenged him. 'I want to get something out of it. Why else would I pick your men for you?

It was over. There was no slow withdrawal. 'No more,' she told him, and he'd shrugged. They turned away from each other then, lived together yet apart. His disappearance had been a relief, had forced her to start again. But even years later, the scent of Camel cigarettes made her nauseous.

Chapter 20

The flat in Praed Street was above a minimart. It smelt of washing left too long in the machine and dirty socks lurking under beds. Two sofas covered in plastic faced each other on either side of a coffee table, and two widescreen monitors, a printer and a paper shredder were set up as a workstation against the back wall. Alex might have sent the messages to Angie from here.

The Avery Brothers sat side by side on the sofa opposite hers. Daniel was studying something on his laptop. Joseph was silent and inscrutable. He looked as if he was grinding his teeth; he caught her eye and flexed his jaw. All four of the dogs were ensconced on a blanket surrounded by rubber bones and squeaky toys.

The Brothers were an enigma; they let people believe they were homeless, yet they owned property, looked like throwbacks to another era yet were comfortable with technology.

'Do you live here?' she asked Daniel.

'Sometimes. Not now.' He didn't look up.

'It's noisy, isn't it? Paddington?'

He shrugged. 'Lively, I'd call it.' His brother slid his eyes towards her and then stared at the wall.

Jen gave up her attempt at social chit-chat. She wanted to open the window to let in light and air, but she'd have to get past the dogs first, and it might alert the Brothers to the men across the street. She'd seen Mike outside the pub opposite, chatting with Lee and Hamid. He was definitely up to something. Gary wasn't with him.

She lit a cigarette, her second in the half-hour she'd been waiting. Where was Alex? Although she was dreading seeing him, she wished he would turn up so she could say what she had to say, do what she had to do. It was one thing to see him from a distance, another to be in his company. He may not be the glamorous man he once was, but ruined beauty told an intriguing story. She had to trust herself; keep her head and not allow him to goad her or lead the conversation; she had to keep her cool.

Alex had kept up appearances until recently. Lenny had mentioned a beautiful suit and an expensive watch, but appearances could be deceptive; the suit might have been the only one he owned and the watch a fake. And what did glamour mean but enchantment? He'd enchanted her and, for a short while, she'd believed in him. How foolish she'd been, how young and greedy, how deluded to think she understood his motives, let alone her own. Even now, years later, she struggled to understand their behaviour then. But she was losing herself in the past. This meeting was about the present, about the future of her daughter, and to find out if Alex had sent the messages; and if so, what he knew about Angie.

The bell rang. The dogs growled, lifted their heads and stared at Joseph. He clicked his fingers, and Gog and Magog followed him out of the flat. Gussy and Flossy stood side by side, ears twitching, watching the door. 'Stay,' Daniel said, and they dropped onto their haunches. He closed his laptop. Jen struggled to swallow, her throat working frantically. She'd forgotten to bring water.

The street door opened and shut, there were two sets of footsteps on the stairs, a low murmur, a laugh cut short, and then they were there, Gog and Magog leading. Joseph hovered in the doorway and Alex shouldered his way in.

He looked at her, a dark flash, his eye a camera. The shock of his gaze was unexpected; she'd forgotten how compelling it could be. He sat on the sofa opposite her, his long fingers plucking fastidiously at his trouser legs.

'Hello, darling.'

'Hello, Alex.'

A drop of sweat slid from Jen's hairline and into her eye, and she blinked it away. The Brothers were fussing with the dogs' leads, clipping chains onto their collars.

'All right then,' Daniel said.

They left, the dogs panting, the thump of the Brothers' boots loud on the stairs. There was a rush of noise from the street as the front door opened, then slammed shut, leaving them alone.

Marooned on separate sofas, they examined each other. The silence was as unnerving as a shout. Alex crossed his legs and rested linked fingers on his thighs. For a moment, he looked as he had in Reg's showroom; dark, beautiful and dangerous. With a shock, she felt the lurch deep in her belly, the thickening of her blood. Her mouth filled with water, and she swallowed. Her mind and her eyes were playing tricks on her, her body replaying old feelings, a mental and physical flashback, a memory of heat and pleasure. But the man sitting opposite her was not the man she'd longed for. Not the man who'd beguiled and manipulated her. This Alex was down at heel and defeated.

'What's all this about then, Jen? I'm surprised you wanted to meet. You've ignored me so far.'

'I didn't recognise you. You've changed, Alex.'

He looked her over, judging her. She was conscious of her market stall jeans and cheap trainers, her naked face, grey with fatigue and stress, and hands reddened by housework.

'You're not doing so well yourself, are you? Working as a cleaner, I hear.'

'Housekeeper,' she said, then cursed herself for correcting him. 'Better than working for the Averys. Or are they your new best mates'

They were goading each other, hoping to wound, to force a reaction. They had fallen into old patterns within seconds of meeting again. After all her determination to stay in control of her anger, she'd lost her better self.

'You left everyone in the lurch, Alex. I'm surprised you had the nerve to show your face back here.'

'What do you care? You did well for someone so bloody uptight. You should thank me. I taught you all you know.'

'Don't kid yourself…'

'You wanted what I gave you. All of it. The sex, the men, the money.'

'So what? I was young and greedy... just a kid.'

Quit while you're ahead, she told herself, before this goes any further. Don't let him lead. Alex was broken, a busted flush, to use his language. He would never be part of her and her daughter's life. She would fight him; she wasn't a lonely, unhappy girl anymore, and she had friends.

'I needed to acknowledge you. We live in the same area; it's too awkward to pretend we don't know each other.'

'I thought you wanted to talk about our daughter.'

It came so suddenly that she thought she'd imagined it. He held up his hand as if to silence any denial and she shrank back into the sofa, her tongue as thick as felt in her mouth. He was smirking, thinking he had the upper hand. She wanted to pick up the heavy glass ashtray on the table and smash it into his face. But her arms were leaden, she couldn't move them. This wasn't how she'd thought it would be; he'd snatched control from her and left her without weapons.

'Did you think I wouldn't find out?'

'She's not yours.'

'Calm down, Jen. I only want to meet her. Just once. I won't even speak to her if you don't want me to.'

He'd changed tactics: from arrogant and threatening to obsequious and wet-eyed with sentiment. He would do or say anything to get his way.

'I told you. She's not yours.'

She turned to leave, but he gripped her wrist.

'Whether you like it or not, Jen. I'm going to meet her.'

She pulled her arm away, and ran out of the room and down the stairs, bumping into boxes of toilet rolls and washing powder, and stumbled into Praed Street.

Supporting herself against a wall, she caught her breath. Oblivious to the traffic or the people hurrying past, she didn't see Gary and Mike standing in a doorway, didn't see Lee and Hamid. Nothing existed for her but the clamour in her head. Gary hurried across the road, followed by the others.

'What happened?' Gary held onto her arms and examined her face. 'Did he hurt you?' She shook her head.

'Are you all right, Jen?' Mike turned to Gary. 'Is she OK?

'He knows,' she said. 'He knows about her. He wants to see her.'

'Is he still up there?' Mike didn't wait for the reply. 'Stay with her, Gary, tell her.'

The door had shut behind her, but he put his shoulder to it and disappeared up the stairs, followed by Lee and Hamid.

Snapping his fingers in front of her face, Gary brought her out of her trance. 'Did he tell you?'

She shook her head and tried to speak, but Gary went on. 'Hayley told him about Angie. I phoned to warn you, but you'd turned your phone off.'

She'd lost before Alex had walked into the room. While she brooded over the past, he had come fully armed and sure of his victory. While she had examined and judged him, he'd waited for the right time to confound her. And he had; he was a skilled poker player, someone who understood the odds and knew the risks and the rewards. But her daughter was not the reward, and he hadn't factored in the threat from Mike, or her closeness to Gary. Grabbing at Gary's wrists, she steadied herself. There was still a chance that they could beat him.

Chapter 21

It wasn't finished yet. She followed Gary up to the flat. Alex was on the sofa, a tissue held to his nose. Mike stood over him. Lee and Hamid looked awkward but held their ground by the door.

'Four of you? I'm flattered.' Alex dabbed at the blood seeping from his nose.

'We need to sort this. Not here. Come on, Alex, we need to talk this through.' Mike was robust and confident. Beside him, Alex looked old and sick. He stood, leaving a smear of blood on the plastic cover of the sofa.

Gary was at the window, scanning the street. He nodded. 'All clear.'

Mike carved his way through the crowded pavement, followed by Lee and Hamid walking on either side of Alex. Anyone watching would see a group of men returning to work after a late lunch in one of the pubs or burger bars. Jen and Gary brought up the rear.

'I didn't have time to let you know,' Gary told her. They were walking fast. 'I only found out an hour ago. Mike has a plan; he's got Liz's keys; he's taking Alex to her flat. You must talk to Angie. We'll keep Alex out of the way until you've had a chance to speak to her. Get to her before he does. Hayley swears she hasn't said anything to her. Sadie took away her phone and is keeping her and Adam in the flat.'

Jen could see dandruff on Alex's shoulders, and an incipient bald spot blinking through the black curls. An ambulance passed them, its siren gasping out a final warning as it neared the hospital. There was too much noise, too many people. She kept her eyes on the men in front of them, frightened that Alex would break away.

'Hurry up,' Gary said, 'we're falling behind. We must keep up with them. Mike thinks he might make a run for it.'

'What's to stop him calling out for help?'

'Mike let him think that they might reach an agreement, some sort of deal, but it won't take him long to catch on, though. He's told him Lee and Hamid are part of his plans, but they're there to distract him.'

They caught up with them at the crossing under the flyover. If Alex was going to break away, he would do it while they waited for the lights to change. Moving closer, they formed a tight little group, curling around him like a fist, Mike blocking his way from the front, she and Gary behind, Lee and Hamid on either side of him. Lee and Hamid were talking, telling jokes and keeping Alex occupied. They all crossed over the road. Alex was walking faster. Hamid caught at his arm and pointed something out to him, trying to divert him.

They reached Liz's building. Mike was waiting by the lift. Alex tried to break away and opened his mouth to shout out. Mike slapped his face.

'Shut up, you idiot,' he said. 'What do you think is going to happen? We just want to talk.'

'You go up, we'll follow you,' Gary said. He waited until the lift doors shut and they were out of earshot. 'Mike's going to lock him up, but he can't keep him there for long. You'll have to talk to Angie tonight.'

The lift returned and Lee and Hamid shot out, grinning. 'We'll leave you to it,' Lee said. 'Call if you need us again.' He was wiry, swift on his feet, a good man to have on their side. Hamid, stocky and muscular, nodded in agreement. 'Heard about him, never seen him. Bit of a let-down.'

The lift juddered up towards Liz's floor. Mike let them into the flat and hurried them into the sitting room. Alex was standing by the window, staring out at the building opposite. Mike went to stand beside him, all heft and muscle and false bonhomie.

'Not much of a view, is it? You could see into the flat opposite if the curtains were open. The family there keep themselves to themselves. Nice little Bangladeshi family.' He took Alex by the elbow. 'They won't help you, and we're on the fifth floor here. Come and sit down.'

He was enjoying himself, and Jen felt uneasy; he'd taken over, and he hated Alex. The men had settled themselves at the kitchen table. They didn't belong there. It was Liz's table, where she sat to do her crosswords. Jen opened a cupboard; the teapot was there, and so was the biscuit tin. Liz would come back, and the men would leave, and take Alex with them. Everything would be all right, everything would return to normal, and she and Liz would sit at the table and have tea and gossip.

The men were talking, taking turns – Gary's voice light and questioning, Mike's deeper, accusing, and Alex's scornful and provocative. It was happening, the scenario she'd imagined; her humiliation of the man she detested. It wasn't how she'd imagined it; she felt removed from the action, apart and alone. Under the harsh light, the men looked like caricatures of themselves: Alex white and clown-like, his features stark, his lips too red, dark rings around his eyes, Mike ruddy-cheeked and confident, Gary detached and sombre. They had taken over, spoken for her; she had to make her voice heard.

'What do you want, Alex?' Her voice broke through the rumble of the men's questioning. They turned towards her.

'You know what I want. I want to meet my daughter. I want you to admit she's mine.'

'Why?'

'I'm her father…'

'What does that mean? What does father mean to you?'

He started to speak, but she interrupted him again.

'Love her. Protect her, support her. Clothe her and feed her, house her. Keep her safe. That's what fathers do. That's what Mike does. What Lee and Hamid do. It's what the dad in the flat opposite does. Brought his kids here so he could keep them safe and give them a future. Is that what you want to do? What sort of future do you imagine for her?'

Alex stared at the wall behind her head. Mike stood up.

'We're done. You'll stay here, Alex. Just for tonight. The phone is off, there's cereal, tea, milk and biscuits. You won't starve.'

'Stand up, Alex,' Gary said. 'Empty your pockets.'

'What for?'

'Just do it.

Alex fumbled in his pockets and brought out his belongings reluctantly. Spread out on the table they were a stark metaphor for all he stood for; a phone, a keyring with two keys, a ten-pound note and coins in a woman's purse, and a betting slip from William Hill. He had no driving licence and no bank cards. Gary checked the phone, then scooped everything up and put it in a plastic zip-lock baggie.

'Now take off your clothes and shoes. You can keep your underwear.'

'Fuck's sake, Gary, there's no need for this. What do you think I'm going to do; kidnap her?'

He looked around the room, as if for an escape.

'Come on, Alex, get it over with.'

Alex kept his head down as he unbuttoned his shirt, struggling with the buttons, his bony fingers shaking. Jen watched the bend and flex of his knuckles, the pale nails. He stripped down to his underwear. She looked away, repulsed.

Gary took his clothes and put them into a plastic bag. He handed back the socks.

'Jen, can you get something for him to wear from the bedroom?'

Liz's bedroom was cold, the curtains were drawn, and the covers on the bed were pulled tight over a sagging mattress. The Alex of bespoke suits and handmade shirts would have hated it here but compared to the damp boat or the threat of the Averys and their dogs in Praed Street, it was dry and safe. An old towelling dressing gown hung on the back of the door.

Alex took the dressing gown from her without making eye contact. Faded and worn, the hem of the gown flapped around his kneecaps. His hands trembled as he tightened the belt. He thrust his feet into Liz's carpet slippers, watched by Jen and the two men. His shins were thin and lumpy with varicose veins, and the kneecaps wrinkled. Mike snorted but couldn't suppress his laughter. Gary remained expressionless.

'Abduction. Unlawful confinement.' Alex found his voice, goaded by Mike's laughter. 'Still the same fucking hard man, you. When did you last have to use your fists? Phoney bastard.' He turned to Gary, blustering and spraying saliva. 'You haven't changed either. Saint fucking Gary…' He stopped talking; his nose had started to bleed again. 'Jen. Please.'

He surely didn't expect her to help him.

'Get into bed if you feel cold,' she said and followed the men out. She shut the door and Mike locked it.

'I didn't hurt him earlier,' Mike said. 'I slapped him, that's all. I must have caught his nose. He was sounding off about his rights. I'm sorry about Hayley. She must have heard us talking.'

They were running from the image of Alex humbled and frightened, dabbing at the trickle of blood from his nose. A man reeled out of the pub on the corner and stumbled into them. Mike gave him a gentle push. The others walked around him. They didn't talk again until they walked into the light and warmth of Mike and Sadie's home, into the comfort of central heating, soft furnishing and warm lights. Liz and Elsie were on the sofa, their feet up, a bottle and glasses on the table in front of them.

'How did it go?' Sadie put down a platter of chicken, and Elsie poured the wine. 'Hayley's out. Adam's dad came to get him, and she went with them. I couldn't stop her.'

Jen's knees gave way, and she almost fell into the nearest chair. Closing her eyes, she fought back the tears; she mustn't give in to weakness now. However uneasy she felt about capturing Alex, they'd bought themselves time. Mike had taken it upon himself to lock him up and he was right; it would keep him out of the way until she could talk to Angie.

He's had it, mate.' Mike stripped the meat off a bone and wiped his mouth. 'He'll never claw his way back to his old self.'

Sadie egged him on, and Liz and Elsie joined in, their cheeks flushed. They sprawled back against the cushions and kicked off their shoes, and talked over each other. 'I keep thinking of him wearing your dressing gown, Liz,' Mike said. They stopped laughing when Gary mentioned the contents of Alex's pockets.

'Is that all? Ten quid and a betting slip?' Sadie said.

Surprised by pity, Jen poured herself more wine. Gary came and sat by her; Mike was still laughing, flushed and exhilarated by success. 'Don't worry about Alex,' he called over. 'He's probably used to being locked up.'

'It gives us time, Jen.' Gary sounded as uneasy as she felt. 'There was nothing to stop him from confronting Angie. We don't know what he would say to her, what he wants from her. It was his message on her Facebook. Retro Boy. Remember? Angie and Hayley in your clothes?'

'As if I could forget. I'll talk to Angie, prepare her. If I let him meet her, I'll tell him it must be official. That should put him off.'

Gary watched as she dialled Angie's number; he listened as she told Angie to get home; she had something important to discuss with her. He watched as she dropped the phone; saw her close her eyes and slump back in her chair.

'What is it? You're scaring me, Jen. What is it? What's happened?'

'We're too late. She knows. Hayley told her.'

Chapter 22

The skaters were sitting on the wall outside the building, their boards leaning up against their shins. They looked up from their phones and watched them walk past.

'Do they know about him? Does everyone know?'

'How could they? Anyway, who cares what they know,' Gary said. 'They're just kids.'

There was no such thing as 'just kids'. Just kids could wreak havoc on their own and other people's lives. Just kids could be dangerous. Adam and Hayley were just kids. Gary led her into their building, and they climbed up to her floor in silence. He unclasped her fingers from his sleeve and held her hand in his. 'Call me when you've talked to her, but this is between the two of you.' He waited until she reached her flat, and then stepped back into the stairwell.

Alone, Jen felt the full import of what she was about to face. Had Hayley told Angie the facts – bad enough – or a spiteful version of her own? The walk down the hall to her daughter's room seemed to take forever. Angie knew she was coming; she wouldn't have gone out, yet the flat felt empty, the silence ominous. Bracing herself, she knocked but didn't wait. She opened the door.

Angie was reading something on the computer and listening to music. Pulling off the headphones, she turned to Jen. She seemed composed; there were no tears, no anger, and no confusion. It was unnatural, and Jen felt wrong-footed; she'd prepared herself for a battle, for accusations and insults.

'Angie? Are you OK?'

'Were you ever going to tell me? Did you think I wouldn't find out?'

Turning back to the computer, she brought up a photo of Alex on the boat, and then scrolled down to a message from Hayley: 'Meet your wasteman dad, you loser.'

The camera had caught Alex unaware and looking straight at the camera. Slouching on an upturned bucket, barefoot and with his trousers rolled up, he looked romantic – an elegant gipsy. Distance lent him glamour and mystery, the father Angie might have dreamt of, even longed for.

'Is that my dad?'

She was nibbling at a nail, her hair hiding the sides of her face. Jen pulled herself together. Whatever was said or done in the next few minutes would affect the rest of their lives.

'Yes, it is. Look at me, Angie.'

Jen reached over and pulled her hand away from her mouth. Angie looked back at her coolly.

'He looks like me. We look alike.'

'I told you that.'

'Not much else, though. OK, Mum. Spill. The truth. All of it.'

Jen told her, and the telling released something in her; the words tumbled out, recklessly. Words she'd hoped she would never have to say. She told her how she'd met Alex, their infatuation with each other and how quickly that infatuation had died. It was a story she'd told her before, forced out of her over the years, word by reluctant word, fragments and sentences. Now it was a narrative, the story unfolding, with a beginning, a middle and an end, like all stories. A story her daughter was old enough to understand. A story that Jen needed to own. But she didn't tell her everything; it was too soon for total honesty. She was entitled to her privacy. And she didn't want to demonise Alex; that could turn Angie against her.

'He didn't abandon you. He didn't know about you.'

She had told her this too, at various times and in diverse ways.

'*He doesn't know you exist, and if he did, he wouldn't care.*'

How cruel she'd been.

'I found out I was pregnant after he left. I looked for him, but he'd disappeared.' Angie was looking at the photo of Alex on the boat again.

'What was he like when you were together?'

Jen went into the bedroom and brought back the photo album. She showed Angie the photo of her and Alex in the nightclub.

'You've got his looks and his brains.'

Angie was turning the pages of the album, and Jen examined the photos with her, trying to see herself and Alex through her daughter's eyes. 'This was us in Paris, and here, in Brighton.' Hand in hand and smiling, they looked happy, young and beautiful, confident that they would be rich and popular, and envied for their looks and their smarts.

'Hey! That's the jacket you gave me.' Angie was looking at the photo of her and Alex sitting outside a café, Jen in her fake fur and Alex chatting up a couple of girls. 'He was gorgeous, you both were. How old were you?'

'Seventeen, eighteen. He was older, in his twenties.'

'What happened to him? How did he end up in such a mess?'

'I don't know. He was unrecognisable when he came back here. Even Gary didn't recognise him, and they'd been friends for years.'

'You said he didn't like having his picture taken. Why didn't you show me these before? Why were you so against him?'

'He was an addict.' Angie looked up, scowling. 'Not drugs. Gambling. He would have messed up both of our lives. I wanted you to have a stable life. A normal life. I knew he was back, but I hoped he'd go away again, and he did for a while. He may be back for good now. Or he may leave. I wish I knew.'

She paused; steeled herself. Angie looked up from the album.

'He wants to meet you.'

Jen recounted her meeting with Alex.

'I suppose I'll have to.'

'Only if you want to. Do you?'

'I don't know yet. I feel a bit numb. Shocked, I suppose. I'll think about it.' She clamped her headphones on.

'Can we talk about this later, Mum? I've had enough now; I really do need to think about it.'

Jen felt rejected and dismissed. She'd wanted to stay, to talk more, but Angie had shut it down and made it clear she wanted to be alone. Jen turned to go, reluctant to leave. She glanced back and tried again. 'Angie…'

'No. Mum. I mean it. Leave me alone.'

Her voice was muffled, but she had turned back to her computer and Jen couldn't see her face. She left then, and walked back to the kitchen, her legs shaking.

She called Gary, and he came down.

'How did she take it?'

'I don't know. She led the conversation and seemed to take it well. She wants to think about meeting him. I hope she decides against it.'

'At least it's out in the open now. Maybe Hayley did us a favour.'

Hayley couldn't have known the harm she would do. Or maybe she did. Whatever her motives, her actions had changed everything. She needed to talk to Sadie.

Sadie sounded as if she'd been shouting or crying when she answered the phone; her voice was croaky. 'I don't know where Hayley is. Ask Angie. Mike's gone out to look for her. I'm waiting for him to call.' She hung up abruptly, cutting Jen off.

'What did she say?' Gary was frowning, clicking his lighter off and on; he was as anxious as she was.

'She's looking for Hayley.'

Ignoring the 'keep out' notice on Angie's door, and hoping to catch her unawares, Jen walked into her room. Angie was sitting on her bed, reading something on her phone. Jen shot a glance at the computer: a screen saver, no messages, no Facebook.

'What do you want, Mum? You're supposed to knock.'

'Are you hungry? Gary's going out for a takeaway. Have you heard from Hayley? Her mum's looking for her.' Keeping it casual, taking her cue from her daughter.

'I haven't, and I don't want to. Amina's coming over. Can she eat with us? Tell Gary she's veggie.' She'd turned back to her phone before Jen had closed the door.

Where were the tears, the accusations? Why wasn't she upset about the news about her father? Jen hovered, uneasy and unsure, then walked back to the kitchen.

'How is she?'

'Says she's hungry and acting as if nothing has happened. Amina's coming over. I don't understand it.'

Amina was with Gary when he came back with the food; they'd met on the way in. Usually so polite, Amina didn't greet Jen and avoided eye contact. Angie came out to meet her, and they spooned food onto their plates and hurried back to her room, balancing their plates of food and whispering.

Gary waited until he heard Angie's door shut.

'Angie has known about Alex for a while. Before Hayley sent the photo of him and the message. I heard Amina talking to her on the phone. She didn't see me, but I was walking right behind her. I heard her tell Angie "At least you know for certain now".

Jen felt sick. It was impossible. 'How? She can't have done,' she said. But she wasn't so sure; Hayley's betrayal might have been a slow process. All it would take would be a hint to the kids on the towpath, in the streets, and at school. Stories told and secrets whispered, questions asked.

'The Creepy White Boys are hiding from the police and social services; they're on the run. The man hanging out on the Brothers' boat is Angie's dad.'

Then gatherings on the canal. Time for mischief, cider, spliffs and stoned laughter. Rumours sent out into cyberspace for 'friends' to pick over and laugh at, to add to and send on. And Angie, aware, if only subliminally, of the hints, the sly looks and pointed remarks. Drip by drip, a slow trickle of malice. Until the photo and the messages, jolted her into awareness, leaving only Hayley's final message to confirm the truth.

Across the table, Gary picked at his falafel, gave up, and pushed his plate away. 'Poor kid, she must have been so confused. She didn't show it. Why didn't she come to you?'

Angie had been testy at times, talking back and arguing, but Jen had put it down to anxiety about her exam results, or petty arguments with girls or teachers.

'I've made a complete mess of things.' She was remembering a child's drawings. Crowns, swords and cloaks. Heroic deeds. My dad. Is this him? Or this? The faces of father figures in drawings were scribbled out and obliterated.

They heard Angie's door open, then shut. Amina was leaving. She passed the kitchen and flung a hasty goodbye over her shoulder before hurrying out.

'I'm going to talk to Angie. I can't wait. I need to know what's going on.'

'Hang on, Jen. Give her time.'

He was right. She switched on the computer and logged on. Gary joined her. An hour later, they sat back. According to all the information websites, the dad forums, the mum forums and the legal sites, Alex had no rights. Jen's was the only name on the birth certificate, and there was no personal responsibility agreement from the father. If Angie wanted to meet Alex she could allow it, but she should have legal backing.

'He's not going to agree to a "controlled and gradual process". Counselling and mediation won't appeal to Alex.'

Jen agreed; Alex's aversion to anything official would work as a threat, a weapon they could use. Everything would depend on what Angie wanted. The thought of her daughter meeting Alex sent her heart spiralling, and she panicked, pushed back her chair and stood up. Gary called out, but it was too late. Jen ran down the passage and threw open Angie's door.

Angie spun around to face her. Her eyes were swollen almost shut and her cheeks were wet and looked raw. She was suffering. Jen went to her, wanting to comfort her, but she pulled away. The photo album was face down on her lap.

'How long have you known, Angie? Why didn't you come to me?'

'I didn't know for sure; no one came right out and told me until Hayley did. I hate him. I don't want to meet him.'

She was lost, her words punctuated by shuddering breaths, her unnatural calm shattered. She scrubbed at her eyes and the photo album slid to the floor.

'Hayley's been saying horrible things about him. Telling everyone…' She choked on the words, unable to go on.

'Telling them what? She's probably making it up.' Jen wanted to put her hand over Angie's mouth and stop her from saying the words.

'Is my dad a sex slave for the Brothers?'

It was so ridiculous, so utterly wrong, that Jen laughed, her laugh verging on hysteria, and cut off when she saw Angie's face. 'She's making it up, Angie.'

'Her dad said—'

'Alex owes the Brothers money. He works for them so he can pay them back. Ask Gary or Mike; the Brothers aren't involved with anything like that.'

'What sort of work?'

'Something to do with casinos and gambling clubs, him and the Averys. He might do other things for them, but nothing to do with sex.'

'She said he was spying on the creepy white boys for the Brothers.'

The boys. Jen had forgotten about them. 'Maybe he was. I don't know. But I promise you, your dad is no sex slave.

Angie blew her nose. 'I don't want to go back to school. Everyone will be talking about it.'

'It will all be forgotten about by then.' Jen picked up the album. 'Don't you want to give him a chance?'

'Why? We've done all right without him. I don't want anything to do with him.'

Chapter 23

Angie had gone to bed early and slept a full ten hours, but Jen had hardly slept. She waited for her to wake up so she could take her breakfast in bed.

'I'm not sick, Mum. You don't have to make such a fuss,' she'd said, but Jen had wanted to spoil her, to treat her like the hurt child she was. She'd left her tucked up on the sofa, watching a film.

Mike was waiting for her and Gary outside their building. He was subdued. His precious little girl could be vengeful and spiteful, and his wife wasn't talking to him. Hurt and disillusioned, he'd lost his swagger and was silent in the lift going up to Liz's flat. He opened the door and she and Gary followed him into the bedroom.

The air in the bedroom was stale. Alex lay on his back, his hands folded on his chest, his profile austere and saintly.

'Is he OK?'

'He is fucking freezing.' Rising like a spectre from a coffin, Alex sat up and reached for the coffee and doughnuts Gary was carrying. He ripped open the bag and bit into the doughnut. 'No proper food, no heat. That's cruel and unusual punishment. I haven't committed a crime.' He gulped at the coffee.

Jen had to admire him. Gary and Mike looked as shattered as she felt, but Alex looked rested. His ability to make the best of whatever life threw at him was admirable. A weaker man would have crumbled by now. Physically weak he may be, but he was mentally tough; he could survive any amount of abuse, rise above it, and still be able to spot weakness in his abusers.

Gary offered him a cigarette and lit it for him. 'It was just one night, Alex, and you look as if you've had a good night's sleep. When did Hayley tell you about Angie?'

'A couple of days ago. I'd seen her around, but she was just another kid until Hayley messaged me.' He looked at Mike. 'Great kid you've got there.'

There was a sneer implicit in the words. But Mike had recovered his bravado and refused to rise to the bait.

'I didn't need her to tell me,' Alex went on. He'd recovered from the humiliation of his capture. 'I would have found out, eventually. It's like looking at you when we were together, Jen. Not now. You've let yourself go.'

She ignored the insult – he was in a far worse state than she was.

'It's not about me. This is about Angie, and she doesn't want to meet you.'

'She said that, did she? You know for sure?'

'We've discussed it. Your name's not on the birth certificate, but if you insist on claiming her you'll have responsibilities.' She handed him the articles Angie had downloaded. They had read and discussed them together. Angie had dried her eyes and blown her nose. 'Maybe I'll meet him when I'm older,' she'd said, 'after uni, maybe. Not now.'

Alex glanced at them and put them to one side.

'You'd better read them before you start making demands. It's what she wants that matters; her needs come before yours, or mine. Give it up, Alex, there's nothing in it for you. If you insist on going through with making a claim, we'll put it in the hands of the courts. You'll end up having to pay child support for the last sixteen years.'

Not that there was much chance of getting any money out of him, and she wasn't sure that what she said was true, but she hoped the threat would be enough to put him off.

'Who's we? You and Gary?'

'Angie and me. She's very mature for her age, she knows her mind.'

'Have you told her everything?' It was a desperate ploy, and one Jen was prepared for.

'I've told her everything she needs to know about either of us. She's still a child, Alex. What were you hoping for, anyway? What did you expect?'

'Nothing. How could I? I've only known about her for a few days. It was a shock.'

Mike had been silent, leaning against the door as if he expected Alex to make a run for it. Now he stepped forward and held Alex's face, squeezing his cheeks until his lips bulged out in a fishy pout.

'Stay away from Angie, and from Hayley. There are eyes on you. Go near either of them or Jen, and you'll be done for. Trust me.'

'OK, OK.' Alex choked out the words. No violence, Gary had said, and she and Mike had agreed, but she could see how effective a physical threat could be. Alex's eyes were popping, and his bare feet slid about on the floor as he tried to free himself. He clawed at Mike's hands and kicked out at his shins. Mike let go, and Alex clutched at his face, coughing dramatically.

Gary handed him the bag holding his clothes. Something shut down in him then. Jen recognised that look. It was how he looked when he gave up on a stubborn punter or an unsuccessful scam and cut his losses: a wry twist of the mouth, a lowering of the eyes. Knowing when to quit was one of his strengths. He rummaged about in the bag, drew out his shirt and started to dress, ignoring them, toughing it out, acting as if he didn't care. It was a brave attempt, but they all knew he had lost. Jen wondered if he had ever been serious about becoming part of Angie's life. If he'd seen an opportunity and tried his luck.

Gary handed him his shoes. 'What do you plan to do?' he said.

'That's for me to know and for you to find out.'

'Whatever it is, take it out of the area,' Mike said.

Alex put on his shoes, ready to go. He turned his back on Mike. Malnourished, he matched Mike in height but was half his girth, half his heft. Mike snorted and shifted his feet. 'Go away, Alex. There's nothing for you here.'

Alex shrugged. Mike was vibrating with suppressed fury, hunched, as if ready to pounce.

Gary stepped between them. 'You've forgotten these.' He handed Alex the documents.

Alex stuffed the papers into his pocket. 'I'll read them later.'

Mike took hold of Alex's sleeve, the material crushed and bunched under his thick fingers. 'We'll walk you back to Praed Street. Joseph and Daniel are waiting for you.'

Alex pulled his arm out of Mike's grip and straightened his jacket, trying to take back control.

'Angie seems a nice kid, Jen,' he said. 'Not sure about the fat one, though.'

'Angie *is* a nice kid. She's doing well at school; she has a future. Don't mess it up for her. Walk away.'

They left him outside the mini-mart and the entrance to the Praed Street flat. Mike had arranged for someone to change the locks. A small turbaned man stared out at them through the cloudy shop window. Mike handed Alex the new keys.

'I've given a set to the Averys. They have plans for you. Good luck.'

They watched him fumble at the lock. His hands were shaking but he managed to open the door and shut it behind him. Upstairs, the Averys would be waiting, sitting on their plastic-covered sofas, the dogs at their feet.

'Sadie wants me out of the way,' Mike said. 'She's going to talk to Hayley. Let's find somewhere for coffee, somewhere quiet, away from here.'

They found a café on a side street and ordered breakfast. Jen knew the street well; she'd been living in a bedsit in one of the squares between here and Westbourne Grove before she met Alex. From where she was sitting, she could see the dome of Whitley's shopping centre. She'd spent hours there, wandering around the franchised shops or sitting next to the indoor fountain. Surrounded by people and yet alone, she'd watched the antics of the groups of teens from the Hallfield Estate and couples window shopping. She'd felt conspicuous yet inconsequential, as if she hadn't mattered to anyone. She looked across the table; Mike and Gary were slumped in their chairs, exhausted. She mattered to them and Liz and Sadie. Whatever happened next, she knew she could count on them.

The waitress brought out their coffees. Mike tore open the sachet of sugar and sprinkled it over the foamy surface of his latte. She'd ordered a double espresso, hoping the caffeine jolt would wake her up.

'I spoke to Kevin last night,' Mike said. 'The Averys are planning to leave for Plymouth soon. Alex is going with them.'

This was good news. It would give her and Angie time to talk things through, to make plans, to protect themselves if they had to.

'He still needs the Averys; they're bankrolling the job on the coast.

'How long will they be away?' Gary rubbed at his eyes; he hadn't slept either and he was smoking too much.

'Don't know. Still, it keeps him away from Angie for a while, at least. I'm sorry she had to find out about her father like that, Jen. She must have heard us talking.'

'She knew, sort of. All the kids did. Nothing stays secret for long. I should have done something about it as soon as Alex came back.'

'It doesn't excuse her. We're thinking about sending her away until school starts again, get her away from Adam.'

Another reprieve. Hayley and Alex would be out of the picture. But distance meant nothing. Jen pictured the computers in the Praed Street flat, Daniel's laptop, and their phones.

'I don't trust Alex. He'll always be a threat.'

Gary was playing with his lighter, clicking it on and off. Mike wiped his lips and threw down the paper napkin.

'True, but you've got breathing space. Anything might happen on the coast. He might give the Averys the slip.'

Not if there's a chance of making big money, Jen thought. He needed the Brothers and they needed him, a synergistic relationship that could make or break them. Their sortie up north might have been small-time, a rehearsal for something bigger. It worked then; it would work again. The gamblers' fallacy. Alex was clever, and he would be relying on this trip to the coast to set him up for good.

'Maybe he won't come back at all.' Gary was turning the lighter around in his fingers.

Mike stirred in his seat and looked sideways at him. 'What do you mean?'

'Not that, Mike. Are you mad? No, maybe they'll make a lot of money, and Alex will go back to his old life, forget about Angie.' He put his cigarettes and lighter away. 'Maybe they'll be caught. Who knows?'

But Jen knew it wasn't the end Mike and Gary thought it was. It wouldn't end until Alex left the area. He would be there, in the flat or on the boat, in the streets where her daughter lived. But now Angie knew about her father, and he knew about her. The thing that she'd feared had come about but it wasn't the disaster she'd thought it would be. Angie didn't want to meet him, and he had other things on his mind. All the same, it wouldn't do to be complacent. Alex was nothing if not predictable.

Chapter 24

Jen hadn't seen Mrs L for weeks; she'd left the house before Jen arrived. It was a relief not to have to face her spite and despair every morning. She'd left another message telling her not to open the door to anyone. Not that she needed reminding. There were too many doors, too many rooms, and the creak of a door or the wind rattling the glass of a window would stop her as she reached up to a cupboard or climbed the stairs. Fixed in place, as still as a child playing statues, she'd wait, her senses alert for the thud of a footfall or the shadow seen out of the corner of an eye. Being on constant alert was stressful but hardened her resolve. She'd decided to give in her notice before the new school term began.

She walked into the kitchen and stopped. Dressed for work, her coat hanging on the back of the chair, her briefcase by her feet, Mrs L was waiting. In front of her on the table was a scrap of paper and some money. She had the tense expectant look that Jen recognised; she wanted a confrontation.

'I owe you for this.' Mrs L tapped the post office receipt. Jen had forgotten about the money she was owed. She reached for it, but Mrs L put her hand over it.

'There's something else. What happened to the clothes you took from the boys' room? Did you take them to the charity shop?' She sat back and folded her arms. 'Or did the cleaners take them? Should I speak to them?'

It was a trap, juvenile but dangerous.

'They wouldn't do that.'

'So where are they? They must have done. Unless you took them. You know you should check with me before you take anything.'

It was a chance for her to confront her boss. If she was wrong and there was no connection between her and the canal boys, she would deal with the fallout.

'I gave them to some kids who needed them.'

Jen waited for a reaction. Mrs L stared back, expressionless.

'What kids? And who are you…' but she stammered to a halt.

'Brothers. Four of them.' Jen scooped up the money on the table and stuffed it into her pocket. 'The two older boys look after the young ones. I thought you wouldn't begrudge them the clothes your stepkids have grown out of.'

She waited to see the effect her words would have. Mrs L kept eye contact as if she hoped to intimidate her into silence. Jen refused to drop her gaze.

'They're starving. The older ones are begging or stealing. They'll get caught or taken advantage of. Something bad will happen to them if it hasn't already.'

'What's that got to do with you or me?' Mrs L shrugged and turned away, her hand groping blindly for the cigarette packet on the table. It was a turning point, and Jen plunged on.

'I thought you might know them. Your father knows them. I've seen him talking to the older boy.'

Mrs L crushed the cigarette packet and made a fist, her knuckles white. She stood up, and her chair fell to the floor. Her briefcase slid under the table.

'You need to leave. Now.'

Jen closed in; it was what she'd been waiting for. She was in control, and she was unforgiving. 'How *is* your dad? What does your husband think of him?' She watched as Mrs L struggled to right the chair. 'Has he met him? Have you had him round for dinner or introduced him to the neighbours?'

Mrs L was kneeling, reaching for her briefcase.

'Do they even know about him, Emily?' Dizzy and triumphant, Jen pushed on. 'About you?'

'Get out. I don't want you in my house.'

'I don't want to be here.'

Mrs L looked up at her, her face contorted, bubbles of spit gathering in the corners of her mouth.

'Get out, or I'll have the police throw you out.' Panting, she grasped the handle of her precious briefcase and started to draw it towards her. Jen kicked it out of her reach. Left her on her hands and knees and walked out.

Her legs shook as she climbed the basement stairs and into the hall. What had she done? She opened the front door, and the transition from the dimness of the hall to the glare and noise of the street felt as shocking as a punch to the head. Weak and dazed, she held on to the railings by the steps. She had to stop and get her breath. Everything in the street was the same and yet looked false, cinematic and unreal. There, on the corner of the square, the police officer kept a lookout for terrorists or madmen. Outside his shop, the coffee merchant smoked a cigarette and chatted with a customer. The Filipino housekeeper sweeping the steps of the house next door smiled at her and nodded, as usual, and she smiled and nodded back, as she always did. They had never spoken. It was too late now to ask her name, too late to learn about her life.

Too shaken to walk home, she went into the café, ordered a coffee, and took it to a stool by the window. It was hard to believe that she had shut the door on the last five years, and so violently. All that preparation, the months of uncertainty; the discussions, and the research into her next move looked ridiculous now.

She wondered if Mrs L was feeling as shocked as she was. Then, as if she had willed it, Mrs L strode past the window, as immaculate as always. No one would believe she'd been crawling about on the floor minutes ago. She paused before she crossed the road and looked both ways, then walked briskly towards the underground station. There was no hint of the trauma she had suffered earlier. Anyone watching her would see a glamorous and successful woman. If they knew her as Jen knew her, and if they passed close to her, they might notice a tremor in the hand clutching her briefcase, and the desperation in her eyes. Jen fought back her pity. Mrs L had brought her misery on herself.

What now? Where to? Her days had been shaped by her job. Every day for five years she'd left her world to become part of the Laurences'. She ordered another coffee, took it outside to one of the tables and lit a cigarette. The Laurences had been decent employers, they'd respected her, and she had admired and respected them; their occasional lapses were forgivable. They didn't pretend to be her friends, unlike their neighbours, who feigned an interest in the lives of their staff but bragged at how little they paid them. Until Mrs L's father had come to the door, she and Mrs Laurence had a good working relationship, distant and impersonal, but one that suited them. But it was done, in the past. There was no going back.

She left the coffee shop and started to walk. Walking calmed her and allowed her to marshal her thoughts. Compassion for Mrs Laurence had replaced anger. Now she regretted her cruelty. Mrs L was a woman weakened by guilt, fear poisoning her every moment. Jen knew how that could taint everything you did.

Her phone rang. It was Mrs Laurence, and she let the call go to voicemail. The message was brief: Could she call around this evening? Or she could come to her. She didn't want their relationship to end so unpleasantly. Jen put the phone back in her pocket. Still raw from their confrontation, she would wait until her emotions cooled before making contact.

Lost in thought, her feet had taken her to the bridge over the canal. She leant over the railing and peered along the towpath; it was deserted, the boats locked up and dark. She remembered the boat where the Brothers kept their dogs and recognised the tin bath full of bricks and rubble. The Averys hadn't chased the boys away. After the fight about the dogs, it would have been the obvious thing to do. They must have their reasons to keep them close. Cardboard covered the windows, but she could hear voices. The voices got louder, and the door to the cabin opened. Jen stood back; they wouldn't see her, but she had a clear view of the boat and the path. One of the older boys stepped out onto the deck. He was wearing the black parka Gary had admired.

Soon the other boys appeared and joined their brother. They were all wearing something she had taken from the Laurence's house. Dressed by Gap, and by Adidas and H&M, they looked identical to any of the boys who hung around outside McDonald's, except the clothes hung off the younger boys, dwarfing them. Their trainers were falling apart, but there was nothing she could do about that. They all needed a bath and a decent meal, but they looked comfortable in their borrowed clothes. The risk she'd taken had been worthwhile, but the unease she'd felt earlier returned. The pay cheque at the end of this month would be the last.

The keys to the house were still in her pocket and she curled her fingers around them. She would post them back through the letterbox, but not yet. She needed to see Angie, to cook her favourite tea, still a fish finger sandwich, despite Gary's efforts to educate her palate. She needed to see Gary. To tell him all that had happened. To mend her friendship with Sadie. Her showdown with Alex had been agonising, but she'd got through it, and she would get through this. All she needed to make a new life was the belief in herself and the support of her friends. Emily Laurence would be fighting her demons on her own.

Chapter 25

For years she'd resented the urgency of her mornings, of getting Angie off to school and the rush to get to work. Now she had more time than she needed, and the novelty of sitting around in her dressing gown, reading and drinking tea had worn off.

Everyone she knew had a purpose. Her friends and her daughter were engaged with something that excited them: Angie was out all day, enjoying freedom before exam results, sixth form and A levels, Liz had left her job in the launderette and she and Elsie were discovering the countryside in Elsie's old Morris, visiting gardens and taking tea in village teashops. Sadie had taken Hayley to stay with relatives in Devon, and Gary was still immersed in his Nomad project.

She was restless, longing to move on but with nowhere to move to. The part-time courses she'd enrolled on didn't start until September and her application for a job in the local theatre had been unsuccessful. Too much leisure was tiring and left her with time to brood, to castigate and then forgive herself for the way she'd left Mrs L, and so she'd set up a routine: exercise, a walk to the market and a visit to Iris before settling down in front of the computer to search for a job.

She finished her breakfast, grabbed a towel and bathing suit and set off for the local fitness centre. Except for the few regulars bombing up and down the fast lane, the pool was quiet, and she ploughed along for twenty lengths, enjoying the power in her limbs, and the strength of her shoulders. Keeping the Laurence house immaculate had been demanding, and had made her strong, but swimming toned her arms and legs and gave them shape and definition. She was less tired in the evenings now, and less eager to open a bottle of wine. Turning onto her back, she closed her eyes against the sun that slanted through the glass panels of the ceiling. The echo of a child's voice from the baby pool and the splashing of water as a swimmer passed her in the adjoining lane chimed like music in the humid air. She surrendered herself and let the water hold her, suspended, apart, and totally at rest.

Later, energised and buzzing from the exercise, she walked to the antique market. Shameless in her need to learn, she'd courted Iris, developed a friendship and responded to her endless requests for tea and cakes. In return, Iris had taken her through the stock and let her examine the clothes and accessories. She'd introduced her to some of the other traders and taught her what defined fifties collectables or sixties kitsch, the difference between streamlined art deco and ornate art nouveau. Today she was mending a lace collar on a blouse. She used a contrasting material and placed it under the hole in the lace, lined up the edges of the tear and pinned them carefully, and then looped her thread in and around the edge of the tear. All while filling her in on the latest gossip. Before Jen left her, Iris gave her a sample of lace with several small rips.

'Have a go at mending it and bring it back next time.' Iris enjoyed teaching Jen – it gave her eyes a rest, she said – and Jen was happy to be taught. She'd never worked with lace, but it looked simple enough. She would like to have a stall of her own one day but it would be a long time before she had the money and the ability to take her place among the dealers and traders.

On her way home, she took a detour past the Brothers' flat on Praed Street. Although persuaded that Alex wouldn't try to contact Angie, she wouldn't relax her vigilance until he left the area for good. The flat looked abandoned, the curtains half-drawn across the windows; she couldn't tell if the Brothers and Alex were there, or whether they'd left for Plymouth. She bought a drink in the shop, and drank it outside, studying the notices for yoga and Pilates classes in the window. The energising effects of the swimming were beginning to wear off. She turned to retrace her steps and was almost knocked over by a man on his way into the shop. She glanced through the open door. Leaning forward and resting his palms on the counter, he seemed to be questioning the storekeeper, who shrugged and shook his head. The man turned to leave and Jen caught a flash of pink flesh, a distorted eye, and a mouth pulled up into a humourless grin. Mrs Laurence's father rushed past her, and she bent to fiddle with the lace on her trainer. He hesitated, looked up at the windows above the shop, and then strode away; he hadn't noticed her. He was going in the same direction as she was, so she followed, hanging well back.

There were men like Ted Mason everywhere in this part of London: men in late middle age with the same build and dodgy geezer swagger, but the shock of his damaged face set him apart. It didn't look like a birthmark, something with which he'd been born. It looked like a burn or the result of a chemical attack. At some time he had suffered a serious accident or injury. It must have changed his life, but he flaunted his disfigurement, used it, and kept his head up as if to say, 'What of it? What's it to you?'

Walking fast, he barged his way through the crowds. Swerving around a couple trundling enormous suitcases, she lost him. The street was popular with tourists and commercial travellers and lined with cheap hotels and guesthouses; he might have slipped into any one of them, might even live there or be visiting someone who did. Or he'd spotted her and given her the slip.

She continued on her way to the village to do some shopping. Gary refused to eat the white sliced bread she and Angie had been used to and thought instant coffee was an abomination. She bought a wholemeal loaf from the bakery and coffee beans from the coffee merchant, then treated herself to an Americano and a croissant in the coffee shop.

From her stool, she could see the Laurence's house. Five years ago she'd stood on the doorstep, hopeful, yet overawed, and nervous. Mrs L had impressed her: her clothes, her hair, the scent she was wearing, and the house itself were the stuff of expensive fashion magazines. She had showed her around and outlined her duties as a housekeeper. Jen would be expected to keep the house immaculate and look after the family's clothes. Mrs L had needed reassurance that Jen would be happy to do some light cleaning. Jen had told her that her mother and grandmother had both worked as housekeepers and had trained her how to clean a house professionally. It was the only lie she'd told. Mrs L was cool and business-like, asked for references, but told her she should start as soon as possible.

Exhilarated by her success, she'd run home, eager to tell Angie the good news and to share it with Sadie and Mike. A decent job, at last, one that she could enjoy and that was well paid. And such a lovely house in a beautiful street! But that was the past, and now the street and the house were symbols of a life she no longer admired. Her love affair with the village was over.

About to leave the café, she saw Ted Mason turn into the street and ducked out of view. He climbed the steps to the Laurence house, rang the bell and stood back to examine the windows, then used the knocker. A man approached from the other end of the street, walking unhurriedly. Too fit and alert to be a resident, and wearing trainers with his smart suit, he had to be one of the security team that patrolled the streets. Ted Mason hadn't seen him.

The man addressed him. Jen couldn't make out the words but she knew the tone, the sarcastic use of 'sir' or 'madam,' the flattened pitch, and the expression in the eyes that didn't match the implications of what was being said. She'd heard it used on her neighbours, on cocky teenagers and confused immigrants. Ted thrust his hands in his pockets as he listened. There was an exchange of words. Whatever version of himself Ted gave must have satisfied the man and he walked away. Ted looked up at the windows of the house, peered down into the basement and then swaggered away.

So, her father was still a threat to Mrs L, and if she and the canal boys were related, he would be a threat to them too. They formed a wretched trio, a relationship that lay at the heart of their unhappiness. Although they lived within streets of each other, they might as well have lived in different countries and different time zones. The boys didn't surface until the late afternoon and kept close to the market and the canal. Mrs L ran in the park in the morning, then took the underground to her job in the city. She left early and returned late. Ted was more elusive and less predictable. Even so, they would find each other eventually, stray into each other's worlds, and come face to face.

It was still early, and she was reluctant to go home to an empty flat. It seemed like years since she'd walked in the park, yet it was only a couple of months. But the park disappointed her as much as the village had. The grass was flattened and yellowing, the trees and shrubs drooping as if as bored as she was. It was too crowded, there were too many rowing boats on the Serpentine, and too many people queuing for tables outside the café.

The path around the lake was quiet. It was here that she'd seen her employer show the first signs of the stress that would undo her. That day had been a watershed moment for them both. Her employer's life had started to unravel, the persona she had built up crumbling under the threat of the past, and Alex's presence hung darkly over her own life. And while she sat in the sun, enjoying a moment of peace, Angie and Hayley had been giggling in front of the mirror, tottering in the slippery clothes she'd worn for Alex, taking turns to photograph each other, innocent of the havoc the photos would cause.

The sky was a hard white, and there was no breeze. Summer was entering the dog days; sultry and airless. Her old life was on its way out. If only her new one would start soon. Not that the present was so bad; she had no complaints.

Chapter 26

Angie would get her exam results today. Jen was sure she'd done well, but she was still nervous. The doorbell rang as she was on her way to wake her up. It was too early for Liz or Sadie, or one of Angie's friends. She glanced into Angie's room. Hunched under the blankets, it looked as if she was still asleep.

She opened the door and stepped back, surprised. Mrs L looked out of place and uncomfortable.

'Is this an inconvenient time?' she asked.

Barefoot and in her bathrobe, Jen felt at a disadvantage.

'You should have rung me first.'

'I had to see you.'

Mrs L was immaculate in her linen suit and Jimmy Choos.

'Are you all right, Mum?'

Angie had come to stand beside her. Yawning, she leant one hip against the door jamb and folded her arms. Wearing an oversized tee over her briefs and luminous with youth, she made the older women look washed out.

Mrs L was staring at Angie. Jen noticed the longing in her eyes. She had never looked at her stepsons like that.

'I'll come back later if it's not convenient. But we need to speak.'

Jen stood aside and beckoned her in; she might as well get it over with. Angie followed them into the kitchen. 'I haven't had my breakfast,' she said. The two women sat at the table and watched as Angie filled a bowl with cereal and poured herself a glass of milk. Coltish and serene, she acted as if she was alone. The light gilded the fall of her hair and slid over the unblemished skin of her limbs. Mrs Laurence watched her, her eyes following every move. Jen felt dowdy and plain between her beautiful daughter and the sophisticated Mrs L. Her hair was unwashed and her toenails needed clipping, the varnish chipped. Alex was right; she'd let herself go. She pushed her feet further under the table.

'I'll leave you to it, then. Remember it's results day today, Mum.' Angie sauntered out, carrying her bowl and glass.

Mrs L turned her gaze back to Jen. 'You have a lovely daughter.' And there it was again, a yearning in her eyes and her voice. She groped in her bag and took out an envelope.

'This is a cheque for what we owe you. And I've written you a reference; I'm sorry you're leaving.'

'You told me to leave. You told me to get out.'

'I'm sorry. I was angry.'

You were frightened, Jen thought. She reached for the envelope. It was for Mrs L to break the silence; she'd said she wanted to talk, so let her.

'I don't care what you did with the clothes you took. I'm glad they were of use to someone. But I've been under a lot of stress. You must have wondered what was going on,' she said, and waited.

Jen let her wait and stared back at her, unblinking. Goaded by the silence, Mrs L started to talk, her words spilling over. Her father had been making a nuisance of himself, she said, turning up at the house when her husband and the boys were at home, or hanging about and making the neighbours suspicious.

'I haven't seen him for years. He left my mother to look after us on her own. I thought he was dead. I didn't want – don't want anything to do with him.'

Jen remained silent. Mrs L glanced up at her and then dropped her eyes.

'My husband didn't know about him; he still doesn't, he thinks both my parents are dead.'

She was still avoiding eye contact, staring down at her clasped hands, her face shadowed by the wings of her hair. 'I told him he was someone I'd exposed for embezzlement and that he'd been in prison. That he blamed me for the way his life had turned out, and he was stalking me.'

She looked up, tucked her hair behind her ears and glanced at Jen as if to check her reaction. 'He showed up outside my firm. We have good security, and he didn't get past reception. I haven't seen him since.' Her smile sat like a sketch on her mouth. She was lying, and any sympathy Jen felt for her disappeared.

'He wants money. So you see, Jen, I've been extremely worried. But I think it's over now.' She stood up. 'I'm sorry to burden you with my problems, but I owed you an explanation.'

Jen saw her out.

'I don't expect you'd come back to work?' Mrs L asked. Jen shook her head. 'No, I didn't think so. Ah well.'

Jen stopped her before she left.

'You said "us". Your father left your mother to look after us. Who else, apart from you?'

Mrs L stared at Jen; her lips tucked over her teeth.

'What's that to you? It's none of your business.'

Jen stepped closer to her. 'You don't fool me. But OK, thanks for the cheque and references. No more than I deserve, though.' And she shut the door on her.

Mrs L had worn out her sympathy. She had tried too hard to convince her of her motives when there was no need and she didn't have to say anything. Their relationship, association, whatever it had been, had ended when Jen walked out.

'So that's the famous Mrs Laurence. You sorted her out, Mum.'

Angie had come into the hall. Jen flinched, Mrs L and her lies were overshadowed by the shock of seeing what Angie was wearing; her shorts almost revealed her gluteal crease. At least her top was modest, although it kept slipping off one shoulder. Jen wanted to order her to change back into something less revealing, but all her friends dressed like that. Instead, she told her how good she looked; she would leave the lecture for another day. Angie hitched her T-shirt up over her shoulder.

'Your boss looks like a rat in high heels.' She laughed, a belly laugh, raucous and intimidating. Had Mrs L heard her, it would have driven her back to the mirror. But Jen could see Angie had admired her ex-boss, admired the way she looked.

'I want shoes like that,' Angie said.

'They cost a fortune; you'd have to take out a loan.'

You're jealous, she told herself. The shoes were symbols of wealth and success. 'Look at me,' they said. 'See how far I've come.' Yet Jen had seen her kick them off and sigh with relief, seen the bunions, the distorted toes and the Scholl foot treatment in the bathroom cabinet.

*

Jen paced, staring at the phone. Angie had promised to call her as soon as she got her results. There was a bottle of wine in the fridge, but it was too early for a drink; she'd wait until this evening; Gary had booked a table at Joe Allen's in Covent Garden. She hoped they hadn't been presumptuous and Angie had done as well as they expected. The phone rang and Jen snatched it up.

'All A's in my core subjects, and French and Spanish, B's for Human Biology and Science. Only one C, but I knew I didn't do as well in Maths as Miss Hanson thought I would.' She was exhilarated, confident and brimming over with hope and plans. 'I might take a gap year after my A levels. I want to travel, Mum. I want to see the world…' She stopped. 'It won't be yet. Not for a while.'

'I'm proud of you,' Jen said, hoping Angie didn't hear the tremor in her voice.

'Amina did brilliantly and so did Zac and Deepak. We're all geniuses! We're meeting up at the Rec. Don't do lunch, Mum.'

Jen heard Angie's friends call out to her and heard her answering laughter before she cut the connection. Her daughter's world. It almost broke her heart. The young move on, but there would be some years with her daughter yet, and she would enjoy every moment of them.

The phone rang again; it was Sadie. Their friendship had survived Hayley's spite, but they were still awkward with each other. They were taking small steps, tentative approaches, mending their friendship a little at a time.

'Congratulations. Hayley told me Angie did well. Her results were awful; she just about scraped through, but she doesn't care. She wants to leave school. I wish she and Angie hadn't fallen out. Still, it's not all bad. Adam broke up with her. He was a bad influence.'

Jen had seen Hayley hanging out with the skateboarders outside the buildings. She'd let the black hair dye grow out and taken to wearing a leather jacket festooned with chains, and jeans with the knees out. However tough the outfit, she had a forlorn look. Her outing of Alex as Angie's father was old news. Now Hayley was the centre of spite. Adam's ex-girlfriend had attacked her in the street. The girls had filmed her getting a beating. Hayley had limped home, her black eyeliner running down her cheeks, followed by a posse of jeering girls holding their phones aloft. The videos had done the rounds among the kids at her school. Sadie believed Adam had goaded the girl into attacking her.

'I'm hurting for her, Jen. She's just a kid, my kid, and I can't bear to see her so unhappy. She came home drunk one night. She told Mike about a man who hangs out on the canal and gets alcohol for them. A freak, she's scared of him. She called him Phanto, after the Phantom of the Opera. Mike thinks it might be Ted. The police patrol down there now, so the kids have moved nearer Camden.'

She'd asked Jen to persuade Angie to become friends with her again. Angie wasn't keen. 'I've moved on, but I'll try, for Mike and Sadie's sake.'

*

Later, over their celebratory meal, Angie babbled on about her plans. She was flushed, happy and a little tipsy. Her exam results and the prospect of sixth form and, later still, university had driven out any unhappiness about her father. She left to go to the toilet, and Gary turned her glass upside down.

'No more for the genius,' he said. Jen watched anxiously as Angie walked back from the toilet, weaving through the tables. Gary was holding his breath – Angie was wearing the shoes she'd bought with birthday money she'd saved. They were her first high heels and vastly different from the Docs or trainers that she usually wore. It took confidence to wear high heels when you were as tall as she was. Her practice had paid off; she walked as if she'd worn five-inch heels all her life, walked as if she owned the restaurant, the street outside, and as if the fates of all the diners were in her hands. A waiter stopped on his way to give someone their bill, his eyes following her. No one was talking at the tables closest to theirs. Unaware of the attention, Angie collapsed into her chair. 'I better not have any more wine,' she said. 'I'll never make it back in these shoes.'

They took a taxi home. The skaters watched them from the wall as Gary paid the driver, Angie's shoes clutched under his arm. Hayley was with them. She looked ill at ease with her companions. Angie stopped on their way in.

'You want to come up, Hays?'

Hayley shook her head and said something to one of the boys. He sniggered.

Angie shrugged and linked arms with Jen and Gary. 'I tried, Mum,' she said, 'but she's such a loser.'

Chapter 27

Jen and Gary had breakfast in bed the next morning. The envelope Mrs L had given Jen was still in her dressing gown pocket. She fished it out and handed it to Gary. He read it and handed it back.

'You seem disappointed. She's been very generous; three months pay and a good reference.'

'Buying me off,' Jen said. 'She had five years of my life.'

'So enjoy your freedom. I'm going to go walkabout. It's how I get my ideas. Why don't you come with me?'

'What about Angie?'

'She's out all day with Zac. She won't miss us.'

Zac. That name had come up a lot recently. Zac had his sights set on Oxford. Zac played drums in a band. His mother was a school governor. It was all very aspirational and a little intimidating. She'd asked Angie who his parents were and whether they lived on the estate.

'They live in St John's Wood. And before you start, he's just a friend.' She turned away, but not before Jen saw her lowered eyelids, her secretive smile. Jen didn't pursue it; there would be no rolling of her eyes, no 'as if', where Zac was concerned. This boy meant something to her. There had been other boys, their names coming up in conversation for a while, then dropped. 'How is Simon or Rolly?' Jen would ask her, showing an interest, only to be met with a shrug. 'How should I know.'

'She likes this Zac. I don't want to leave them.'

'You need a break, we both do. They'll be fine. Trust her.'

'I do. It's him I'm worried about.'

*

Gary had bought travel cards and they chose a different café for breakfast every morning. 'They might make a good subject for a photographic essay. Most of these places won't last. Chains take over. Costa, Starbucks, or hipster indie cafés,' Gary said. 'It may be our last chance to experience them.'

He took her to a greasy spoon in Deptford, where they drank tea in the company of silent men whose dull work clothes and grey faces stood out starkly against white tiled walls, and where the radio droned away unheard in the corner. 'That was depressing,' she told him later. 'It felt like a time warp.' She wondered where the men went when they left the café, where they lived. Did they have families?

'That's the story,' he told her. 'The men's faces, their hands, their overalls. Their lives. I would have loved to photograph them, but it would have been an imposition. And it's been done by better men than me. All the same, I might go back and talk to them later.'

They went to parts of London she only knew by name, jumping on and off buses, or swaying among the commuters on the tube. They took coffee in a Formica café in Bethnal Green and ate *millefeuilles* in a French patisserie in South Kensington. She put herself in his hands; trusted him. Let him dazzle her with his love of London. They followed the river from Putney to Tower Hill, leant side by side over bridges to watch barges glide past old warehouses, and tottered down cobbled alleys where jazz leaked through dusty windows and the smell of Japanese food fought with the tang of urine. Holding hands, they dodged grumbling traffic to get closer to any interesting building.

And they talked; told each other secrets, and revealed a little more of themselves. Talked about what they saw, the people they passed, about Angie and Zac, but not about Alex or Mrs L. When they were hungry, they found a park or green space, spread their jackets on the grass and ate their sandwiches with office workers on their lunch breaks.

The rhythm of walking and the constantly changing streetscape made them talkative. They sped up when they talked about themselves – her stride as long and as swift as his – interrupting each other in their eagerness to reveal their desires. Slowed down when they talked about their past.

'I slept rough when I came to London,' she told Gary. They were lying on the grass in Hyde Park, all talked out and watching the soldiers from Knightsbridge Barracks exercise their horses. 'I'd left home and didn't have anywhere to stay, and no money. I slept near here somewhere, under a tree.' She glanced at Gary, then looked away and traced her initials in a patch of dry earth.

'You must have been frightened.' He passed her a can of Coke. 'How old were you?'

She'd been sixteen and terrified. By day, the park was a green oasis where people strolled or jogged or walked their dogs, but at night it was a theatre of alien sounds and movements, a place of illicit meetings and assignations, of flitting shadows and whispers. Cowering, her imagination out of control, she'd listened to the snapping of twigs, rustles in the undergrowth, and the unearthly scream of a fox. She'd screwed her eyes shut – if she couldn't see it, it wasn't there. Despite her fear, she must have slept a little and woke damp and stiff, and with the torn and frayed look of the rough sleeper, her hair full of twigs, her jacket grass-stained and muddy. A few weeks had been enough to eat the flesh off her bones and stiffen her joints and teach her humiliation. Pride's not important when you're hungry and frightened and she had teamed up with Stickman.

'He was begging outside the station and he chatted me up. He was skinnier than you and crazy, but he taught me how to live out on the streets and didn't ask too much in return,' she said and watched his face. He looked back at her and she turned away. 'I swallowed my pride and phoned my mother. She'd been glad to get rid of me and hadn't reported me missing. Bought me off with enough money to rent a room for a month or two. Anything rather than let me come home again. Not that I wanted to.' She added a question mark to her initials.

Gary crumpled up the paper bags their sandwiches had come in and lobbed them into a nearby rubbish bin. 'Most kids try to escape, in one way or another. I did. The police picked me up in an amusement arcade. I was thirteen and thought I knew how to look after myself.'

She watched him fumble a cigarette out of a crumpled packet and turn away to light it and imagined him as a skinny adolescent, playing the machines, ignorant of the men eyeing his slender back and the tender nape of his neck. How vulnerable he must have been then, how street smart and knowing, and yet how innocent.

'My dad had to get me. I felt like an idiot, but I was glad to see him. He didn't say much, just took me to a café and fed me, then took me home.' He stood and brushed his palms as if to brush away the memory. 'I wish my dad were still around. I'll always miss him.'

Talking about his father pained him. She didn't press him; he'd accepted her story without comment and she'd allow him the same respect. Their past was theirs, for them to reveal or to keep to themselves. We learn who we are, people like us, like me and Gary. Alex too. We learn to accept ourselves. She, the mother, but also the runaway, the beautiful failure, the Zombie girl. Alex, the archetypal trickster, the gambler and the addict, Gary, the lonely boy, the urban walker, the artist. All escapees. A week in our shoes, she thought, eying the office workers and tourists around them. But they would have their stories too.

Gary was photographing a decaying wooden boat, squatting down to take a close-up of the name on the hull. Angie had accused her of not taking an interest in his work. 'You never ask him about it. It's all about you, and about your job,' she'd said.

It wasn't true; she was in awe of his art and had seen his photography as something mysterious, and apart from their life together. His unique way of seeing the world around him resulted in more than a portrait or an image, more than a decisive moment. It drew you in and asked you to see the truth. Nothing was so banal that he couldn't tease out the drama behind even the most obvious of images. His work had an eerie quality; clean, sharp images, yet permeated with mysteries. He caught reflections of the past in the windows of steel and glass buildings in the city and heard history in the wind that blew between the concrete walkways of the estates. He loved his city and the people who lived there. It was his world, not hers and she was grateful that he'd shared it with her.

They spent the last day of their walkabout in Richmond, explored the Lanes and the Green and had lunch at an Italian café. The park was a challenge, wild and hilly. Gary had to drag her past a stag standing stock still and staring, his will stronger than theirs, his odour ripe. Looking into that ancient gaze kept her rooted. 'He won't hurt you,' Gary said. She wasn't so sure.

Later, tired and hungry, they took tea and cakes in the garden of Pembridge Lodge, then queued to look through the telescope on King Henry's Mound; through the trees and the past to the dome of St Paul's Cathedral rising above the present. Giggling like teenagers, they sat on Ian Drury's memorial bench in the corner of the garden. Reasons to be cheerful.

Coming back on the underground, they were relaxed and silent. He examined the photos on his camera while she watched the pretty streets lined with trees flow past the window. Another world, she thought, surely not as peaceful and safe as it appeared, and too like the world she'd run away from.

Back home, she studied the photos he'd taken. Some instinct allowed him to see through to the real story. The rotting wooden rowing boat in front of the fleet of fibreglass Bluebird boats that had left it stranded and redundant. The weary slump of the chef's back outside his kitchen, shoes off, the hole in the heel of his sock, his dirty fingers clutching a cigarette. The soiled rags wrapped around the ankles of the homeless woman, her cracked glasses, the tattered open book face down on her lap. Her eyes were closed, her hands folded, as composed as a nun at prayer.

'I wanted her permission to use the photo,' he'd told her. 'It's an intimate moment, and I needed to know if she was OK with it.'

The front door slammed shut and Angie rushed in. Jen started to reproach her, but Angie spoke over her. 'You two have missed all the drama,' she said. But Jen was staring at the boy who was trying to hide behind her daughter.

'Oh, this is Zac,' Angie said. Zac looked through the heavy fall of jet hair that hung over his eyes and smiled. Angie was impatient to tell them the news. 'Social workers took two of the boys off the boat. The police were there.'

'Which boys?' Gary sounded concerned.

'The ones squatting on the canal. The police took the young ones away. Luke and Sam tried to stop them, but they couldn't.'

When had Angie learned their names? They were the canal boys, the creepy white boys. Knowing their names humanised them.

'Where did they take them?'

'Probably to a care home or back to their foster parents, I don't know.' Angie turned to Jen. 'Can we watch TV?'

Jen nodded, better trash TV than more talk about feral boys. Gary was texting someone, his thumbs jabbing at the keys on his phone.

'Mike might know what happened.'

'They'll be OK, Gary. Stop worrying about them.'

It had taken a while for social services to catch up with them, but now the young ones would be safe. Doctors would examine them, psychologists would interview them, and administrators would fill in forms. Eventually, social workers would take them back to their foster parents and their brothers would no longer have to protect them. Gary's phone pinged. He read the text. 'That was Mike. He hasn't heard anything.'

'It's for the best, surely. The little kids are safer with their foster parents, and the other two can get on with their lives now and stop abusing old women.'

'They stopped abusing anyone a while ago. Hadn't you noticed? And the younger boys were separated and put with families miles away from each other. That's why they ran away.'

He knew too much about them, and Jen wondered how and when he'd found out.

'Why do you care?'

'Why don't you? Why are you so harsh? Their lives must have been a nightmare. Make that Laurence woman admit they're related somehow. She should help.'

He took his jacket from the back of the chair.

'Where are you going?'

'Where do you think? Don't wait up for me.'

'You're wasting your time. Those kids don't want your sympathy. Leave them alone; let the authorities deal with them.'

They both knew that they would disappear before turning to the social.

'I'm going to find out what's happened to them. And I wish you'd use their names. They're not "those boys". And not the creepy white boys, or the canal boys, that is so insulting. Their names are Luke and Sam. The little ones are Nate and Tony.'

He slammed the door on his way out. Jen stood at the window and watched him walk away. She was stunned. Why couldn't he see how wicked the boys were, how amoral? What they'd done to Liz was unforgivable. They'd humiliated her, almost broken her. With a pang, she remembered her tough, loyal friend wringing her hands, avoiding eye contact. How she'd hesitated before speaking. Outwardly she'd recovered, but what they had done had damaged her, had stripped her, not only of her clothes but of her dignity and her sense of self.

Their circumstances were no excuse. Gary had been left to fend for himself, yet he'd grown up to be a good man; he'd never stolen anything or harmed anyone. Neither had she. Being homeless had been hard, and if she hadn't found refuge when she had she might have become a predator or a victim herself. The boys were both. The sooner they were locked up in the young offenders' detention centre with all the other evil little bastards, the better as far as she was concerned.

Chapter 28

It had all fallen apart, their plans for the evening aborted. The ingredients for the meal they'd planned were still in the carrier bags and the wine was chilling in the fridge. Gary had abandoned her to look for the boys. He'd demanded that she used their names; he cared more for them than for how she felt. After their week together, the closeness and the truths they'd shared, his abandonment was shocking.

The flat door slammed. Jen checked the time. Eleven o'clock. Angie was sticking to the rules Jen had set her, determined to prove that her friendship with Zac wouldn't distract her from her studies. She sauntered into the room and threw herself down on the sofa.

'Zac's dad drove me home,' she said, 'right up to the door as if I was a child.'

'Be grateful that he cares enough to see you home safely.'

Angie eyed the bottle on the table, the single glass.

'Where's Gary?'

'Out. Obviously.'

Angie sniggered. 'Lovers' tiff?'

By midnight the bottle of wine was empty, and Jen was worried. It wasn't like Gary not to call; he'd know how anxious she'd be, how sorry for what she'd said. He'd left so suddenly and with so little reason – surely he could have waited until the morning. She regretted her outburst, but they would talk. Gary wouldn't let anything fester; he dragged any disagreement out into the open for discussion.

She started the ritual of preparing for bed, her phone on the side of the basin, glancing at it every few seconds as she cleaned her face and brushed her teeth. Their being together for twenty-four hours out of twenty-four might have been too much for him. They had never spent so much time together. Sometimes they didn't see each other for days, one or the other of them busy with work. She had loved their walkabout and had thought that it had brought them closer, but it might not have been the same for him. When she gave in and rang his number, her call went to voicemail.

In bed, she opened her book, but her eyes slid over the lines without registering the words. Instead, she saw him, thirteen and confused, under the gaze of the men in the amusement arcade. Remembered his reaction when he'd thought Ted Mason was propositioning Luke. '*Predators see kids like him and think they're theirs for the taking.* He cared and she'd taken his compassion and fashioned it into a weapon to use against him.

The hiss and thump of the landing door closing alerted her; he was back, and she could apologise, make it right between them again. She threw her book down and waited. Unsteady footsteps continued to the end of the landing. Picking up the book again, she listened as her neighbour fought to get his key into the lock.

Where was he? How could he leave her like this? If he cared about the boys so much, why had he kept his distance from them? He'd made a point of not contacting them. He was a phoney, a fool, a do-gooder who did nothing. He *was* pathetic. But then, she reasoned, she hadn't wanted him to get involved, even counselled him against it.

Pummelling her pillow, she turned over in the bed. Oh, how she hated this constant introspection, always questioning her motives, or his. It did no good and undermined their happiness. What did it matter if she didn't know him as well as she thought she did? Who knows anyone else, anyway? Neither of them had laid out every moment of their lives for the other's inspection. Some truths are damaging.

She had to do something, to look for him, to find him, tell him how sorry she was and bring him home. If he wasn't in his flat, she'd look in all the places where the boys might be found. Even if it meant braving the drunks and the addicts hanging out by the canal, even if she had to rouse Luke and Sam on their boat, she would find him. Maggie might know where he was, she might have seen him pass her doorway. Street people saw the world from a different angle; they saw things that others didn't, heard things, knew things and had ways of passing information on to each other.

She dressed hurriedly. It was two a.m. but the streets never slept. Punters would be leaving the casinos and clubs, some looking for women or trouble or on the lookout for victims. Police in unmarked cars would be kerb-crawling, their eyes skimming the side streets and doorways. On her way out, she sorted through the cutlery drawer in the kitchen – Gary kept her knives sharp. Living on the streets had taught her how to keep out of danger, to recognise the flicker in the eye of a predator, the silence and stillness that comes before a violent act. A word, a gesture, even a 'dirty look' was enough to spark off mayhem. A smile was as dangerous as a sneer; neither meant what it seemed. She'd kept a sharpened nail file in her sock. Hoping that she hadn't lost her street smarts, she slipped a knife into her pocket.

She took the stairs two at a time. There were no lights on in his flat, but she leant on his bell, banged on the knocker and shouted through the letterbox. Go home, she told herself before you do something you'll regret; go home, open another bottle. Go to bed. But her anger burned hotter, and she thundered down the stairs and into the street. She ignored the drunk sitting on the wall outside the building and the fox pawing through the rubbish on the path. The knife in her pocket felt dangerous.

Then a murmur, a soft laugh, and she saw him, talking to Daniel Avery, his hand on Daniel's shoulder. He turned to look at her as if he had never sat at her table, cooked for her, or slept in her bed.

She rushed him. Punched him in the mouth with enough force to mash his lips against his teeth. *Now see what you made me do. Your fault.* Panting, she clawed at his face. He held her wrists. She could hear Daniel laughing. The drunk cackled and shadowboxed from his seat on the wall, and the fox streaked past them, in a flash of orange. Weakened, her rage draining away, she leaned her head on his chest.

'Finished?' Gary said. 'Can I let you go?'

She pulled away and turned to Daniel. 'You can fuck off.' He gave a mocking salute, bowed and left. The fox looked back, decided they were no threat and returned to paw over old chicken bones and eggshells.

'Are you coming home, or what?'

She looked away from the blood on Gary's lip. They climbed the stairs in silence, as wary of each other as strangers. She watched her muddy trainers until they reached her floor. He caught at her arm. 'Never do that again, Jen,' he said. 'I can't talk to you now. I'll see you tomorrow.'

He left her. Her legs shook as she walked along the landing, and her hands shook as she tried to open the door, but it flew open.

'Where have you been? I was worried.'

In PJs and rabbit slippers, Angie was red-faced and tear-stained, eight years old again. 'You woke me up when you went out. Why did you bang the door? Where did you go?'

Snuffling, she followed Jen to the bedroom, almost treading on her heels. Ashamed and sickened, too numb to comfort her child and weary beyond words, beyond thought, beyond care, Jen bent to pull off her shoes and threw her fleece on the floor. The knife fell out of the pocket. Ignoring her daughter, she climbed into bed.

'Mum, you haven't got undressed. What happened? Shall I get Gary?'

Pulling the duvet over her shoulders, Jen rolled away from her and kept her eyes shut.

'Are you hurt? Why isn't Gary with you? Please don't go to sleep.' She sat on the bed and the mattress sagged. 'Mum?'

That last word. *Mum*. It was too much. Jen sat up and reached out to comfort her, but Angie pulled away. The knife was in her lap.

'Not before you tell me why you went out with a knife in your pocket. Is Gary all right?

'He's upstairs. You'll see him tomorrow. We had a row over the boys.'

'Over Luke and Sam? Why?'

'Because of what they did to Liz.'

Jen stood, wincing at the ache in her knees and her back. Angie took hold of one of her hands and turned it over. There was a trace of blood on her knuckles.

'Did you hit someone?'

'I fell. Go to bed, love. I'm exhausted. It's all right, we'll talk about it in the morning.'

'How can you say that? It's not all right.' But she left reluctantly, her head down. 'If you've hurt Gary, I'll never talk to you again. I'll leave home.' She turned back. 'Why are you always so angry?'

*

There was a text from Gary in the morning; he would come to her flat for breakfast. Jen read it repeatedly. The tone was cold. She would have preferred anger. They'd never had a serious row; their arguments had been without rancour. Even her hatred of the boys had never caused anything more than a heated exchange between them. She dreaded their encounter, yet she was desperate to see him. Angie was at the table, her knee jerking in an involuntary jig.

'How long does it take to come down from his flat? He's not coming. You've driven him away. It's your fault, Mum.'

The bell rang; why wasn't he using his key? Jen steadied herself and opened the door. He had his back to her. He can't look at me, she thought and walked towards the kitchen. He caught at her arm.

'What have you told Angie?'

'The truth. We'd had a row and I went out to look for you.'

She pulled away and he followed her. Angie ran to him, a child again, innocent and hopeful, grabbing at his hands and then dragging off his jacket. He laughed and kissed her on her forehead. His bottom lip was split. There was no kiss for Jen, just a quick acknowledgement, a brief look into her eyes. Angie reached out and touched Gary's lip.

'What happened... it was you, wasn't it, Mum? You hit him.'

'It was an accident, Angie. Your mum didn't mean to hit me. It's not as bad as it looks.'

They pulled out chairs, sat, and reached for the cups, for the croissants. Angie watched them anxiously, looking from Jen to Gary, and filling the silences with chatter about moving into sixth form. Aware of their surreptitious glances at each other, she stumbled to a halt.

'Do you two need to talk?'

'Later,' Gary said. 'Let's enjoy our breakfast first. Tell me, how's Zac?'

Angie ignored his feeble effort to divert her.

'I know you rowed over what Luke and Sam did to Liz. She's over it, Mum. Why aren't you? You shouldn't hate them, especially if it comes between you and Gary.'

'It won't come between us,' Gary said.' Your mum and I will sort it out. You're stuck with me.'

Settling back in her chair, Angie was all cool teenage nonchalance again. 'OK, I'm glad, and I'm glad you care about Luke and Sam. Someone must. What happened to their brothers?' Angie looked sideways at Jen, checking her reaction. 'Were they sent back to their foster parents?'

Gary drew Jen into the conversation. 'If they were, they'll run away again; they want to be together. Your Mrs L must take some responsibility. Talk to her. Jen. We know she's related to them somehow; make her admit it.'

'What then? Drag her to social services?'

'Mum. Why are you still arguing?'

'Because Gary's forgotten that I did confront her. It cost me my job.'

'So you've got nothing left to lose. Anyway, I'll be in my room. You two can talk.' She left, and Jen and Gary were left facing each other over empty coffee cups.

'Does she know what happened last night? What if she'd seen?' He didn't wait for an answer. 'Don't ever do that again. How would you feel if I'd hit you?'

She was too ashamed to meet his eyes, to say she was sorry. Sorry was what violent men said to the women they lashed out at, what they said the next time and the time after that.

'I didn't know where you were. I was frightened.'

'You've no reason to be frightened. I know what can happen to kids left to cope on their own. So do you. You and Angie come first, but there's room in my life for other people, whoever they are. I want you to know that. If you don't trust me, there's no point in our being together.' He was cool and distant. 'Another thing; I've got to go away for a few weeks. It will give us both a chance to think about things.'

Chapter 29

The kitchen was fragrant with the aroma of good cooking. Angie had chopped the onions and prepared the garlic, sprinkling the cloves with salt and crushing them under the blade of a knife. She'd watched as Gary trimmed rashers of bacon and added them to the pot. Happy that he was back from Somerset and that they were going to be eating together, she watched everything he did.

She'd missed him, and her move into the relative independence of sixth form was wearing her out. As well as the stress of coping with an unfamiliar environment, she'd had to face jokes about her father, the sex slave. It was a lot to take on, and anxiety and exhaustion had made her supercilious and snappy or anxious and needy. She was trawling through the photos on his camera. Jen looked over her shoulder and saw men tending fires and women watching kids playing.

He'd read about the New Age Travellers in an article in a Sunday paper. Their independence had attracted him, and he'd decided to make them part of his project. Coming so soon after their fight, Jen wondered if he'd joined up with them because of it. She'd avoided talking about the night before he left and hadn't asked him why he seemed so friendly with Daniel Avery. Nothing good would come from being close to the Averys.

Liz had defended them. 'No one gets close to them. They grew up hard, and rumours grow around outsiders like them. They're not all bad. But I didn't call to talk about the Averys. What's this I've heard about you hitting Gary. I didn't believe it at first. What were you thinking? He would never lift a hand to you, Jen, to any woman.'

'We'd had a row over the boys who attacked you. He makes excuses for them all the time. I can't forgive them for what they did.'

'Why should you forgive them? I haven't. Don't let what they did come between you and Gary, though. He's a good man, and he must see something in them that we can't. He's no mug, he wouldn't let anyone make a fool of him. Trust him, Jen. And think about Angie. At least she didn't witness it. Did you talk about it?'

Jen had tried to explain herself to her daughter, stuttering and pausing, and beginning again. Angie had listened, her eyes never leaving her mother's face.

'You never hit me, Mum. I never thought you would, and I was horrible to you when I was younger.'

'I was so mad at him, Angie. I was never that mad at you, whatever you said.'

'You were jealous. You've always been jealous of the boys.'

Her perceptive daughter gave no quarter. After the meal, Angie went to her room. Gary was making coffee. He always made it too strong, but a caffeine rush would make her brave enough to say what she had to.

'I spoke to Liz the other day,' she said. 'She'd heard about our fight. I suppose Sadie knows as well.'

'They've heard worse. Not about me, mind.'

'What was going on between you and Daniel that night? You looked like you were best mates.'

He looked at her, held her gaze. She prepared herself. Whatever he had to say, let him say it, get it over with.

'I was going to tell you; I was waiting for the right time. I knew you wouldn't be happy about it,' he said, and Jen shut her eyes.

'Just tell me, Gary.'

He poured the coffee, emptied the jug and took it to the sink. He was stalling and she waited. He sat down facing her.

'I was looking for the boys,' he said. 'I'd tried the boat first, but they weren't there. The Brothers wouldn't like the police and social services nosing around, they must have made the kids leave.'

The light was on in the Praed Street flat, and he'd rung the bell. Daniel had come out to talk to him. 'He's usually more forthcoming than his brother and it was worth a try. I asked him if he knew where the boys were.'

He was drumming his fingers on the table. Jen cupped her hands over his; he wasn't immune to Joseph's brooding presence and Daniel's sly innuendos. Daniel's offhand attitude barely concealed his contempt, and Joseph didn't disguise his. Withdrawing his hands from under hers, Gary sat back.

'Daniel was guarded at first, but listened to what I had to say, then led me up to the flat. Joseph was there, and Alex, and a man I hadn't seen before. They'd had the flat decorated and set up as an office. The Brothers are going straight, concentrating on their rentals.'

'Wait.' Jen stopped him. 'Aren't they going away? I thought they were going to Plymouth.'

'That's off. Alex will be the frontman, running things from Praed Street. He was smirking at me. He's fallen on his feet, for now at least.'

No wonder Alex had given up his demands to be part of Angie's life; he'd had other plans. He'd seen the possibility in the houses behind Harrow Road, the shops and flats in Kilburn, and the boats on the canal. He'd skim whatever he could from the Averys and disappear again. If Angie had wanted him in her life he would have left her and broken her heart.

'The other man there was Kevin, Mike's friend, the ex-squaddie. He'll oversee doing up the properties.' Gary paused to light a cigarette; he was smoking more than usual, even smoking at the dinner table. Angie had coughed ostentatiously – she'd shamed her mother into giving up some time ago. 'And I know this is going to make you angry. I told them what I knew about Luke and Sam, how they'd been looking after their brothers until the social took them away. I persuaded them to let them stay on the boat. They could help Kevin with the refurbishments. Smartened up, they'd fetch a decent rent; the boys will have to move eventually, but they'll be there for a while. Kevin said he'd be happy to take them on.'

He drained his coffee and put the cup back in the saucer carefully. 'Daniel walked back with me, and he asked about Alex. He was checking him out. I fobbed him off, and then you appeared.'

He didn't look at her, and she was too angry to look at him. His intervention meant the boys would stay in the area. When would he learn that Luke and Sam were evil little bastards? What did it take?

As for the Averys', they'd always been mysterious, always nomadic. How long before they decided the straight world was not for them, pulled on their boots and marched away? They'd lived on the margins too long. Alex might coach them on how to act the part of respectable landlords, to give up their greasy jackets and big boots and strut around in suits from Marks and Spencer's, but he would be the face of their business. The Brothers had bought cheap, ridden out the housing crises, and now they would be set to make a decent profit. Until Alex cheated them out of it.

'Who knows what they're up to, really?' Gary said. 'I suppose we'll find out soon enough.'

'Does Mike know about their plans?'

'I'll tell him. He's not going to like it. He still holds a grudge against Alex. He won't be happy to see him succeed.'

Pushing his chair back, Gary stood. 'I'm fed up with the whole business. Alex, Mrs L, her dad, and the boys. I couldn't wait to get away from it all, to tell you the truth.'

It was as if he'd thrown his coffee in her face. She'd been hurt by his coldness, hurt when he'd drawn his hands from under hers as if her touch offended him. They hadn't slept together since his return from Somerset; she'd expected it would take time to get over her violence, but she hadn't seen this coming.

'I'll help you clear up, then I've got to work. I'll sleep upstairs again. Don't wait breakfast for me tomorrow; I'll snatch something on my way into town.' He was clearing the table and hadn't looked at her. 'Actually, I might—'

'Might what?' She heard herself; surly, belligerent.

'Nothing. It doesn't matter.'

She shrugged and turned away. Hold on, she told herself, don't let him see you care. The kitchen was still warm, the table littered with the remains of the meal he'd cooked. Together, they gathered up the plates, the glasses and the cutlery. It was their usual routine, the time when they talked about their day or discussed their plans for the evening. She washed, he dried, she cleaned the surfaces; he folded the tea towel and hung it up. Then, with their chores completed and their hands empty, they stood facing each other, waiting.

'I'll be off then, Jen.' His voice cracked. He put on his jacket and patted the pockets for keys and cigarettes. A peck on her cheek, a clumsy pat on her shoulder, and he left without another word.

Jen watched him go as if rooted to the floor. With the paraphernalia of cooking cleared away, the kitchen seemed cold and bleak. The bulb in the central light was buzzing and flickering. It would go out soon, and she would be in the dark, but she couldn't move. She'd done nothing to stop him. What could she have said – don't go, stay the night with me? I'm sorry? The words would have stuck in her throat. He was punishing her by his absence, but she wouldn't beg; she'd done without him before, and she could do it again. What did she care if she never heard his key in the lock, never watched him move around in her kitchen again, never ate the meals he prepared? Never slept with him again or woke with him beside her.

But she was bereft. He'd brought colour to her days. The weeks without him in her kitchen, or her bed, had felt like winter. His presence had filled the spaces in her home; now the rooms would be full of dead air and silence, her days too long, her nights too dark. Even eating breakfast together had been an event. His return from Somerset had been a reawakening.

Grabbing the keys from the dresser, and stopping to tell Angie she was going out, she left the flat. Taking her time to climb the stairs, she calmed herself; she would forget her pride and tell him how much she'd missed him. He was still wearing his jacket when he opened his door.

'I was just about to come back down,' he said. 'We need to talk.'

Chapter 30

We're not breaking up,' Jen told Angie. 'We need time to think about how we go on. Gary will be working away, and I've got to concentrate on getting a job. Being apart will give us time to make some important decisions.'

'That doesn't make sense. Why can't you work things out together? It's your fault he's left again. You shouldn't have hit him.'

Angie was holding her mother to account, refusing to let her off the hook. It took a while to convince her censorious daughter their separation was temporary. She wasn't sure it was. They hadn't been together long, but long enough for her to feel that their relationship might become permanent. He called regularly but talked about his work and apart from asking how she and Angie were, avoided the personal. He'd made it clear before he left. 'I need to think about what I want. I need some time to myself.'

But he'd shocked her. She hadn't expected this of him. She'd absorbed the blow and agreed that it was for the best. It was up to her now; she wouldn't let his leaving weaken her. She would find a way to make a living. For now, she'd keep to her daily routine: exercise, a visit to Iris in the market and then home and a trawl through the internet in search of a job.

*

A group of Japanese tourists were dawdling through the fruit and veg stalls. The tour leader held a pink parasol above her head and waited for the stragglers to catch up. Jen was glad to see them. The turmoil caused by Brexit – the marches and demos, the changes in the government, and the terrorist attacks had meant fewer tourists coming to London. Sales in the Antique Market were down.

Iris was keeping her eye on a couple examining the frocks hanging on the rails when Jen arrived. She ushered her into the cluttered space at the back of the stall. 'I need a favour. Can you fill in for me for a couple of hours? Something's come up and I'm desperate. I know it's short notice...'

'Go' Jen said, 'I'll be fine.'

'You know where everything is. Record any sales and keep an eye out for shoplifters. Call me if there's a problem. I'll be back before closing.'

Elated, Jen took Iris's place on the stool behind the counter. This was what she'd been hoping for. All those trips to the café, all the little jobs she'd helped with – sweeping, tidying, keeping Iris company – had paid off. Although she'd looked after the stall while Iris popped out for a minute, it was the first time she'd left her in charge.

At first, Jen watched nervously as people riffled through the rails or picked over the fragile scarves and costume jewellery, poised to leap from her stool and wrestle any thief to the ground. After a while, she relaxed and began to enjoy watching the people and chatting with potential customers.

Iris was impressed when she returned later; Jen had made four sales to the party of Japanese tourists: a silver evening purse to a couple looking for a present for their daughter, and a scarf to a man who'd spent a long time describing the forties suit he wanted to accessorise. There had been a furious row between two women over a fifties dress; the smallest woman won, and the other went off in a huff but returned later to buy a blouse.

'You've taken more in an afternoon than I did for the last two days,' Iris told her. 'Can you do the whole of next week? I've got a house clearance and stock that needs sorting. I can't pay much, but it will be an experience and you should make some useful contacts.'

The week turned into an unspecified time – 'if that's OK with you' – and 'watching the stall' became helping to prepare the new stock for sale or rental. Jen was grateful for the extra money and glad that she had more responsibility; playing store detective had become tedious. Sewing buttons onto fragile blouses, taking up hems and mending lace was simple work, and although she had experience working with garments, vintage clothes had to be approached differently, with more care. Shoppers were scarce during the week and the sewing machine, steamer and ironing board at the back of the stall were in almost constant use and showed the other stallholders how useful she could be. They stopped by to bring her tea, or just to chat, and although she wasn't yet part of their world they knew her name and knew what she could do. She had taken another step towards a future she was beginning to see for herself.

Looking back, she realised that even her short-lived career as a model hadn't been the disaster she'd thought it was. Talked into believing she had a future in fashion, she'd gone along with it. Anything was better than the series of soul-destroying jobs she'd had until then. That she felt a complete phoney, had failed and felt the failure keenly, didn't matter anymore. She'd learned about fashion and how to wear clothes and it had led to her job with the Cousins. They had been good teachers and collaborating with them had sparked an interest in the garments, their care and their construction. Even the job with the Laurences had expanded her horizons. Their furnishings and artworks, the food they ate, and the wine they favoured had been an education. And Alex had introduced her to a world few people had access to; louche, dangerous but enviably smart. Putting it all together made her a suitable candidate for the sort of job she wanted: something creative yet practical, something that would fulfil her; a dealer in vintage fashion, like Iris, or a wardrobe supervisor for a theatre, or in film and TV. It would be a while before she felt confident enough to strike out on her own, but she wanted to be her own boss, to do or die by her own efforts.

She needed to learn the best way to present herself. Talking it over with Gary would have helped. His common-sense approach to any problem had helped her in the past, but her grief at his leaving had turned to anger and bitterness. And then back again. Love and hate tattooed on her knuckles.

She blinked away the images she and Angie had seen on his camera: sleeping kids splayed like so many multi-coloured starfish around a bonfire, arms and legs akimbo, men and women passing jugs of cider between them, a girl with her head against her man's shoulder, his fingers in her hair. Imagined Gary, his long legs crossed, his head bowed over his camera, or the spliff he was rolling. Why would he want her, with her problems and her anger, when he could live so freely? Well, she would let him go, she told herself. Let him lock himself away with his cameras, or go walkabout without her and cook his complicated dishes. She would rather eat ashes.

It was time for Iris to come by, and for them to pack up, and she folded the blouse she'd been working on. A woman caught her eye; Jen had noticed her earlier.

'Can I help with anything?' she said and moved to the front of the stall. The woman ran her gaze over her.

'I thought it was you. Didn't you used to work for the Laurence's?'

'I left a while ago.' Jen straightened the gloves the woman had been handling. She recognised her, she was a regular in the shops in the village. Hearing the Laurence's name shocked her; she still felt something for her ex-boss. The slightest thing would bring her to mind. The scent of her cigarettes, the click of high heels on the pavement, and the trace of her perfume drifting in the wake of a passing woman would make her turn her head, her heart leaping.

'How are the Laurence's'? We hardly see them anymore and you could set your clock by them.' The woman was pretending she cared.

'I don't know. As I said, I left some time ago.' Jen put the gloves back in the drawer and slammed it shut. The woman didn't take the hint.

'We thought you must have left. The house is looking shabby; you'd kept it immaculate.'

What business is it of hers, Jen thought, and who is this 'we'? Who has she been talking to? Didn't she have anything better to do but gossip? Thankfully, she saw Iris coming towards her, her arms full of garment bags.

'Sorry, we're packing up now. Can I help you with anything else?' she said.

Iris stood aside to let the woman leave. She unzipped a bag, took out a jacket and hung it up.

'You look angry. Did she try to steal something?'

'I thought she might, but she was just killing time.'

'Well, it's chucking it down outside.' Iris threaded a padded hanger between the shoulder straps of a beaded evening gown. 'Help me hang this lot up, and then get on before the rain gets worse.'

Within minutes of stepping into the street, Jen was drenched. Angie was home and making herself and Zac a sandwich when she burst through the door and into the kitchen, dripping water onto the floor. 'Is it raining, mum?' Angie said, and she and Zac fell about laughing. Later, showered and in dry clothes, she sat in the kitchen with them and ate the sandwich they'd made her.

'Gary phoned while you were in the shower. He'll call back later and send some photos. We're off to drama club. Zac's the actor, not me; he thinks he's the next Robert Pattison.'

They were in high spirits and as playful as ten-year-olds. Her daughter and Zac were in tune with each other. Jen had had the 'conversation' with her, struggling along and trying to ignore Angie's rolling eyes and pleas to shut up.

'You don't have to, Mum; we did all this at school. I know what I want,' she'd said, 'and it isn't a baby. I'll sort out my birth control when I need to. I want to be in charge of my body. We both want to get a good degree. Please don't talk about it anymore. It's too embarrassing.'

She'd plotted her career path: a good degree in Modern Languages, then a year abroad, all leading to a job that involved travel. And she'd been equally certain about her and

Zac's future together. 'We may go our separate ways after sixth form, but we'll always be friends.'

Despite his pretty-boy looks and his obsession with his hair, Zac was loyal and serious and had come into her life when she most needed it. Jen was envious of their relationship; she'd always found such intimacy difficult, and she hoped that her daughter would always be as happy as she was now. Not so long ago she'd learned about her father, only to reject him, and had been bearing up under the malice of a girl who had been her best friend since nursery. Instead of breaking her, it had made her stronger.

Warm, dry and fed, she relaxed and waited for Gary's call. Her phone buzzed: a text, bland and impersonal. What did she care about noise in the camp? Disappointed, she texted him back – 'you like your music loud, so stop complaining,' and pressed send before she disgraced herself and embarrassed him by asking him to come home. Tell him how much she missed him. Or telling him to fuck off.

The phone rang. Gary's call, at last. The line was bad; he sounded as if he were calling from the seabed; all she heard was crackling and whooshing. If he insisted on gallivanting around the countryside he couldn't expect a good connection. 'Stop playing around, Gary.' She could hear him breathing. But the breathing was too shallow, too fast, almost panting. Gary wouldn't mess around like that. Someone whispered into the phone. 'Please, please…' A man shouted something in the background. The line was cut.

She checked her logs; she didn't recognise the number. Hands slippery, she dialled Angie's number.

'What is it, Mum? We're in the middle of something here.'

'Sorry. I wanted to…

She heard Zac call her name and Angie interrupted her. 'Got to go, sorry, Mum, sorry' – and cut her off.

Jen hadn't thought the call was about Angie, it could have been anyone on the end of the line, she reasoned. Somewhere, though, a woman was begging. *Please, please.* Please help me? The line was so bad it was hard to judge the tone. She told herself the woman wasn't pleading but asking. A wife nagging her husband: Please don't forget to pick up the dry cleaning. Please don't be late again. A misdial, innocuous, normal. The phone rang again, and she grabbed it.

'Jen? I'll have to be quick, I'm standing in a field, mud up to my ankles. It's the only place I can get a signal.' Gary paused, and Jen imagined his furrowed brow, his long fingers clutching the phone. 'You OK? Give my love to Angie.'

She didn't tell him about the phone call. There was no point, and he'd joined up with the Travellers again to get away from such dramas. Instead, they'd exchanged small talk, saying nothing of any real interest. It had been a duty call, a call made because he'd promised he would.

Chapter 31

Sadie held on to Jen's shoulders, and her kiss was a mere breath against her cheek. Groaning, she lowered herself onto the chair in front of the stall and lit a cigarette. Surely she hadn't forgotten that there was no smoking inside public buildings. If she had, there were NO SMOKING notices on every floor. Jen plucked the cigarette out of her friend's fingers and put it out. 'You can't smoke in here, Sadie.'

Without any preamble, Sadie launched into a complaint against her daughter. 'She stays in her room. We bribe her to go out. No one calls for her; all her friends have dropped her. She doesn't turn up for work at Greggs. It's breaking my heart, and she won't talk about it. At least she's not drinking anymore. Mike is beside himself. I worry about his blood pressure. He's thinking about leaving the market.'

Sadie had sung this song too often in the last few months. Despite the care and the love they had lavished on their daughter, Hayley was slowly crushing her parents. Not deliberately, or with malice, but blinded by self-pity, she couldn't see how her behaviour was hurting them.

'When did you start smoking again?' Jen examined her friend. Big-boned and strong, Sadie had carried her extra pounds proudly, but now she had the slack-skinned look of someone addicted to fasting.

'Are you eating?'

Ignoring Jen's question, Sadie went on. 'She plays awful music, about death and suicide. Adam is back with his ex and sends her photos of them together. How can someone so young be so cruel?'

They both knew how ruthless teenagers can be. Angie had shown little sympathy for Hayley. 'What goes around comes around,' she'd said. 'Now she knows what it feels like to be the victim.'

'Maybe you should get help for her. Counselling,' Jen told Sadie, her eyes on a man hovering by the dress rail.

'Sorry, love, you're working. I'll go,' Sadie said. She raised her chin in the direction of the man examining a sixties dress. 'He'll never get into that.'

Jen relented. 'Stay. Keep me company,' she said, glad that her friend hadn't lost her sense of humour. 'You can sort through these buttons for me. I want the little mother-of-pearl ones. All the same size.'

'It's nice in here, cosy,' Sadie said, picking through the buttons. There was a ring on each of her fingers. 'I get fed up sitting at home.'

By the time Jen was ready to pack up the stall, Sadie had cheered up. 'What's going on where you used to work?' she said as she was leaving. 'There was an incident there the other day. The road was cordoned off, police all over the place.'

Jen hadn't been near the village for some time; that part of her life was over. It wasn't unusual for there to be police activity in the area. It could have been a traffic accident, a theft from one of the shops, or something to do with any of the residents.

She had her own problems. Her job for Iris would end soon. What then? She had bills to pay, and a daughter to feed and clothe. Angie didn't nag her for 'things' anymore, but there were school trips and equipment to pay for. There would be more expenses when she went to university. It was time to shut up the stall, and she hung up the dress she'd been working on and left.

It was getting dark, and the air was sharp. Autumn was making way for winter. It was a short walk to her flat from the market, but her feet hurt and she had a headache. She might need glasses; the lighting in the market was designed to show the stock at its best, and not for the intricate work that she'd been doing all afternoon. Catching a glimpse of herself in a shop window, she straightened her spine and threw back her shoulders. Angie mustn't guess how tired and worried she was. The stairs up to her flat seemed steeper, the light on the landings dimmer, the shopping she'd done on her way home heavier.

She wasn't looking where she was going and almost tripped over a backpack in the hall. There were camera cases next to it. She waited, her heart hammering; Gary was back. His leather jacket hung from a hook on the back of the door, and she could hear the murmur of conversation from the kitchen. The handles of the shopping bags were cutting into her palms. She put them down, took a deep breath and straightened her shoulders.

The conversation stopped abruptly when she walked into the kitchen. Angie's smile was tentative. 'Gary's here, Mum,' she said and gave a nervous giggle. Zac sniggered and blew air through his nose. They were watching her, waiting for her reaction.

'I haven't got enough food for everyone.' How lame she sounded.

'Takeaway then,' Gary said. 'Celebrate being together again.'

Angie flashed a thankful smile at him and her mother, and then she and Zac were arguing about what food to get, talking over each other and shouting their preferences. Stiff-jawed with resentment, Jen occupied herself by putting away the shopping, anything to avoid looking at Gary. So little to say to her when he'd called her, and yet here he was, walking into her life as if it was his right.

'We'll go,' Angie said. 'Come on, Zac. I haven't had fish and chips for ages.' He followed her out, grumbling about high carbs – he'd voted for healthy Lebanese.

Gary came round the table and stood behind her, his hands on her shoulders. 'You look tired.' He massaged the muscles, easing the tension. 'I'm sorry I left the way I did,' he said. 'It wasn't fair to you.'

The image of herself she'd seen in the shop window flashed before her; a worn-out woman, downcast and defeated. She wanted to spin around and face him, spit her resentment into his face, but she was too tired. Instead, she leaned her head back and rested it against him. He put his fingers in her hair and massaged her scalp, and her temples, and tugged gently at the strands of hair that had escaped her plait. Jen wondered if this physical contact was a ruse to avoid looking at her. If we can't look at each other, then there's no hope for us, she thought.

The kids rushed back in, carrying the grease-stained bundles of their fish supper, and she moved away from him. The room was filled with the smell of hot oil and vinegar. Gary had brought bottles of Somerset cider, the real stuff, aromatic and tart, and he poured them all a glass. They ate the food straight out of the paper it came in. Angie and Zac monopolised Gary, eager to hear about the Travellers, asking him questions, demanding to see the photos he'd taken.

She tried to concentrate on what Zac and Angie were telling Gary about the play they were working on. The food and cider made her lethargic, and the kitchen was hot and steamy. Gary glanced at her occasionally, puzzled at her silence. Part of her dreaded being alone with him – he seemed changed. The phone rang, interrupting her train of thought. She turned it off. Whoever it was would leave a message. The phone's ringtone had woken her, and she opened the window and started to gather up the remains of the meal. Angie and Zac helped clear the table, dumping glasses and cutlery onto the draining board.

'We're off,' Angie said. 'Rehearsals.'

'She seems happy,' Gary said when they'd left.

'She is. She and Zac are good together. They're almost too sensible.'

'I'm glad about Angie, but what about you? I haven't had a chance to apologise properly. Can we start again?'

*

He wanted to make their relationship permanent, and official. Not marriage, neither of them was ready for that, but he wanted them to live together. To make a life together.

'Let's not wait. Why don't we talk to Angie and see how she feels about moving up to my flat? It's big enough for the three of us.'

He was taking too much for granted. Her resolve hardened. She wanted to concentrate, to put all her energies into finding the right sort of work. The upheaval of moving, the commitment to sharing her life so completely with someone other than her daughter, was too distracting. If she decided to move in with him, she wanted it to be an equal partnership. To pay her way, to keep her independence. So hard fought for, so proudly won.

'I don't want to move now. The next few months are going to be difficult for me. I've got to find regular work. We can go on as we were. Wait until Angie goes to uni, as we'd planned. We're OK for now.'

He hadn't tried to persuade her; he took her rejection well – so well that she wondered if he was as ambivalent about them living together as she was. Instead, they talked about her work at the market and his plans for his project. Safe, ordinary conversations that comforted them, and let them find a way back to each other. They were still talking when they heard Angie's key in the lock. Gary caught Jen's hand. 'I'm serious,' he told her. 'I want to commit to you and Angie. I hope that's plain enough.'

He waited until they were in bed to ask about Alex. 'I sort of missed him and the boys; I even missed the Averys. I kept wondering how they were getting on.' His phone rang and he glanced at it and turned it off. Trouble with the Travellers, he told her. Scuffles with the police, raids on their camps by resentful locals. He sympathised, but they'd chosen to live the way they did, he hadn't. He'd been glad to come home.

His call reminded her of the one she'd had earlier. She didn't recognise the number, and she played the voicemail: Crackling, breathing – then silence.

'What's up?'

'It was someone from the market. I promised to look after his stall, and I forgot.' The lie came easily, she didn't want to plunge him straight into another situation.

'Are you sure it's all right? You looked upset. Is he giving you a tough time?'

'No, no, nothing like that. I'll call him in the morning.'

She was making it worse, piling up the lies, building a wall between them. Gary put out his cigarette. 'Something's up, Jen, I can tell. You're upset.'

'I lied, I'm sorry, she said. I didn't want to drag you into it,' and the relief was a blessing.

She let go of resentment and anger. Despite their differences, their opposing ways of looking at the world and despite her anger, he wanted to be with her, he would listen, and he would support her. So she told him everything, the incident in the village, the woman pleading, a man shouting, the silent calls.

'Check your logs. See if the numbers are the same and see who picks up. Could it be your old boss?'

'If it's her, she's in trouble. If it were just an argument with her husband, she wouldn't have tried to call me. But her father's been stalking her.'

Gary watched as she dialled Mrs L's mobile and her landline. Both phones went straight to voicemail.

'Something's wrong. I can't ignore it. What if it is Mrs L, and she's in danger?'

'What about her husband or her friends? Try them.'

'I don't know how to get hold of her husband, and I don't know any of her friends.'

'If you're so worried, go round, see if she's OK. Make an excuse.'

They talked it over and decided on a plan.

Chapter 32

The Laurence house looked unoccupied and unloved, the immaculate facades of the other properties a silent rebuke. The brass letterbox and knocker were dull and smeared and the bell wasn't working. Jen pushed aside a discarded crisp packet with the toe of her shoe. It was not her responsibility anymore and she ignored the greasy takeaway box stuck between the railings. Before she knocked, she felt in her pocket for the photo of the boys Gary had downloaded.

'She might admit she's related to them. It's worth a try,' he'd said, and she agreed; it was a way to prove she was letting go of her resentment of the boys.

She used the knocker and was about to knock again when the door opened. Mrs L was barefoot and in her dressing gown. Her features were shrunken in her puffy face and her hair was unwashed, the dark roots showing. The skin around her eyes looked bruised and crusted with last night's makeup. It wasn't the first time Jen had seen her with a hangover, but she looked as if she hadn't bathed or showered for days. She ran her fingers through her hair and looked anywhere but at Jen.

'What do you want?' She glanced over Jen's shoulder; they were attracting attention from passers-by. 'You'd better come in.'

Jen stepped over a pile of mail on the doormat and followed her into the hall. Instead of taking her down to the basement, she led her into the drawing room. The air was thick and dust motes span giddily in the shafts of light from the windows. Despite the luxurious sofas and Oriental rugs, the silk-shaded lamps and the artworks, it was devoid of character. Mrs L stood in the middle of a Turkish rug like an uninvited guest. The odour of stale alcohol on her breath and seeping out of her pores hung around her like a mist.

'Why have you come here? I have no business with you anymore.'

She was struggling for authority, but her voice shook.

'Someone phoned me, asking for help. I thought it might be you.'

'What are you talking about? Why would I do that?'

'Whoever it was sounded frightened. I thought you might be in trouble. You told me your father was stalking you.'

'I said no such thing. Don't be ridiculous. And anyway, what business is it of yours? You need to go.'

The light from outside intensified as the sun slid past the window. Mrs L turned her head away, blinking as if the brightness hurt her. Her legs gave way and she sat down on one of the chairs. Her face looked greasy and she was swallowing, her hand over her mouth. Jen grabbed a wastebasket and watched as her boss threw up into it. The gagging and retching went on for a long time. Jen didn't know whether to laugh at her or help her, hold her hair back. Instead, she opened the window to let in the fresh air. The retching stopped and Mrs L dabbed at her streaming eyes, wiped her mouth and apologised as primly as if for an escaped burp. 'So sorry about that,' she said and tried a little laugh.

'Where's your husband? Is he at work? Shall I contact him?'

'I need to clean myself up. Don't come here again.'

It was as if Jen hadn't spoken. Holding the basket close to her chest, she walked into the hall with exaggerated care. Jen followed her and caught hold of her arm.

'It was you who made those calls, I know it was.'

Mrs L tore her arm away and staggered towards the front door. 'Leave me alone.'

As she reached to open the door, she slipped on the pile of envelopes and circulars and fell heavily. The fall winded her; she was gulping for air. Jen wanted to step around her and escape into the street, but she couldn't leave her lying there. She helped her up; her arm felt as if the bones were hollow.

The fall had taken the fight out of her. Still clutching the wastepaper basket to her chest, she let Jen lead her down the stairs to the basement and the downstairs toilet. Wordlessly, she handed the basket to Jen. Gagging herself, Jen emptied it into the toilet and rinsed it out.

When she returned, Mrs L was sitting on a chair in the kitchen, her head down, her hair hanging over her face. The kitchen smelt of spoiled food and garbage left too long in the bin. Empty wine bottles stood against the skirting, dishes crammed the sink and tottered on the draining board, and dirty glasses, plates and empty takeaway cartons littered the table. The pedal bin had overflowed, and eggshells and chicken bones lay scattered on the tiles. The neglect felt personal, a deliberate eroding of the years of care Jen had lavished on it. Mrs L and the household were falling apart.

'Let me call your husband. You're not well.'

'Go away. I thought I told you…'

'I'm going. But one thing. Look at this.' Jen gave her the photo of the boys on the deck of the boat. 'When I worked here, you were looking for someone. I wondered if it was your father or these boys.'

'What boys? What are you talking about?'

'The ones I told you about; the ones I took the clothes for. At least have a look.'

Mrs L took the photo, dangling it between two fingers as if it were dirty. Shaking her head, she gave it a cursory glance, and then put it into the pocket of her gown.

'If you've come to tell me where they are, I know.' She was boasting as if she'd achieved something momentous. 'It took a while, but I found them.'

'If you knew where they were, why didn't you try to help them? You must have seen the state they were in.'

'I did help them. I told social services where they were.' And there it was again, pride at prevailing over hungry, frightened children.

'Do they know it was you?'

'I didn't give them my name.'

'I mean the boys. Do they know you turned them in?' Jen took a risk, trusting her instincts. 'You're their sister, don't you care about them?'

'I didn't talk to them. I don't want anything to do with them. I haven't seen them for years. What was I supposed to do? I'm not responsible for them.' She stood up, but she staggered and looked as if she was about to faint or vomit again. Jen caught her up.

'You'll feel better when you've had a shower.'

Jen led an unresistant Mrs L up to her bedroom. Mrs L stripped off her robe and staggered into the bathroom. There had been no evidence of Mr L in the kitchen, no cigar stubs in the ashtray, no carelessly abandoned *Financial Times*. Jen waited until she heard the shower running and did a quick check of the bedroom. The bed was unmade, the sheets and duvet on the floor, but there were no books on his bedside table, no pyjamas under the pillow. She peered into his dressing room. Apart from a couple of old suits, it was empty. Mr L had taken his clothes, even taken his squash racquet and gym kit, and moved out.

The sound of running water stopped, and she waited for Mrs L to come back into the bedroom. She should be feeling better, and Jen could leave with a clear conscience. There was no sound from the bathroom, and Jen peered through the open door. Mrs L was sitting on the toilet, her robe at her feet. The photo of the boys was face-up on her bare thigh, and she was stroking it repeatedly, pressing it with the palm of her hand as if to ease out the creases. Jen watched as she knelt by the bowl, tore the photo into pieces, and flushed them away.

Jen turned away in disgust. Mrs L – *Emily* – could drink herself into a coma, fall and knock herself out or set the house on fire for all she cared. She stepped past her and scanned the open cabinets and the shelf over the washbasin. There was no razor or aftershave, no male grooming products. Mrs L was alone in the house. Jen left her kneeling by the toilet and escaped into the relative sanity of the streets.

The atmosphere in the streets was bracing; home-going crowds swarmed past her, traffic belched out fumes, and loud music pumped out of car windows. People ran for buses or hailed black cabs. Jen breathed in the polluted air and smiled at anyone pushing past her. These were the normal hassles and minor annoyances, the price you paid for living in the heart of a dirty, noisy, rumbustious city.

There was no one hanging out in the courtyard outside her building and she ran up the stairs and along the landing to her flat. Gary came out of the kitchen to greet her, a tea towel over his shoulder.

'You OK?' he said.

'I am now. I could do with a drink.'

Jen pushed her plate away and eased off her shoes. 'No more, Gary. I'm finished with her.' He refilled their glasses. 'I hated seeing her in that state. The house was filthy, and the kitchen stank. She can't be going to work, and she's alone. I'm sure it was her who made those phone calls, but she didn't admit it. Mr L has left her. It must have been him I heard shouting when she phoned. I wouldn't have put him down as a violent man, but I hardly knew him.'

'Did she admit she was related to the boys?'

'Not in so many words, but she didn't deny it. She refused to take any responsibility for them. She was gloating about turning them into the social.'

'Anyone could have turned them in,' he said. 'Adam's parents weren't the only ones worried about them. People were talking. They caused a lot of trouble.'

Gary was more interested in the boys than he was in Mrs L, but Mrs L had been her problem, and the boys his, so she held her peace. That fight was over. And Nate and Tony were the real victims. Jen didn't know what they looked like and had never examined their faces, floating like pale moons inside their hoods. Luke and Sam could look after themselves, but the younger ones were helpless. They had been so small, so thin. She didn't know if they had ever laughed, had fun, or been loved. She hadn't tried to find out. They were better off now; a foster home was better than the damp boat, and foster parents better carers than Sam and Luke. Alex wouldn't be a threat while he was swanning around as head of Avery Rentals, and Kevin would keep Luke and Sam busy, impressing them with his war stories. Northern Ireland, Kosovo, Afghanistan: Gary had told her he'd served in them all. If anyone could manage the boys, he could.

They were free now, she and Gary. Alex might become a problem again, but for now, they could live their lives and help each other step out of the cage of their past. Mrs L and her marital troubles, her alcoholism and her despair were out of her life for good. She'd demanded to be left alone, and Jen was happy to oblige her. She could leave Mrs L and her problems behind with a clear conscience. Finding a job, and being with her friends and her family were what counted now.

Chapter 33

There were no abandoned boats in Little Venice, no squatters, no reeling drunks or comatose druggies, just silence and the reflection of lights quivering on the water. On the other side of the canal, windows framed interiors as warmly lit and mysterious as paintings by Dutch artists – a man reading at a table, a woman playing with a kitten. Other people's lives, and not so different from her own. Iris's smart little flat, and the workroom crammed with clothes, was a break from the stall in the market, and Jen would never tire of the view from the window.

She was happy in her new role as Iris's assistant. Full-time and official now, stamps paid for, contract and terms and conditions in place. It was more than she'd hoped for. A job she loved, and one that could be the start of a career. Iris was training her; she'd taken her to auctions and estate sales, and Jen was learning how and what to buy. The thought of bidding frightened her.

'What if….she'd asked Iris, but Iris hadn't let her finish.

'No such thing as what if,' she'd said, and Jen accepted that she had found her place at last.

A cabin trunk and suitcases were waiting to be unpacked. Iris had bought the contents from a woman who was selling the family house and her and her brother's belongings. The house had been in the family for generations and, judging by the style and quality of his belongings, her brother had enjoyed the privileged existence of his class until the war ended it.

'Shot down over Germany,' Iris had told her. 'Poor woman had tears in her eyes while she helped me make an inventory.'

Unpacking a dead man's clothes was sad and dirty work. The sharply tailored suits and jackets, the wide-legged flannel trousers and the cashmere sweaters had been packed lovingly and folded between layers of tissue paper. Jen pulled on the gloves Iris insisted she wore. 'Scabies, darling,' she'd said. 'You wouldn't want them. Trust me, I've had them twice.'

An hour later, the trunk was empty, and the clothes had been examined for flaws and hung on the rails. Searching through the pockets of a tweed jacket she'd found a toffee and an old George VI half-crown. The coin went into a box with the others, the jacket into the pile for the clothes bank. She cleaned the inside of the trunk and closed the lid. A corner of the label for the Grand Hotel in Naples had come unstuck, and she pressed it down; vintage travel labels were desirable. There were others, for Rangoon and Delhi, for Berlin and Madrid. Little works of art, gifting her a glimpse of another time, of other cities, other worlds. She would buy a couple for Angie to put on her pinboard.

The old leather cases yielded a couple of real treasures: a fifties Pucci blouse in immaculate condition and a sixties pillbox hat. Both objects had a history and were culturally important: Marilyn Monroe had been buried in a Pucci dress, and Jackie Kennedy was photographed wearing a pillbox hat. Bob Dylan had written a song about one. Iris would sell them to collectors, and Jen could use them as subjects for an essay she was writing for her course: 'Iconic Fashion in Popular Culture.'

She stacked the empty cases against the wall and scrubbed her hands. Gary had asked her to pick up a goose from the organic butchers for their Christmas lunch. Once, the tradition had been Christmas lunch and booze with the Longs at their place. Mike would be at his expansive best, Sadie running from kitchen to sitting room, her raucous laughter rising above the music. Liz would be there, with Elsie, and Mike's friends from the market would drop by. Gary had come with a different woman every year.

All that had ended; now Mike and Sadie fled London for the Canary Islands every December; Mike's aching joints hurt less in the sun. She and Angie celebrated the day on their own with a chicken from Tesco and watched television in their dressing gowns. This year, though, Christmas would be at

Gary's flat. Liz and Elsie were coming for lunch, and Amina would drop by to spend time with Angie.

*

Gary's lunch had been eventful. Everyone had eaten and drunk too much. The empty wine and spirit bottles had piled up, and the music and conversation had got louder. Liz started an argument with Gary about the council's plans for the regeneration of the area and the market, and Elsie had fallen off the sofa and cut her lip. Gary had to help Liz take her home. Jen had fallen asleep fully dressed and face down on the bed.

It had been fun, sort of, but now Christmas and Boxing Day were a memory and she and her daughter were getting on each other's nerves. Inertia was making them snappy. Slumped at opposite ends of the sofa they were supposed to be watching a talent show Angie had recorded. She'd Skyped Zac and chatted to him all through the programme, ignoring the tedious sympathy-seeking stories, the caterwauling of the competitors and the posturing of the judges.

Yawning, Jen took another chocolate from the box and another sip of wine. The waistband of her jeans dug into the flesh of her waist. Too much food, too much sitting around, too much flesh.

The fitness centre was open, and Jen jumped up. I'm going for a swim, do you want to come? You could do with the exercise.'

'You go mum.' Angie didn't look up from her screen.

Jen collected a towel from the bathroom and pulled open the drawer where she kept her sports gear. She retrieved her swimsuit and goggles from the pile of discarded leggings and sports bras. Amongst them was a set of keys, and she drew them out. There was a tag on them; Jen recognised Mrs L's neat handwriting from the lists she'd left for her.

Recognising it gave Jen a pang. There would have been no celebrations in the Laurence house this year. No beautifully wrapped presents under the Norwegian spruce in the hall. No teenage boys stomping up and down the stairs, noisy with excitement. Friends wouldn't have come to visit, and neighbours wouldn't have come for drinks. The paperboy would ring the bell expecting his Christmas tip, but he would be disappointed; the Laurences had been generous. The bonus they gave Jen every year had helped pay the winter bills.

Making a fist, she felt the metal of the keys digging into the palm of her hand; they were cold and hard. A key inserted between each finger, the tips protruding, made a sort of knuckleduster, a trick Mike had taught her when the threat posed by gang fights on the nearby estate had leaked into the surrounding streets. 'Jab at the eyes,' he'd said, 'or aim upwards into the soft flesh under the jaw.' Thankfully, she'd never had to use them that way. She put the keys back in the drawer and wriggled into her swimsuit. It felt tight.

An hour later, she was back home, re-energised from her swim and ready to work. There was reading to do for her course, and an essay to write. She turned on her computer and took out her books. Angie stuck her head around the door.

Zac's coming back tomorrow, Mum. Can he and Amina come over?

*

Zac's return signalled the end of sloth and gluttony. Mike and Sadie had come for breakfast bearing gifts – saffron and wine for her and Gary, a beaded bracelet for Angie. Tanned and rested, they were less desperate about Hayley.

'She didn't want to come with us this year and grumbled and misbehaved until she teamed up with a Spanish boy. We promised she could go back to see him if she took a few courses and maybe learned Spanish. It will give her a goal and she might forget about him in the meantime.'

Sadie kept glancing at Mike as she talked. He seemed distracted. A big man, stout but hard-bodied, his limbs thick and muscular, he'd let himself go. Now he looked soft and flabby, his muscles slack. He'd finally given up his stalls, but he wasn't enjoying his freedom. Love for his trade had kept him active and working long after there was any need to. He seemed at a loss, his hands curled loosely in his lap.

Shamefully, Jen realised she had never paid much attention to his work. She'd accepted the little gifts: the fruit put into a paper bag and tucked into her carrier. The grapes, the aromatic melons, and the peaches warm from the sun in the summer. The courgettes and the asparagus. 'Try this, tell me what you think.' Disguising his generosity as a need for her opinion.

She'd never thought about how hard it must have been to leave his wife and child warm in their beds to drive down to Nine Elms while it was still dark. To unpack his van and dress his stall while the rest of the world was waking up. To wait for customers in winter, clapping his hands in fingerless gloves and stamping his feet while the wind blew refuse along the gutters. To keep the faith and smile while summer visitors squeezed the fruit asked patronising questions, and then left without buying. Despite that, his work was part of his identity. It had kept him fit and engaged; it must have been hard to let it go.

'You know, Hayley was good at languages at school,' Angie told Mike. 'We were in the same group. She liked Spanish.'

It had taken her insightful and compassionate daughter to do what she should have; praise their daughter and give them hope. Sadie was watching her husband. Sensitive to his wife's mood, Mike roused himself.

'I need something to do. I'm bored. The guys in the market are fed up with me hanging around.'

'We could take a drive out to the country; visit some of those stately homes Elsie and Liz are always going on about.' Sadie looked hopeful, but Mike didn't look convinced.

'That lot get enough of my money.' He launched into a rant about the aristocracy. 'But thanks, love, I know I need to do something.'

'You could come with me tomorrow,' Gary said. Mike drew his chair closer, and Gary showed him the photos he'd taken of the river and the containers taking waste up to Wandsworth.

Jen started to clear the breakfast dishes. They'd had their break, let loose, and now they were ready for whatever came next. New year, new life. Or so she thought. Later she would look back on that time as the time before.

2017

Chapter 34

Jen knew a good suit when she saw it. The man walking in front of her was wearing a suit that was the result of hours of discussion, measurements taken and fittings arranged. Rolls of material had been unfurled and examined, draped, and held up to the light. After weeks of adjustments and tweaking, the suit would be ready to wear. But not by the man wearing it now. The fine wool struggled to hold his heavy limbs and square trunk. She didn't need to see his face; she recognised Ted Mason's exaggerated, rolling gait, the broad back, the thick neck.

She followed him as he turned into the village and watched him climb the steps to the Laurences' house, take out a key, open the door and walk in. As if he lived there. As if he owned the place. She continued walking, unable to take it in. How had it happened? Ted Mason had gone from intruder and stalker to living with his victim. And he was wearing one of the suits Mr L had left behind. She tried to imagine him sitting in one of the chairs in the drawing room or opening a can of beer in the dining room. Did he sleep in the house? And if so, where?

Surely Mrs L wouldn't have let Ted into her life voluntarily. It had been a while since her last confrontation with her ex-boss, and she hadn't seen anything suspicious during her visit. The kitchen had been so squalid she might have missed something, but she'd seen enough to convince her that Mr L had left his wife and that she was alone.

But why should she care? Mrs L was out of her life. Jen was content now, even happy. Her daughter was immersed in college life, making friends, and looking forward to her next steps into the world, and she and Gary were learning how to navigate their new relationship. There were still moments when the shadow of her anger and her violence hung over them, but they were working through it. Life was good and peaceful. She felt safe.

But then she remembered Ted Mason's swagger as he walked up the steps to the Laurences' front door, the disturbing phone calls – a woman pleading, a man shouting. Sadie had mentioned a commotion in the village; she was seeing her and Mike for lunch on Sunday, she would quiz her, and try to jog her memory.

*

Sadie remembered the disturbance. The police had blocked off the entrance to the street and a crowd had gathered. Everyone had thought it was terrorists or something to do with the politician, but the boy who delivered their papers had told her that he hadn't been there at the time. The newsagent had seen a couple fighting in the street. Someone else said there had been an attempt to break into the jewellers; a window had been broken, and a motorcycle was seen speeding away. No one knew anything for sure. Trying to weed out the rumours from the truth was like untangling a nautical knot with gloves on.

'I don't remember anything else, Jen. Why, what's up?'

'Ted Mason's got a key to the Laurence house. I've got a bad feeling about this. What should I do?'

Mike interrupted her. 'Why do you have to do anything? Stay away from him. The barman in the Sussex Arms told me he got that face setting a fire for the insurance. He fucked it up and went to prison, but his accomplice nearly died. He brags about it. You don't know that he's moved in. He could have been visiting. Don't go near the house, Jen.'

'Of course, he's moved in. He's got a key. He's wearing one of Mr L's old suits.'

Sadie thought they should go to the police. Mike said the police would have checked him out already; they'd be keeping an eye on him. They would know everything that goes on in that street, he said, and if Mrs L hadn't complained, the police couldn't or wouldn't be able to do anything. 'He's her father. What makes you think she's in danger?'

She told them about the phone calls, the woman asking for help, the man shouting.

'Not your problem,' Mike said. Stay out of it. Leave it to me, I'll get talking to him. Buy him a few pints.'

He had perked up. Jen could almost see the energy surging, firing up the synapses and hear the snap and fizz of life returning at the thought of some action. Jen was relieved; Mike's interest would allow her to put her concerns about Ted to one side; she could leave him to inveigle his way into the man's confidence, and leave her to concentrate on her own life.

*

Walking fast, her mind on the evening ahead, Jen was stopped by someone calling her.

'Miss. Miss. Tall lady.'

The housekeeper from next door to the Laurence's was running to catch up to her. Jen stopped, puzzled; the woman looked frantic.

'You were her friend. You must help. The poor lady is frightened.' She was flushed and out of breath.

'It's OK…' Jen tried to calm her, and pulled her into a doorway and away from the curious glances of the passers-by and the noise of the traffic.

'You saw her every day. No more running, no more work. There is shouting. I never see her now. The mister and his boys don't come anymore. Only him, with that face. I don't know what to do.'

Before Jen could react, she pressed a scrap of paper into her hand and whispered, 'Call me. We talk.'

She scuttled off. Jen looked at the barely legible name – Jaslene – and a telephone number. At home, she rang the number and left a message. Rang again before she went to bed, and left another message. Jaslene didn't return her calls.

She must have regretted talking to her. Despite her better judgement, she was going to be dragged back into Mrs L's sordid drama. She couldn't ignore what she'd been told. She rang Mike.

'What about the husband? He should know another man is living in the house,' Mike said. 'He should contact the police; they might act if it comes from him.'

*

Mr Laurence was an enigma. She'd picked up his underwear from the floor, ironed his shirts and collected his suits from the dry cleaners, but only saw him occasionally. He was amiable and polite; he'd kept his distance and didn't seem the sort of man who would walk out on his wife, and then frighten her into making desperate phone calls. Google revealed the name of his company, but he'd left it months ago. He'd been friendly with the owner of the estate agents in the village, and the man who owned the coffee merchants and some of the neighbours; he might have told them his plans.

On her way to work the next day, she took a detour through the village. It was a waste of time. The barista in the coffee shop was cold and unresponsive, and no one she spoke to knew anything. She had made herself conspicuous by asking questions in an area where there was still a police presence, and she turned to Google again.

His ex-wife, the lawyer, was easily traced. She may be the ex-wife, but she was still part of the family, still sharing responsibility for her sons, and so must have to consult with her ex-husband. She had sent her voicemails and texts telling her she needed to speak to Mr L, but she was either away or was ignoring her. Jen was determined to pass on the burden of Mrs L and her troubles; Mike was right; it wasn't her problem. She'd combine a trip to town with a visit to the V&A and drop into the ex-wife's offices and tell her what she knew and ask her to pass it on to Mr L.

Her office was in a soot-stained building behind Russell Square, her name one of six on the brass plate by the door. A bored receptionist asked her if she had an appointment and shrugged when Jen said she had information of a personal nature, but rang and announced her. Jen could hear an irritated chirruping from the other end of the line and felt a tremor of doubt; had she overestimated her connection with wife number one? The receptionist handed her the phone. Jen was halfway through her explanation when Mrs Laurence cut her off.

'If you don't have legal business with me or my firm, please don't turn up here without an appointment. You were my ex-husband's cleaner. What business could you possibly have with his family? Stop interfering in things that don't concern you. And don't contact me again.'

Jen was left holding the receiver and looking foolish. She felt the receptionist's eyes on her and imagined her smirk as she walked out. Back in the street, she thought of all the clever things she could have said, but the first Mrs L was a tougher proposition than the current one; she doubted she could have outsmarted her. A criminal lawyer knows how to use words to confuse and undermine her opponents. Contacting the family had been a bad idea. If they knew anything, they were hardly going to tell her. She had no standing in their eyes. Cringing, she recalled how she'd introduced herself. 'News of a personal nature.' So pompous. Who spoke like that? She'd been slapped down, put in her place and made to feel she was not worth a minute of a busy and important woman's time. Made to question her behaviour. She fantasised about throwing a brick through the window of the offices and felt better.

*

Sadie laughed when she told her and Mike about her visit to the first Mrs L, and at her pompous way of introducing herself, but Gary was serious. 'You've done your best. It's not your responsibility.'

'Don't underestimate Ted; he's dangerous,' Mike said. 'He's an arsonist and a petty criminal. He's got nothing to lose, and prison is no deterrent to someone like him. Seriously, Jen. Keep away.'

Sadie was looking anxious. 'Keep out of it, both of you. You don't know what's going on. He's her father, after all.'

'Don't go to the police. What will you tell them? They might suspect you of something. They suspect everyone, it's their job.

'If you're that worried, keep trying Jaslene,' Mike said. 'She must see what's going on in the neighbourhood. Is she friendly with any of the other housekeepers or au pairs in the street? They all gossip about their employers. But stay away from Ted. He's my job.'

Sadie was unhappy. 'It's none of your business, Mike. Tell him, Jen.'

Jen understood why Sadie was anxious, but Mike could look after himself. If he wanted to get involved, it was up to him; he could get close to Ted and was big enough and shrewd enough to deal with him. He and Sadie stopped on their way out, and Gary was watching her. She told them what they wanted to hear. 'I'll wait until I hear from Jaslene. I won't do anything reckless.'

Chapter 35

Mike was meeting Ted in a pub near Paddington station. He saw Ted as a small-time villain but recognised that he was dangerous. Jen felt there was something more, something dark and powerful under the villain persona. Something that made her want to step out of his eye-line. 'Know your enemy' was a useful maxim in any battle, but for that, she had to see him up close, and for her to see him up close, she needed a disguise.

She dressed in the clothes and shoes she'd bought for job interviews, and used a beige foundation on her skin, darkened her eyebrows and lashes with mascara, then shrugged on an old coat. Tucking her hair up under a floppy hat was the final change. Before she left the flat, she checked her appearance in the mirror. The unadorned and stark beauty that attracted and repelled, the 'six-genes away from the albino' look that was part of her image, was lost under the make-up and silly hat. There was nothing about her now to offend or challenge. Keeping her head down, she hurried into the street. Mrs Asan, Liz's neighbour, was walking towards her. Usually eager to talk, she passed her without a second glance. Jen swung through the crowds, enjoying her anonymity.

She pushed open the door to the pub and a blast of heat and noise almost blew her back onto the street. Workers desperate to get a drink before returning to the suburbs packed the tables. People shouted at each other or into their phones and stood two-deep at the bar. A couple of men inched their way past her and then stood in the doorway, put off by the mob inside. Startled, Jen turned her head away. 'Let's try somewhere else,' Mike said. 'Excuse me, love.' Then he was on the pavement, holding Ted by the elbow.

They were walking towards Bayswater, and Jen followed them. She was sure that Mike hadn't recognised her, and Ted had the blank look of a sleepwalker. Queensway was busy, the tat shops and cheap eateries doing a good trade; she wouldn't be noticed. They turned into a pub and she gave them time to settle down and then entered.

They were watching snooker on the television, their backs to the door, pint glasses on the table in front of them. She ordered a glass of wine and found a table where she could watch them without them seeing her, and opened her newspaper. Hopefully, she looked like an office worker killing time before going home to a lonely bedsit and the cliché cat.

Ted was shovelling crisps from a giant bag into his mouth, his arm rising and falling like an automaton. He lifted his tankard, washed down the crisps and then stared blankly at the screen. For the first time, Jen could examine his face properly; ignore the burns that made him grotesque and see the man. Even before his accident, he must have had a threatening appearance. His profile was blunt and flat like a snake's, his ears small and as if pasted on, his features nondescript and the skin that was not scorched and puckered was pockmarked and sallow. His hand dipping into the bag of crisps was plump and featureless. She imagined those unblinking eyes watching the kids on the canal, that hand touching them.

Beside him, Mike radiated power and strength. He sat upright in his seat, his face impassive, and drank slowly, pacing himself. Ted finished his beer and wiped his mouth. Mike got up and went to the bar. As he walked back to his table, he nudged hers with his hip. He'd recognised her.

An hour later they were ready to go. Ted could hardly walk straight. Mike was unaffected; he could hold his drink. Once in the street, Ted staggered over to the side of the road and threw up. It was doubtful that he could even see her, and Jen watched from a doorway. He finished spluttering and wiping his mouth and stood on the kerb, swaying.

How vile he is, she thought. Men like him. What a waste of blood, breath and skin. It would take a second to pass him, her shoulder brushing his. Watch his face as he fell under the wheels of a car. Or better still a bus. It would be an accident;

he was drunk and unsteady on his feet. It would take the slightest touch to send him reeling into the road.

Jen clenched her fists, shoved them deep into her pockets and screwed her eyes shut. Pincer fingers. Light glinting off the lens of spectacles. Not him, she told herself. Not under a bus for her father. For him something cold and lingering. But perfect for the one in front of her now. Brutal, clashing, grinding. Metal and burning rubber. Could she do it? Did she have it in her? She stepped out of the doorway. Mike hailed a taxi, and she moved back and away from the kerb, her hands slippery.

'He's not going to be sick, is he?' The taxi driver was doubtful, but Mike reassured him.

Ted collapsed into the back of the cab and it drove away. Mike waited until it was out of sight and joined her. 'He gave the Laurence's address. If he's not living in the house, he's confident enough to turn up drunk.' He linked his arm through hers. If he noticed she was trembling, he didn't comment. 'Come on, I need to eat.'

He'd recognised her outside the pub in Paddington. 'It only took a second; it's your shape, the long, spare leanness of you, like a sketch. Your hands in your pockets. You're magic, girl. I'd know you anywhere. All the same, I'm impressed.' He led her back into the pub, and they settled themselves at a table.

'Ted was already pissed when we met,' Mike said. The waiter brought their drinks, and they ordered. 'He was bragging about his daughter, saying she's going to come into some money. Her husband is divorcing her. There'll be a settlement. To hear him talk, he's on good terms with her. Not that I believe him. He brags about the house and said the place is a gold mine. He'd worked for an antique dealer when he was young and learned how to spot the good stuff. Said the place is stuffed with it.'

Mrs Laurence might get the house, and her father would do his best to get his hands on it. He must have forced his way into her life or convinced a weakened Mrs L that she needed him. As sick and vulnerable as she was, it wouldn't have been difficult.

The waiter brought their food. Jen waited while Mike tackled his steak; she enjoyed seeing him eat and drink, happy that he was himself again. 'I wouldn't be surprised if he's sneaking some of the smaller items out of the house.' He paused to drink. 'Eat up, Jen, the steaks are good here.' He filled her glass. She wasn't hungry and felt too agitated to eat, but she took up her knife and fork.

Ted would be impressed by the contents of the house. She'd been impressed by the artworks and ornaments herself, but over time they became just items that she looked after. She did have her favourites. A painting of a vase of poppies on the landing and a bronze figurine of a greyhound in the drawing room had touched her. They were beautiful, perfect, and small enough for Ted to smuggle them out of the house. His pudgy hands would unhook the painting from the wall, and lift the bronze greyhound from where it had rested for years. Oh, how she longed for that car, the crushed and broken skull. But not by her hand. She knew that now. Murderous as her thoughts were, as strong as her hatred was, her self-preservation was stronger. They had finished eating. Mike signalled to the waiter. 'Any luck with Jaslene?'

Jen had given up leaving messages to her; she suspected that the housekeeper had blocked her calls. It was frustrating. Why had the woman given her a phone number if she wasn't going to answer? At the very least she would be able to tell her if she'd seen Mrs L.

'Where does your ex-boss work? Have you tried there? You could contact her. Whatever you do, don't go near the house. He might be a drunk, but don't underestimate Ted; he's dangerous. Promise me, Jen. I mean it.' He was sincere, sure that she would be in danger if Ted spotted her.

'Hand on heart, Mike,' she told him. 'I won't go near the house.'

They split up then, Mike to go home, she to walk off her jitters. Mike had noticed her agitation while they were waiting for their meals. 'You look hot and bothered,' he'd said. She'd been folding and unfolding her napkin and had snatched at her drink when it came and gulped it down. 'Slow down, girl. Don't let him get to you. He gets to me. Something about him. We'll sort the bugger out. Don't do anything daft.'

Observing Ted Mason had hardened her resolve, yet she felt uncertain. Mrs L hated him, had said he wanted to drag her down, and yet he was living in her home. Alone, abandoned by her husband, she may have let him into her life. Or, more likely, he had a hold on her, something in their shared past that let him control her.

Chapter 36

Jen spread the contents of a file on her bed. She remembered seeing something about Mrs L's workplace among the jumble of receipts, old postcards and newspaper clippings. She found what she was looking for; an article and photo from a magazine of a group of men and women, one of them holding a trophy. And behind them, a board with the name of the company emblazoned across it. The men looked triumphant and puffed up, the women stood at either end of the line-up like punctuation marks. Mrs L looked resentful, her arms hung down awkwardly, and she wasn't smiling. The other woman wore a hijab with her business suit and looked tense, her shoulders rigid, her face stern. Jen had cut it out to show Angie, who had glanced at it and yawned.

She fired up the computer and loaded the company web page. Speech ready, she dialled the number and asked for Emily Laurence. Emily Laurence wasn't available.

'Mrs Laurence is on leave at the moment.'

It was as if she was talking to a machine. They weren't at liberty to tell her when she might be back, but Jen had learned enough. Her boss would struggle to work through flu and food poisoning episodes, and, later, through vicious hangovers. It took more than an illness to keep her at home. Her job gave her status and proved how far she'd come. But her status, her marriage and her family would mean nothing to Ted. His brutal appearance hid something more complicated: disconnection from the world around him. He charged through life, she thought now, not caring if anyone was in his way. Other people didn't matter to him; he would take what he wanted without feeling pity or shame, without feeling anything.

Except for rage. Rage fuelled him. She remembered the force with which he'd slammed the drawing-room door, the lamp upended on the floor, its ivory silk shade dented and split. He'd used the doorbell like a weapon, leaving Mrs L hunched in the chair, her hands over her ears like a child. Ted Mason was a sociopath, a vicious man, someone who could set a fire for money. Someone who could abandon his wife and his children when it suited him, but later seek them out to get what he could from them. His daughter was as devious, but she had a conscience. Ted had no conscience, but he was reckless and clumsy – he'd set fire to his face.

They had to find proof that he was stealing from his daughter, get him out of her house, and hopefully out of her life. She needed eyes on the street. An idea was forming; neither she nor Mike had reason to hang around the village and she was too well known there. Ted would get suspicious if he saw Mike. She would check the stalls in the market to see if she recognised anything Ted might have taken. She put the newspaper clipping in her bag and stuffed the rest of the papers back in the folder. It was getting late, and she hurried to open the stall.

An hour later she watched Sadie make her way toward her. She settled herself on the chair in front of the stall and Jen gave her the newspaper clipping.

'Have a look at this. I found out where Mrs L works, but she's on indefinite leave. Keep an eye on things. I'll get the teas.'

Ignoring the lift, she climbed up to the top floor. While she waited for her order she walked out onto the terrace and stared over the chimneys and rooftops. Sadie would fit in anywhere. Her appearance was conventional, her clothes were quietly fashionable, and her shoes and handbag excellent copies of the real things. There was nothing to mark her out as different from any well-off woman of her age. No one would guess she'd spent her youth selling cheap sweets from a stall in Shepherd's Bush Market, or that her husband was an ex-con. Formidable, yes; an angry Sadie could turn a drunk or an arrogant teenager into a quivering marshmallow, but not enough to draw attention to herself. Jen took the lift back down to her floor, carrying the teas.

Sadie handed her back the newspaper and took her tea. 'Is this your old boss? She's good-looking. Glamorous. Nice shoes.'

'She might not look like that now; it was taken some time ago.' Before stress and fear etched lines around her eyes and thinned her lips. 'I've had an idea,' she said. 'Do you take a shortcut through the village when you take Foo to the park?'

Foo would be the perfect cover. Old and fat, he stopped every few yards to sniff and snuffle. He would give Sadie the perfect excuse to glance around and take note of anything unusual. Jen wrote down the number of the house for her.

'Just see if it looks cared for. It looked neglected the last time I was there. Don't ask any questions; everyone's a bit jumpy because of the security in the area. Maybe have breakfast at the café some mornings.'

Sadie had heard enough about Ted to know him if she saw him, but Jen described Jaslene. 'You can't miss her. She works for the couple next door to the Laurences. Don't go near Mrs L or Ted if you see them but take a photo if you can do it discreetly. I'd go myself, but I'm too well-known there.'

Sadie examined the clipping again. 'Nice looking, your Mrs L. Can't miss her, with that hair, that bod. She's fit.'

Not anymore, Jen thought and again felt the tug in her chest, the flush of guilt.

'Jen, I have to ask. Why are you getting so involved?'

Because she knew something fateful hovered over Emily Laurence, and she knew Ted was the catalyst that would bring her down. Knowing all that, and trusting her instincts, she had to act. How could she not? Gary had asked the same question, and she gave Sadie the answer she'd given him.

'I think she's in danger.'

The rest of the day dragged on. Customers were scarce. While she waited for Sadie to come back, she did a stock check, adding items to the inventory and marking those that had been in stock too long. There was a hard copy somewhere, and she rooted around in the drawer. Digging it out sparked a memory; Mrs Laurence had given her a similar one, recording all the contents in the house for the insurance company. She had a copy at home. It would be out of date now but it might help if they had to check for missing items from the house.

She'd finished serving a couple of tourists when Sadie returned from window shopping. She had several shopping bags.

'I managed to take a few photos of the house. It looked a bit shabby, the windows were dirty and the curtains half-drawn.'

'Did you see anyone in the street?'

'The bigwig in the house next door was getting into a car while I was having my coffee. A nice car, a Lexus, and a chauffeur in a smart uniform.'

The 'bigwig' was someone important in the city; the chauffeur was Jaslene's husband. Jen had seen him holding the door open for his boss or sitting in the car waiting for him. He had the closed-off look of anyone who worked for the rich, meant to discourage contact.

'I tried to see into the basement, but the blind was down. There was no sign of Mrs L or Ted. Mike told me about Ted nicking stuff from the house. He thinks there's something seriously wrong with that man. Kevin told Mike he'd been harassing one of the boys working on the boats. The kid was upset, shaking and as white as a ghost, but he wouldn't say why. The boys were doing well. Kevin is going to ask the Brothers to take them on permanently. He likes them, thinks they're good kids.'

Good kids were not how Jen would describe them, but they deserved a chance. Now it looked like Ted Mason was going to ruin it for them.

'I bought a couple of things from the used designer shop. The bag was a bargain. A Ralph Lauren.' She held up the beige tote.

'Can I have a look?' Jen opened the bag and examined the lining. Sadie watched.

'Is it a fake?'

'Mrs L had one like it. I was looking for a little tear on the lining. This could be hers.' She showed Sadie her mending of the rip, the tiny stitches.

Sadie was eager to continue her observation of the street. 'I'll take my laptop and sit in the window, working. Pretend I'm writing a bestseller.'

'Don't approach the chauffeur.'

'Are you kidding? As if.'

That night she told Gary about the handbag. 'If we can prove he's taking other things from the house, we might be able to get rid of him.'

Gary uploaded the photos Sadie had taken onto his computer. 'Is that someone at the top window?' He enlarged it and Jen drew back as the shadow became denser, the outline bolder, but featureless, like a child's drawing: a round head floating above the rectangular shape of the trunk. There was no mistaking the malignancy of that thick torso, that cannonball head.

'He's been down to the canal again. Sadie said he frightened Luke.'

'I heard. Kevin told me. He threatened to throw him in the canal. He would, too.'

'That would be a result,' Jen said, 'Save us a lot of trouble.'

Chapter 37

Two days later, Sadie was waiting for her outside the market. She was playing with the clasp of her handbag, snapping it open and shut. Jen led her up to the rooftop café and braced herself for unwelcome news.

'I was in the village yesterday, taking Foo to the park. Jaslene likes dogs and she stopped to pet Foo. We got talking, about Foo at first, and then I mentioned you.'

'At last...' Jen said.

But Sadie went on. 'She was suspicious, but once she was convinced that I knew you and that you meant well, she relaxed. I think she was relieved to talk to someone, although she kept looking around as if she was scared.'

She was restless; she hadn't sat down. 'You can smoke out here if you want to,' Jen told her, but she shook her head. 'I haven't got long. Let me tell you.'

'Her husband works late and wakes her up when he comes in. It's quiet in the street then, and they can hear raised voices from next door. One night they heard breaking glass and a man shouting, and a woman crying. She couldn't make out the words, but she said his voice frightened her. She'd wanted to call the police, but her husband told her to mind her own business.'

Jen steadied herself, holding on to the back of a chair. Her worst fears. But Sadie hadn't finished.

'He's forbidden her to get involved with what was "going on" in the Laurence house. Those were his words exactly, "going on". He refused to tell her what he meant. Jaslene doesn't know if Mrs L is there or not. She hasn't seen her, only Ted going in and out, and when he's out she can't hear anyone moving about. It's quiet, too quiet. She's sorry she blocked your calls, but her husband made her. I think she's scared of him. Don't call her, in case he finds out, and don't try to contact her. I hope he's not bullying her. He looked like a cold fish to me.'

'He might be protecting his wife. She's more visible in the area than he is. And we don't know about their status. They might not want to draw attention to themselves.'

Sadie wasn't convinced. 'Her husband is a piece of work. I don't trust him. I've got to go, we're off to visit friends. I'll bring Mike up to date with everything on the way and take Mr Foo for a walk past the house when we get back tonight. I'll call you if I notice anything.'

As she left, she turned back. 'Do you remember that woman on the canal? The one who got killed by her old man.'

'You don't think…'

'We all knew he was abusing her.'

They hadn't known for sure, Jen thought. And then felt ashamed. They had known and did nothing. She remembered seeing the woman in the market. She often had a black eye or visible bruising and was once seen with a cast on her arm. They had all been guilty: the market traders who served her and gossiped about her, the neighbours who'd heard the rows but turned up the television and ignored the sound of fighting, the muffled thumps and crying. The police had been called to the house several times but left after talking to them. Nothing came of it, and so a woman died. And then the report in the paper, the shock of it, the excuses they all made. Her death hung over them all for months and then was forgotten.

'Not this time, Sadie,' Jen said. And meant it. Sadie nodded, but Jen could see how disturbed she was.

'I'll think of something; we can't just sit back,' Jen said. 'Not again.'

It was a promise she hoped she could keep. The news about the chauffeur was revealing. Chauffeurs may be discreet about their employers to outsiders, but they talked among themselves. Alex had made it his business to be friendly with them; they saw and heard things that were part of the night-time world, things that the daytime staff didn't. They heard stories from security men outside hotels, bouncers outside clubs, porters in hospitals and detectives in Paddington nick or West End Central. They knew which married politician or celebrity had a lover stashed away in a flat in Pimlico or Fulham, and who trawled for trade in public toilets, or frequented brothels in dingy basements or boutique hotels. They had ears and eyes in banks and restaurants, in gyms and massage parlours, as well as in pubs, clubs and bars. Alex would charm them and even the most guarded of them would let something slip eventually. His genius was in knowing what was important and how he could turn it to his advantage. But she wasn't Alex, and neither was Mike. Either of them approaching Jaslene or her husband for information would get them nowhere.

She was late opening the stall, but business was slow. By noon, she'd sold a twenties sequinned skullcap that had been in stock for too long. Iris turned up, looking tired, her eyes puffy, and only nodded when Jen told her they'd got rid of the skullcap.

'We're overstocked. I'm going to take some of it to my friend's shop in Greenwich. We need the space. I'm glad for an excuse to get out of the house. I'm tired of sitting in front of a computer.'

Jen was learning how complicated Iris's business was. The stall was the first choice among casual buyers and tourists, but some of the traders in the market had left, preferring to work from home, selling online. She and Iris spent the morning searching through the stock and putting aside anything Iris thought her friend could sell.

Leaving the woman opposite to watch the stall, Jen helped Iris carry the garment bags down to her car. She dawdled on the walk back, enjoying the fresh air and daylight; she would be working under artificial light for the rest of the day, and she turned her face up and felt the weak sun on her skin.

'Oi, Jen!' Maggie was sitting in the doorway of a vacant shop. 'Gonna buy me a tea?'

Jen had walked past Maggie without seeing her.

'Where've you been?' she asked her. 'I haven't seen you in ages.'

'Here and there. Out and about. Where do you think I've been? What about this tea then?'

Maggie was in a confrontational mood. 'To answer your question, as if you cared, I've been in hospital. I went to A&E, but they kept me in. I had pneumonia. It was OK in there, warm, and the beds were comfy. I even liked the food. Some of it.'

A law unto herself, Maggie was a mystery. She came and went on either a whim or a necessity. It was a sort of freedom, Jen thought, but not one she envied. Pasty-faced and greasy-haired, and with dark shadows under her eyes, she could have been any age from thirty to sixty. Someone had made sure she had warm clothes when she left the hospital. Her coat looked old, but it was lined and had a fur collar. A poorly knitted orange scarf hung down past the hem of the coat. Jen stopped at the nearest café and bought back tea and cheese rolls. They ate in silence, Maggie sitting cross-legged on her blankets, Jen leaning against the wall.

'I might be getting a place to live. Not round here, though.' Maggie sounded unenthusiastic. Unique among the rough sleepers, she'd been around so long that she had her regulars; people who remembered her family. People who looked out for her and bought her food and drinks. If the room was miles away, she would be cut off from all she knew, and from all who knew her. No one would see her for who she was, remember her from before, buy her a tea or take her for a meal. This was her area, where she had lived with her family, where she'd gone to school. It was where she returned to when she needed to be in touch with her past. These were her streets, her people.

'Will you take it?'

'I don't know. I hated living inside, staring at four walls. I didn't know what to do with myself. I was lonely. Maybe if Monalula came with me.' She gave a short bark of a laugh. 'But anyway. You're OK. Back with Gary. I like him, he's real.' Maggie finished her roll, drained the last of her tea and lobbed the plastic cup into a litter bin. 'I meant to tell you.

I've seen a bloke following you. I'd seen him before. Arsehole. Burns all over his face; he kicked Monalula. Lula can't fight back, he's almost blind.'

Maggie was playing with the fringes on her scarf, looking across the street, her attention wandering. Jen touched her shoulder and she flinched.

'How do you know he was following me? When was this, Maggie?'

'Before I went into hospital. Ages ago. And if I say he was following you, he was.'

'Where was it? Where was I?'

Maggie tugged at her scarf, but she was attentive now. 'By that café over the canal. You were with your kid. He followed you from under the flyover. You stopped on the corner, and he watched you until you split up. He watched your kid for a while, then walked back the way he came. I would have told you before, but I didn't see you around. I got sick. Forgot about it, until now. Shocking news, aye? I wouldn't want him following me.' Maggie struggled to her feet and picked up her backpack.

'Wait. You said you saw him before. When?'

'Months ago. He was hanging around the squat in Kilburn. I only go there if the weather is bad. I'd rather sleep out than with the toerags there. They steal your stuff, nick the shoes off your feet when you're asleep.' She was off on one of her rants. 'There's something about that bloke, he freaked everyone out in the squat, and there's some real nutjobs there. Everyone left him alone. He used to hang out with the kids on the canal, bought alcohol for them until some of the dads went down and saw him off.' She wrapped the scarf around her neck and sank her chin into the fur collar.

Ted looking at Angie, or any child, made Jen want to seek him out and press her thumbs into his eyes. She was as certain as she could be that Angie and her friends hadn't been among those drinking on the canal, but her daughter wasn't the only kid. There were other kids, vulnerable kids. The kids Hayley called losers. How long before Ted crossed the path of one of those kids, and his desires became actions? Ted Mason was creeping into every part of their lives; someone had to sort him out soon.

'Do me a favour, Maggie. If you see him again, can you let me know? I'm working in the antique market.' She reached into her pocket for a card and saw Maggie's jaw tense.

She thinks I'm going to give her money, she thought. Why not? Why didn't she ever give her money? Money would give her independence and let her buy food. Or drink. Probably drink. But she wasn't sure how Maggie would react if she offered it now. Remembering her genteel table manners, and her defiant dignity in front of the college tutors who'd failed her, she might go all haughty on her. She handed her the card and fingered a ten-pound note. 'I can't ask you to follow him, just let me know if you see him.' She handed her the money.

'OK. Will do.' Nonchalantly tucking the money in her pocket, she squared her shoulders as if about to undertake a mission. 'I might follow him if I feel like it. I hate the fucker. He kicked Monalula,' she said again. 'Woke him up.' She was putting on her backpack, struggling with the straps. 'I heard the Averys and Alex have gone straight,' she said. 'Posh landlords now, office, and the rest of it. Suits and ties. That's Alex for you, the tricky bastard.'

Maggie trudged away, leaving her cardboard mattress and blankets in the doorway. Her tracksuit bottoms looked warm but were too short; her ankles were mottled above a pair of battered but sturdy boots. She needed warm socks and gloves. She'd survived the winter, but March was the cruellest month, the month of harsh winds and sudden showers, the time when the homeless were most at risk. Giving Maggie money had broken a rule she'd obeyed without thought. She didn't regret giving her the tenner, though she would buy alcohol with it. Who doesn't like a drink or a spliff to relax in the evening? There was a bottle of white wine in her fridge, and Gary enjoyed a joint when he needed to relax. If a few beers kept out the chilly wind and helped Maggie ignore the insults of the people walking past her doorway, then let her numb herself out. But despite her bravado, Maggie was vulnerable; she was too old and ill to survive sleeping out for much longer.

On her way home, she bought socks and gloves. Maggie's blankets were still in the doorway, and she slipped the gloves and socks under them but hesitated before adding a carrier bag of food. Leaving it there made her uncomfortable; she'd bought food for Maggie in the past, but they'd eaten it together. But it wasn't about her. The gloves and socks would keep Maggie's hands and feet warm, and the food would give her nourishment. If it didn't get stolen.

Chapter 38

For someone who admired the freedom of the new-age hippies and activists he'd spent so much time with, Gary had too many possessions. There were rugs on the painted floorboards, shelves of books everywhere, and his kitchen was well stocked with knives, pans and complicated machines that turned out bread, pasta or espresso coffee. His flat was so warm, so shabby-chic and comfortable, that she'd wondered why he spent so much time in hers. But she and Angie were his family, a borrowed family, one that he loved. A complicated man, her lover. Jen knew people would say the same about her.

Their meal that night was a beef casserole, left to braise for hours in a slow cooker, served with Lyonnais potatoes, and followed by a crème Brule he'd made himself. After eating, they collapsed onto his enormous sofa. Tucking her feet under a knitted blanket, she waited for Gary to fill their glasses. He'd taken trouble over the meal, lighting candles and bringing in the dessert with a flourish. She hadn't wanted to spoil the moment by talking about Ted Mason. They were both relaxed now, and she mentioned what Maggie had told her.

'She saw Ted following me and Angie. Some time ago.'

'I wouldn't worry. He didn't approach you then, so I don't think he will now. Angie hasn't said anything has she. He won't get to you in the street or the market,' Gary said. 'You're well protected there. Tell security about him. Whatever you do, don't approach him. Call me or Mike. Is he still living with Mrs L?

'I think so. He's got a key.'

'Whatever is going on with her and her father might be her choice,' he said.' She might be colluding with him, letting him take stuff and sell it. I don't think you're in any danger, but be careful. I'll tell Mike what you told me. We'll sort him out.'

She believed him. Their capture of Alex had been exciting, and it had been successful. Alex had backed off. Angie was safe from him. But tricky as Alex was, he wasn't a psychopath. Ted Mason was, but she was sure that if they pooled their strengths and resources, Mike and Gary would get rid of him.

They moved into the study, taking the bottle and their glasses with them. Going to a shelf, he took down a book. A Post-it note marked a page. 'You'll want to see this.'

Jen was intrigued. She reached for it, but he held it back. 'Something was nagging at me, something about Kevin. Then I remembered that I'd seen this. It was a long time ago, Jen.'

She opened the book at the page marked. A group of men standing outside the forecourt of a vacant office block stared out at the viewer, feral, dangerous, and with the hectic look of fanatics. Wearing combat trousers, army-issue boots and vests or T-shirts, they looked like an offshoot of a paramilitary organisation. A shopping trolley piled high with someone's belongings, a bike festooned with checked laundry bags hanging from the handlebars and saddle and a battered child's pram formed a barrier between the street and the square. Behind the barrier, the blank walls and dark windows of the abandoned building soared above the huddle of men and women and their animals. Sleeping bags and bedrolls lay in rows like beds in a school dormitory and a group of people sat in a circle drinking, their dogs on blankets beside them. Others slept or read in the light from the streetlamps. Gary pointed out one of the men.

'That's Kevin. I'd forgotten about the photo. It was published a long time ago and I didn't know him then, so I didn't make the connection.'

The man in the photo stared out at the viewer, his face set against the world, bombs exploding behind his eyes. This man would throw Ted Mason in the canal and hold his head under while he had a conversation with a mate. Opposite the photograph was Kevin's story, banal and familiar: brought up in care, then the army and war, war, until invalided out to a life on the streets. A man's life, a tragedy, a cliché.

'He was one of the lucky ones. The Averys took him on, gave him work, and a place to sleep.'

Jen looked at the photo of Kevin again. Now it was anger she saw. The rough sleepers and the homeless had gathered together for safety, and Kevin and his cohorts were protecting them. There were always attacks on street people, some random and some planned and targeted.

Angie phoned – she was making hot chocolate, did they want some? Gary took the book from her and put it back on the shelf.

As they were walking down to her flat, he caught her arm. 'Don't worry about Kevin. He's as straight as an arrow. He's on our side.'

They were watching a film when Sadie phoned later; she had little to report. 'Nothing doing in the Laurence house, the blinds are down and the lights out.' Mike and Gary talked for a while, and then Gary put the phone down and turned up the sound on the TV.

'Mike tried to get an invite to the house, but Ted keeps putting him off. There's nothing we can do for the moment.' Jen turned the sound down again and dropped a file into his lap.

'Don't you want to watch the film?'

'Look through that.' She was already sorting through hers.

'What am I looking for?'

'An inventory. I had one for the Laurence house, for the insurance. It listed all their belongings, even their clothes.'

Ted would be taking jewellery, small ornaments, and even the smaller paintings. If Mike got into the house, he could use it to check if anything was missing.

Angie came in. 'I'm going to bed.' She picked up a leaflet that had fallen on the floor. 'What are you doing?'

At midnight, Angie gave up and went to bed. She'd spent the time reading anything that caught her interest. Jen was about to give up herself when Gary handed her several sheets of paper stapled together. It was a list of everything in the house. Jen shook it triumphantly. 'This will help us check what's missing. If Mike can get into the house, that is.'

Things weren't looking good for Mrs L. Lurid visions of her locked up at the top of the house like the madwoman of Victorian novels, or her body mouldering away in the basement, haunted Jen. The truth would be less melodramatic, but as disturbing: either she wasn't in the house at all – no one had seen her for weeks – or she was a shut-in, hiding inside the house of her own volition, or a prisoner, forced by her father. Certainly, she was too broken to function. She'd been ruthless enough to desert her siblings, but it had been her way of surviving, and she must have hoped Ted wouldn't find them, or her. Jen believed she was a good person, and if she was a good person her pain and guilt might be because of something done to her, rather than what she had done to others.

The way she had broken her connection with her ex-boss still haunted her. It wasn't the guilt at the harsh words she'd flung at her, or the spite with which she'd taunted her that made her ashamed; that was normal, they had been at war. It was remembering the good things between them. The way she looked away when she gave her a bonus, then looked back to see her reaction. It was the shared complicity of a raised eyebrow and an ironic smile over the heads of her neighbours. It was the trust she'd placed in her. It had hurt to see how nervous she was with her stepchildren and the offhand way they'd treated her. More than once, Jen had caught them smirking at each other behind her back and had seen them gang up on her.

Emily Laurence was tough, as hard-faced and combative as Maggie and she'd built defences; she needed them. And so she acted: got herself educated, worked to change a body brought up on cheap meat and white bread, dressed it in expensive clothes, and painted false confidence onto her hungry face. Spoke in an accent that she'd borrowed. Her neighbours, the women whose clothes sat easily on bodies nourished from birth, who owned their accents, knew an imposter when they saw one and found subtle ways to show her they weren't fooled. A smothered grin when she mispronounced a word, a coldness in their eyes as they watched their husbands' surreptitious glances at her. As hired help, Jen was invisible and could see and eavesdrop with impunity, and she'd heard those husbands discuss her boss. They talked about her and competed to tell the most toxic joke about her. Mrs L must have sensed their contempt – they didn't try that hard to hide it – but she answered them with a smile. I see you, I know about you, her smile told them. She frightened them.

She was almost asleep when she remembered the keys to the Laurence's house. Careful not to wake Gary, she crept out of bed and opened the drawer carefully. They were there, under her swimsuit. She took them out and weighed them in her hand. They fitted into her palm and felt familiar. Mrs L had given them to her so she could go in and out of the house. She couldn't put it off much longer; she had to act, to know. They weren't 'sisters under the skin,' her and Mrs L, or different sides of the same coin. They had fought similar battles in diverse ways, and with different weapons, but they recognised each other. Gary turned over in the bed and flung out his arm. Jen hid the keys under her pillow and slipped into bed beside him.

Chapter 39

Jen navigated the littered steps to the door of the Laurence house with care, then peered over the railings and into the basement. The blind over the window was crooked, but she couldn't see in. She rang the bell and then stood back to see the windows on the upper floors. The house looked deserted. Turning the key and opening the door felt dangerous; stepping inside took all her courage.

The air in the hall was frigid and dank. She pressed her hand to the radiator. It was cold; the central heating had been cut off or had broken down. Taking an uncertain step was like cleaving through a solid mass, and Jen held her hands out in front of her, feeling her way, then stood still, listening. She checked that her phone was set to vibrate; Ted was out drinking with Mike, and Sadie had parked in the street outside, alert and ready to warn her if he came home early. She switched on her torch and angled the shaft of light downward.

Her familiarity with the house surfaced; she knew it as well as her own home. She knew which of the treads on the stairs creaked, which door stuck and needed a push, and which rug slipped under a careless foot. Her footsteps clattered on the wooden floor, and she took off her shoes. Pausing before taking the stairs down to the basement, she called out. There was no reply; she hadn't expected one, but she paused again before walking into what had once been her territory.

The kitchen had been where she had felt comfortable. Now it felt cold and alien: a stranger's kitchen. Two bulging bin bags stood against the door to the terrace, but the floor was sticky underfoot and there were dirty dishes in the sink, and foil cartons on the draining board. She checked the fridge. It was filthy; no food, apart from a carton of milk and a six-pack of beer. On the table, a mug with the teabag in it stood next to a plate smeared with grease and egg yolk. Yesterday's

Sun newspaper lay open next to a full ashtray. She took a photo: Ted must eat his breakfast here, but there was no evidence that Mrs L did; there was no organic wholemeal loaf in the bread bin or Jamaican coffee beans next to the coffee grinder.

There was mail on the dresser, some envelopes already opened, and she rifled through them. Anything that looked official or interesting went into her pocket to read before she left the house. Glancing into the utility room, she saw there were dirty sheets in the washing machine. Greying boxer shorts and two pairs of black nylon socks were airing on the clothes horse. If she needed proof that Ted was living here, she had it. She took another photo and then peered into the chest freezer. It was packed with joints of meat wrapped in plastic and family-size bags of frozen vegetables, but there would still be room for the body of a slender woman.

Anything valuable would be in the drawing room or the formal dining room on the ground floor, and she climbed back up the stairs with the same stealth with which she'd climbed down. If Mrs L or anyone else was in the house they would have heard her moving about by now, but she opened the door to the drawing room carefully.

Immediately, and without checking the inventory she'd brought with her, she noticed that the trio of prints that had hung over the mantel had been removed, leaving faded rectangles on the wallpaper, and the bronze greyhound wasn't on the table under the lamp. She remembered the feel of its sleek lines under her hand. The silver candlesticks in the dining room were missing, and an art deco bowl from the sideboard. A car passed in the street outside, the tyres hissing on a wet road. It must be raining. The house seemed to shift, to ease its joists and beams, then settled.

Avoiding the creaky treads, she climbed the stairs up to the bedrooms. The painting of the vase of poppies was still on the wall outside the master bedroom. Despite the cold, tendrils of her hair stuck to her temples and her hands were sweating. These were the rooms she dreaded entering. The bedroom was where the Laurences stood naked, where they kept their secrets. The clothes they wore to show how they wanted to be seen were discarded here, and the creams and lotions that covered their natural odours cluttered the shelves in the bathroom. She waited, listening again, straining to hear a breath, the rustle of bedclothes, the sound of a shower running or a phone ringing. She wiped her sweaty hands on her jeans and opened the door.

Intense heat from the red glow of an electric heater stopped her on the threshold of the room, and then the smell: sweat, stale nicotine and beer, and something clammy, like damp towels or dirty laundry. There was someone in the bed. Jen stood utterly still; she could hear the ticking of the clock.

The person in the bed turned her head towards her, her eyes closed. Emily Laurence was asleep, her legs apart and relaxed, one hand holding the sheet tangled around her thighs, the other resting on her navel. Jen stepped closer to the bed and looked down at her. She was thin and wasted, her belly sunken between jutting hip bones, her breasts flattened above the primitive arch of her ribcage, but there were no bruises, no signs that she had been hurt. She turned her head again, muttered something and sighed, stretched her legs, then let them fall apart. There was another smell here, powerful, intimate and familiar.

Jen turned on the lamp by the bed. Emily opened her eyes and blinked, her eyelids lowering and lifting mechanically. They stared at each other, motionless. Comprehension came for them both; Jen stepped back and stumbled, and Emily's eyes widened in horror. She sat up and scrambled back towards the headboard, pulling the sheets with her, tugging at them frantically, then holding them bunched to her chest. 'Jesus Christ! What are you doing here? How did you get in? Did he... is he here?'

'I let myself in,' Jen said, her voice cracking.

Emily spoke before she could go on.

'You can't be here. Does he know... who let you in?'

'No one—'

'Why are you here? He said he'd be back.' She wiped her face with a corner of the sheet, then leant to retrieve something from the floor by the bed, groping among the tangle of bedclothes and used dishes. She almost fell, gripped the side of the bed to steady herself, and then found her cigarettes and lighter. She scuttled back against the headboard. Jen felt unable to move.

'I could ring the police. Turn you in for unlawful entering.'

'I didn't break in; I had the keys; you gave them to me.'

Emily's hands were shaking so much that she almost dropped the cigarette. Her nails were filthy. Jen had recovered from the shock and stepped nearer the bed, ready to reach out to help her, but tripped over a pair of shoes.

She knew those shoes. Dull, cracked leather, worn down on one side. She held them out towards the woman in the bed. Emily stared at them, her mouth working. The heat in the room was intense. Emily was still watching her, her expression hard to read. Fear? Scorn?

'He wears your husband's suits.' Jen threw the shoes onto the bed. 'Has he taken his place in your bed too? You disgust me,' she said.

Emily shrugged, but Jen had seen her flinch.

'He's stealing from you. I can prove it.'

'You've got it wrong. You can't prove anything.'

Emily lay down and turned to the wall. Her shoulder blades were prominent and the hair on the back of her head was matted, the blond dye growing out. She drew her knees up to her chest and wrapped her arms around them. 'Please go away.' Her attempt at taking control had failed, and her voice was weak. 'He mustn't get my kids. Don't let him get my kids. Look out for them.'

'The kids are OK. You turned them in, remember.'

Jen had heard enough. In her panic to get out of the house, she almost fell down the stairs and left the front door open. Sadie opened the car door and Jen threw herself into the passenger seat. 'Drive,' she said, and now she was shivering. Sadie turned up the heat.

'Where are your shoes? What's going on, Jen. What happened in there?'

'She lied to me,' Jen said. She was clutching her shoes in her lap. 'Ted's not her father, he's her lover. She was in bed... the room reeked of sex.'

Sadie drove, hunched over and gripping the steering wheel. Jen wound down the window, breathed in the rain-soaked air, and tried to make sense of what she'd seen. The car stopped, and Sadie put on the handbrake and turned the engine off. 'Did she see you?' She reached into the back seat for a blanket and wrapped it around Jen's shoulders. 'Let's get in and have a drink. Mike won't be back yet, we can talk. The walk across the deserted courtyard seemed to take forever. Jen's legs were heavy, and her bare feet were cold and wet. She stopped to put on her shoes, holding onto Sadie's arm. Once inside the flat, she dropped into the nearest chair. She was exhausted.

'I'll get you a hot drink; you're shivering.' Sadie hesitated. 'Lying cow, your Mrs L. I can't believe she's having sex with him; he's repulsive.'

'I hardly recognised her. He's fucking her, stealing from her, and she's letting him. How could she?' Jen remembered her hands, her dirty nails. Her rings were missing. 'She fooled me. I believed he was her father, he's old enough. How could she let him...?'

'Fear maybe. He might have threatened her.'

'She talked about the kids. Asked me to look out for them. But she knows they're safe; she turned the young ones into the social. Luke and Sam can look after themselves.'

'What kids?'

Jen hauled the mail she'd taken from the house out of her pocket.

'What kids, Jen? The canal boys?' Sadie was a stuck record.

The sound of a key missing its mark distracted her. Mike was struggling to open the door, and Jen jammed the letters back into her pocket.

'Couldn't get my key in.' Mike lumbered into the room and stopped. 'What's up with you two?'

Sadie deflected him. 'I'll make some coffee; you look as if you need it.'

'That's it. The last time. If I spend another minute with that arsehole, I'll strangle him. He left me waiting in the pub, then talked filth about his daughter.'

'We've got news for you,' Sadie said. She didn't know; she'd heard the words, but the words didn't tell the story. You had to see the room, the woman in the bed. See the dirty plates and glasses, and the discarded underwear on the floor. They lived in that room, her and Ted. Had sex, ate and slept there, like junkies in a squat. Ted must bring her food she didn't eat, wine, and cigarettes she smoked when he lit them for her.

She left Sadie looking after Mike, walked home and crept into bed beside a sleeping Gary. Exhausted, yet restless and unable to sleep, she was kept awake by the memory of Emily, leaning against the headboard and smoking, or lying curled up, her arms hugging her knees to her chest. Her wasted body, her switch from fear to arrogance and then to despair. And too far gone to know Ted was stealing from her. Unless they were in it together.

She reached for the bottle of water by the bed, wrestled a sleeping pill out of the foil pack and swallowed it. Disturbing images flashed on and off in front of her mind's eye, a flick book of unsettling images: Emily's breakdown on the morning Ted had slammed out of the house, leaving her crouched on a chair, her hands over her ears like a child. And later, appearing in the kitchen, breaking down, false confidence stripped away, and her confession: 'He's my father,' she'd said. 'He's my father, but I fucking hate him.'

Emily had lied to her about Ted; but why did she feel she had to explain herself? Why tell her anything at all? Either he was her father and, stressed out and fearful, she'd blurted out the truth in the kitchen, or he was her lover, and she was ashamed of him. Rising above a terrible childhood and making something of yourself is admirable; taking a low life like Ted into your bed isn't. She must have thought he was out of her life, but he'd found her. Passing him off as her father might have been an impulsive decision, one that would haunt her.

Gary muttered something in his sleep. She envied his ability to sleep anywhere, any place. He wasn't a worrier. She tucked her knees behind his and breathed with him, counted each inhalation and exhalation, and soon her breathing became deeper and slower, and she slept. And woke an hour later. Her kids. Sadie was right; Emily *had* said "my kids". "Don't let him get my kids." Luke and Sam might be too old to be hers, but Nate and Tony? How old were they? She tried to do the maths, but she was too tired to work it out and gave up trying.

Chapter 40

Jen groped for the bottle of water by the bed. She'd fallen into a deep and dreamless sleep and woke with a clear mind. 'Running late, Jen, see you later,' Gary called out, and she heard the door slam behind him, and Angie patter into the bathroom. She'd be in there for a while. Between them, Gary and Angie had brought her back into her world. A shower, a coffee and a walk to the market, and the pleasant routine of her day would replace the awfulness of what she had seen and heard the night before.

She would talk to Gary tonight. He and Mike may be angry about what she had done, but it was her decision and her responsibility. She had known there would be consequences, and she was ready to face them. Hopefully, Sadie would feel the same. She left a message for her, made herself a coffee and sat down to read the letters she'd taken from the house.

In formal legalese, a letter from a solicitor to Mr L confirmed the breakdown of his marriage to Emily. The house was up for sale, their divorce was going through, and they were working out a settlement. Mr L was in France, overseeing the sale of their property in Normandy. Mrs L was refusing to let the agent show the house to prospective buyers.

'I've been told that the house looks neglected. What the hell is going on, Emily,' her husband had written. 'We'd come to an understanding. What changed your mind?'

Ted Mason changed her mind, Jen thought. The longer it took to sell the house the longer they could squat there and the more items he could take to sell. She'd read of thieves clearing out houses of everything, even the furniture, but the neighbours were curious; they would be watching. Jaslene and her husband wouldn't be the only ones who suspected something was 'going on' in the Laurence house. Someone would notice if Ted overreached himself. He would have to limit himself to the smaller items, things he could stuff in his pockets or a sports bag. Jen put the letters in her pocket to show Sadie, showered and walked to work, enjoying the weak sunshine and fresh air.

*

Ignoring the greetings from the stallholders, Sadie shouldered her way through the early browsers and settled herself on the stool opposite Jen. She rejected Jen's offer of coffee; she was in a belligerent mood.

'How's Mike?' Jen asked her. 'What did you tell him?'

'Never mind Mike, he's OK. Tell me what happened last night to make you so angry. I was almost frightened to talk to you.'

'She lied, Sadie—',

'Yeah, you said; she lied. I get it. He's not her dad, he's an ex-boyfriend or whatever. But what's all this about the kids? I didn't know she had kids of her own.'

'She doesn't; she meant her brothers.'

'That's not what you told me. You told me she asked you to look out for her kids.'

'Did I? I must have misheard. She was mumbling. The boys are her brothers, she doesn't have children of her own. I would have known.'

Sadie kept her eyes on Jen, searching her face. 'Will you do it?' she said at last. 'Look out for them?'

'There's no need. They're OK, they're safe; she turned them in herself.'

'So why does she want you to look out for them?'

'Maybe she doesn't remember. She's out of her mind.'

'OK, Jen.' Sadie looked away, her mouth set in a grim line.

'I've got to get on. Stay if you like, but Iris is coming over,' Jen said. 'I need to get things ready for her.'

It wasn't how it was meant to go. She'd wanted to ask Sadie what she'd told Mike and to show her the letters. To talk it over with her, to share their thoughts. The best friend she'd ever had, the friend with whom she'd shared so much of her adult life, yet she watched her go with relief.

Later, Mike rang her at work. He was shouting, and Jen held the phone away from her ear. 'What were you thinking? And involving Sadie. What will you do if Ted finds out you were in the house? I don't care if he's her father or her ex, he's a nutcase. He'll come after you.'

As if she hadn't thought about all the ways Ted could seek revenge or punish Mrs L. Mike read her silence. 'We won't let it happen,' he said. He made her promise to tell Gary. 'I didn't expect this of you, Jen. I thought we were in it together.'

She waited until they were getting ready for bed before speaking to Gary. He was pragmatic.

'Tell me why you got so involved again, and why you invaded someone's home. Why go there at all?'

'He isn't Mrs L's father. He's her lover, an ex-boyfriend or husband, and he's stealing from the house.'

She described the missing items. 'I was worried about her; Ted may have been abusing her. Jaslene heard a woman crying coming from the house. If I could prove he was stealing from her, taking things out of the house, valuable things, we could turn him in, get him away from her. Or Mr L could. I didn't tell you, because you would have tried to talk me out of it.'

He leant back on his pillow and regarded her.

'Not her father? How do you know?'

'She's sleeping with him.' Having sex, she should have said and shrank at the memory of Emily tangled in the grubby sheets.

'What a mess. You're better off out of it. Forget it, leave them to it. She and Ted won't get past Kevin to Luke and Sam, and Nate and Tony are back with their foster parents. If you like, I'll talk to the Averys. They'll know where he's selling the stuff. It's up to her husband to get it back, and the police will take notice of him. If I was you, I'd chuck the keys away and forget about it.'

He reached for his book. She wished she had his ability to distance himself, but something was bothering her. Something had been said that she'd forgotten, something she'd seen that she hadn't taken in, something she hadn't understood.

*

Gary kept his promise to talk to the Brothers and went to see them at the Praed Street flat the next day. Jen waited for his return anxiously.

'Daniel was playing a noisy video game and Alex was talking on his phone,' Gary told her. 'Joseph was brushing one of the dogs; I had to shout over the racket. The atmosphere in the room changed when I mentioned Ted's name.'

The gunshots and music had stopped, and Daniel spun around to face the room. Alex put his phone away.

'They looked as if they were holding their breath. Even the dogs were staring at Joseph.'

'We know all about him,' Joseph said. 'What he is. Leave him to us.' He fondled Gog's ears, then took up the brush again and continued brushing him.

'He doesn't say much, but when he does it usually means trouble. I couldn't wait to get out. They're up to something.'

Of course, the Averys would know about Ted. The *Big Issue* sellers, the rough sleepers and the street people, and even the kids skidding around on bikes or skateboards would bring them information. Leaving Ted to the Averys would keep Mike and Gary out of it. Their plan for dealing with Alex had been bold, they had been fearless, but Alex knew when to give up. And he wasn't a violent man. He had a conscience, albeit one he ignored at times. Even his threats to meet Angie had been half-hearted – a throw of the dice to see how they landed, how Jen would react. Ted was different; he had no conscience, and his brutality was primitive, his ruined face a metaphor for the menace he brought with him.

*

Mike's anger was always short-lived. 'Let the Averys sort him out. They must have their reasons,' he'd said, but Sadie was still angry. She'd skimmed the letters Jen gave her, then put them aside. 'I'll post them back through the letterbox. Do it when I take Foo out.' She didn't care if Mrs L or Ted saw her. 'I don't give a flying fart if he's her father or her lover. So what? Sod them; they can't afford to make a fuss. It's over, Jen. She's not worth worrying about. Let her go. She's out of your life.'

But Jen was struggling. She told herself that Emily Laurence had chosen to take Ted back. The bedroom door hadn't been locked and she wasn't tied to the bed; she could have walked out at any time. There was no sign that she'd been beaten or abused, but her brief attempt at bravado had failed and left her looking and sounding broken. And he'd abandoned her. Ted, father or lover, had disappeared.

So, the finale. The end of Mrs L's marriage, the expensive lifestyle. The glamorous friends would be the first to reject her once word got around. Jaslene had seen Mrs L get into an Uber with her cases. What now for Emily. Where to, and with whom?

Mike thought she would be with Ted. They were bound together, he said. 'He'll be the death of her.'

Chapter 41

The distant thrum of police helicopters had become ever-present. The recent spate of terrorist attacks meant that security in an area known as Little Beirut had been beefed up. Jen imagined the village residents had stockpiled goods in case of civil unrest, riots and looting, empty shelves at Waitrose, and the wine merchant closing down. Otherwise, everyone went about their business as usual.

The Laurence house had been spruced up; it looked smarter than the houses next to it. Two conifers trimmed into perfect spheres stood on either side of the pristine front door and the steps leading up to it were clear of rubbish, swept and scrubbed. New owners would move in soon. It felt strange to climb the steps and ring the doorbell. Her feet no longer felt for the steps with the same assurance. The door had been painted a deep grey; she couldn't remember what colour it had been before. She glanced up at the high-end security system that had replaced the outdated set-up that had been there before.

This was her last chance to find out what had happened to Emily, her last chance to assuage her guilt. She feared Mr L had already moved out, but the door was opened before she rang the bell. Mr Laurence looked her over with red-rimmed eyes. Behind him, boxes stamped with the name of a moving company were stacked against the walls on both sides of the hall.

'What do you want, Jen?' His face was sweaty, his hair plastered to his forehead. But then his shoulders dropped. 'Sorry. As you can see...' He stepped aside and beckoned her in. 'I'm moving out in a few days. I can't talk for long.'

He led her into the empty drawing room. The paintings and mirrors had been taken down, and stains marked the carpet where the matching sofas had stood.

'The decorators are coming on Monday; I've got to be out by then.' He made a show of staring out at the street through the window and rubbed a smear on the glass with his sleeve. 'If you've come to ask about Emily, I can't help,' he said. He turned away from the window and leant his meagre buttocks against the sill, crossed his ankles and folded his arms over his chest; he wasn't going to tell her anything. 'I didn't have you down as the nosy sort.' Hot and sweaty and in joggers, he still had the authority of his class.

'Your ex-wife did. I wanted to ask her to contact you. To let you know Emily was in trouble, but she wouldn't listen to me. She sent me away.'

He shrugged; he didn't care. 'She did the right thing. My connection with that woman is over.' That woman. His wife. 'So why are you here?' Spoken through a smothered yawn. Waiting for her to say what she had to say and leave.

'I've brought back your keys. And I heard Emily had a breakdown and I wondered how she was.'

He shook his head, uncrossed his arms and pushed himself away from the window, his gaze somewhere above her head. Everything he did, every move, was false, clumsy and meant to show how little he cared.

'I told you. I don't know what happened to her, or where she is. She was a drunk, out of control.'

'Do you have an address for her?'

'No. Now if you don't mind.' He gestured towards the boxes. 'I'm busy.'

Dismissed, she followed him out. He opened the front door and waited for her to leave. Put in her place again, but this time she was quicker with a response. 'You've been very careless with your possessions. Still, no harm done; I'm sure you can replace anything that's been taken from you.'

Let him ponder that, she thought, let him panic, check his inventory, dredge his memory, wake with a start and realise that he hadn't seen the silver candlesticks or the bronzes he spent years collecting. Never mind his wife; he was probably on the lookout for the next one or had one in his sights already.

'Wait!' he called out. 'The keys.'

She was already walking away and pretended she hadn't heard him. She turned the corner and threw the keys down the nearest drain. He must know where his wife was; there'd be legal issues that would need her participation, papers she would need to sign, but he wasn't going to tell her. Skirting around groups of people blocking the pavement, she hurried on. If Mrs L wasn't with Ted, and if he stayed away from her, Mrs L could rebuild her life, and re-invent herself. She'd done it before; she could do it again.

Once under the flyover, the crowds thinned, and she sped up, she was anxious; Angie and Zac were out with friends and hanging out in Covent Garden or Oxford Street. Jen hadn't wanted her to go; both those places would be vulnerable. The Manchester Arena bombing was still making headlines, and the attacks on Westminster Bridge were not forgotten, but Angie was working hard at college and needed to have some time with her friends. 'Stay alert,' she'd told her. Angie had laughed it off. 'Can't let them win, Mum,' she'd said.

Jen checked her phone for messages. There was a text from Angie. 'On our way home. See you later.'

She was about to text her back when she saw the Averys and their dogs ahead of her. Curious, she waited to see where they were going. The lights changed, and by the time she'd crossed the road, they'd disappeared.

Angie and Zac were drinking tea in the kitchen with Gary when she got home.

'It was OK at first,' Angie told her, 'but our bags were searched every time we wanted to go into a shop and Zac and Deepak were getting dirty looks because of their colour. It got a bit edgy, so we left.'

Gary's phone buzzed, and he listened for a moment, then put on his jacket, and picked up his camera. 'The police are on the canal. Something's kicked off. I'm going down there. Are you coming?'

Jen turned to Angie.

'Not you two, you stay here. Promise you won't go out; or if you do, stay away from the canal.'

'I'm not twelve, Mum. Why? What's going on?'

'Swear you'll stay in.' She didn't care how paranoid she sounded. Angie rolled her eyes. 'OK. I'll stay in. We were going to anyway. Stop stressing.'

*

The streets were less crowded than was usual for a Saturday, but Jen had to step into the road to keep up with Gary. A group of girls wearing fairy wings and tutus had captured him, curious about his camera. Hen-night fluffies, out for a laugh, and determined to have their moment, she guessed. He broke away from them and pulled her into a doorway to let a group of men pass. They were striding along purposefully, self-contained and oblivious of anyone or anything. 'Kevin's mates,' Gary said. 'Ex-army.' He checked his camera. 'Come on, we'll follow them. We'll be OK. They've got no business with us.'

'I hope you're right.' Kevin's men crossed the road and disappeared among the throng. A crowd had gathered on the bridge overlooking the canal. Gary and Jen joined them.

'What's going on?'

The woman standing next to Jen looked fed up. 'There's a fight or something further up. The police are there. It's about time they did something.' Her flat overlooked the canal, she told them, and street people had taken over the towpath under the bridge and kept her awake at night with their music and drunken antics.

'Filthy buggers,' she said, 'muck everywhere, theirs, and their dogs. Needles and used condoms left for the kids to find. The police raid them, cart some of them off, but they creep back, and it starts all over again.'

Gary was leaning over the balustrade, taking photos. She tugged at his arm. 'Let's get back.' But Gary was training his camera on the boats moored further up the path and was fiddling with the zoom. 'Here, look.'

He held her hand steady, and she looked through the viewfinder. She trained the camera on the towpath, and the men leapt into sharp relief. Kevin and his mates were talking to the street people. She couldn't see if Maggie or Monalula were among them. Hopefully, they'd found somewhere safe to sit out the commotion. It would be dark soon and the rough sleepers were an easy target.

She was about to hand the camera back to Gary when she saw him. He had his back to her, but she knew that thick neck, that cannonball skull. He turned his head and she stepped back, fumbling with the camera, almost dropping it. Gary steadied her and she gave it back to him. 'Ted Mason,' she said and waited as he held the camera to his eye.

They walked back to the flat in silence. Music and the babble of voices hit them as they opened the door to the flat. It sounded as if more of Angie's friends had come over.

'Turn the music down, please,' she shouted, not that she minded. Ted bloody Mason was back, but her daughter and her friends were safe; they could play the music as loud as they liked. Gary was restless. 'You need to see this.' He handed her the camera.' I took this earlier today.'

In the video, the Averys were on the bridge over the canal, the dogs at their feet. They seemed to be watching something. Joseph raised his hand and signalled to someone below them. They watched for a while longer, leaning over the bridge, and then turned away.

'I saw them earlier,' Jen said. 'They're up to something. Is it something to do with the boys?'

'The boys and Kevin aren't living on the canal anymore.'

Gary was avoiding eye contact, searching his pockets for a cigarette, and Jen's heart plummeted. 'OK, Gary. What?'

'Ted was seen watching Angie and her friends on Paddington Rec. Pestering them. He was drunk. He offered one of the girls money. Weeks ago. Alex heard about it, and he and the Averys found him. They told him to leave the area and not come back.'

Watching Angie. Pestering, offering money to a teenage girl. She shook off Gary's hand on her arm, elbowed him out of the way, and went to stand outside Angie's room. Slow down, breathe. She's with her friends. Don't embarrass her. Don't frighten her. She was saying the words out loud, repeating herself. 'Don't frighten her. Don't frighten her.'

Gary was beside her. 'Hang on, Jen, she'll hear you.'

If he touched her, she would scream. Not his fault. But he should have told her. Her legs turned watery, and she let him lead her back to the kitchen.

'Hang on, Jen,' he said again. 'Angie's safe. Ted won't hurt her. He won't get near her again.'

'You should have told me. You had no right to keep it to yourself.'

'What would you have done? Or me, for that matter.'

'She's my daughter; it's not up to you to make decisions about her.'

'She's my friend, and I love her. I acted as her friend. You were still riled up about your boss. The Averys and Alex saw him off. Or they thought they did.'

Angie breezed in. She rooted about in the fridge and took out a tub of ice cream, bowls and spoons from the cupboard, and put everything onto a tray.

'Stop arguing, you two. You're as bad as a married couple.'

Stiff with embarrassment, Jen waited until she heard Angie's door shut.

'I don't need protecting, Gary.'

'You need to speak to Alex.'

Chapter 42

Sitting behind a desk and wearing a well-cut suit, Alex was the embodiment of the successful executive. He'd moved up in the world and had recovered his confidence. The drab Paddington flat was now an office – bright, fresh and fit for purpose. An IKEA sofa and coffee table for customers now stood in for the plastic-covered sofas, and an espresso machine and a water dispenser replaced the games consoles and dog toys. Photos of properties for sale or rent were displayed on the walls.

Playing with a pen, turning it in his fingers, Alex looked up at her. Deep lines bracketed his mouth and there was a weariness in his eyes she hadn't seen before. Age and disappointment had diminished him, and she felt a fleeting sadness; for him, and her, and their lost youth. He put the pen down, carefully lining it up beside a notebook. He came around the desk and sat next to her. She fought the urge to move away from him.

'You're not here to rent a flat, are you? Before you say anything, I haven't contacted Angie. I've kept my promise.' He was about to say something else, but she cut across him.

'Ted Mason…'

'That nonce with the burns? Is that why you're here? We know about him.'

Despite his street savvy, he didn't get it. Ted was like an old bare-knuckle fighter. He'd take the punches and the insults, get knocked down, get up again, and stagger back to the fray. What did he have to lose, after all? He'd lost half his face and his access to a home and money. Thinking about him, talking about him agitated her. She had to stand, to move around.

'He's a pervert and a thief. He stole from my boss and threatened the boys who work with Kev. And he's back on the canal.'

'It's all right. Don't upset yourself. We know about him. Maggie told us. We know he's back.'

'But—' she tried again.

'We know everything. Everything, Jen. What he gets up to. Trust me. Leave him to us.'

He wouldn't go into details about what Maggie had told him and why he and the Averys believed her. 'Trust us, Jen, and trust Maggie. She's OK. We've put her and Lula in one of the flats. We've had trouble with kids breaking into the empty properties and squatting. The Averys don't care who lives in their flats as long as they get the rent. They've got other social tenants.'

Clever Maggie had bought her way into the Averys' good books with info about Ted. They were of more use to her than Jen and her handouts. Alex stood up and offered his hand. And she took it. Despite their past and her contempt for him, she let him lead her to the door.

'Speak to Gary. He's a good man.'

*

She didn't need to be told that Gary was a good man, an honest man. A man she could trust. She'd never really doubted him, even as they'd argued.

'*She's my daughter, it's not up to you to make decisions about her.*' Words she'd wanted to take back.

'*She's my friend, and I love her; I acted as her friend.*' His answer, knowing she didn't mean to hurt him. She'd asked him if Alex ever talked about his daughter.

'I'd expect him to, but he doesn't. Until this business about Ted, he hadn't seemed interested. He's doing well now, taking the property business seriously. He's living in one of the flats above the shops; the boys and Kev are doing up the others. Daniel said he can read the market. They're expanding out of the area. Buying and selling property has an element of chance. He seems excited about it, anyway. He may have changed, Jen.'

Gary, and his need to see the best in everyone, was defending her enemy. An addict doesn't throw off his habit so easily. His addiction had informed everything he did in the past, and as far as she knew he still gambled. But Alex wasn't the issue; Ted was. Alex – he of the devious mindset – had asked her to trust Gary, which she did, and to trust him, which she would try to do. As she walked home, she rehearsed ways to tell Angie about Ted, then changed her mind – why frighten her? Gary would say she was overreacting and maybe she was.

Still unsure about how she would approach Angie she paused outside the kitchen. They would be waiting for her, talking, teasing, and arguing while they prepared a fancy dish. Gary was in a retro stage, experimenting with bistro food or French classics, and reading Elizabeth David in bed at night.

They were deep in conversation when she walked into the kitchen. Gary wiped his hands on a tea towel and poured her a glass of wine. He raised his eyebrows and she nodded; they would talk later.

'Lay the table, Mum, and then sit down,' Angie said. 'It's almost ready. Sole Veronique. That's with grapes. Yuck.'

Later, she watched Angie separate the flesh from the bones of her fish with finesse. It seemed as if no time had passed since she was a five-year-old making a sandwich from white bread and three orange fish fingers, or a surly teenager dangling a stalk of Watercress from a fork, her lip curled. 'What's this green stuff?'

She'd laid the delicate skeleton of the fish in the centre of the plate and arranged the green grapes in a circle around it and was taking photos. Satisfied, she sent the photos off to one of the social media platforms she was on and finished her wine.

'I'm going out, you two. Mum can wash up. I did the cooking.'

'Where? You're not to go to the canal.'

'I haven't been there for ages. Someone threw a cyclist in the other day. Hayley told me. I'm going round to Zac's.'

'Eleven o'clock, Angie, no later. Will Zac's dad drive you home?'

'Yeah, yeah. He always does. He's worse than you. Paranoid.' She collected her plate and scraped her artwork into the bin. The flat door banged shut, and Angie clattered along the landing, already chatting on her phone.

Jen paced, wandering from the sofa to the window and back again. It was her duty to know where her daughter was, and with whom. Angie knew the rules, but teenagers think they know better than adults and protect them with lies and evasions. Finally, unable to bear it, she took out her phone. Gary waited while she spoke to her daughter, and told her not to be late; they wanted to talk to her. He tried to reassure her, but Jen suspected he was as anxious as she was.

'Ted followed her weeks ago and nothing happened then. Nothing's going to happen to her now.'

'It was twice, though. Watching her, following her. Pestering the kids.'

'Nothing's going to happen, Jen. She's with her mates. Let's go out,' Gary said. 'Walk off your jitters.'

They walked the streets she knew so well; she'd walked down them for years. People she knew lived in these streets, yet night made them sinister. She'd shopped at that minimart, bought her cigarettes in that corner shop, and chatted with the owner. Now, Ted Mason lurked in every shadowy doorway, swaggered under every streetlight. The sound of a door shutting quietly, or the rattle of a window opening, the sudden clatter of footsteps made her heart beat faster, and she quickened her step. Beside her, Gary kept pace.

'She knows to stick to well-lit streets at night, but does she do it?' Jen had seen people walking, heads down, faces lit by their phones, oblivious to anything going on around them. Gary tugged at her arm to slow her down, but she pulled away and continued walking. Walking helped, movement, any movement was better than waiting, blood pooling. If she saw Ted now, she would rush him, knock him down. She left Gary standing and ran. Legs pumping, heart pumping, blood pumping. She wanted to howl like a wolf. Her phone buzzed and she skidded to a stop.

'Mum, I'm home. Where are you? You said you wanted to talk.'

Gary caught up with her. 'Jesus, Jen.' He was laughing. 'Let's go home.'

Back on the main roads, there were people, voices and music, and they turned in and out of the shops, bought pistachios from the Arab supermarket and the jalebis Angie liked from the takeaway and a bottle of wine from the off-licence. They'd come up with a plan to tell Angie why they were worried, without frightening her, and stress vigilance when out with her mates.

Angie was waiting for them. Zac was with her.

'What's up?'

They looked at each other and laughed when Jen mentioned Ted.

'If you mean that old man that hangs around, we all know about him. He's just an old drunk, Mum. He can hardly stand up.'

'He's a dick,' Zac added.

Stunning them into silence. To Angie and her mates, Ted was an old man, drunk and incapable, a dick. But what about the vulnerable kids, the rudderless? To them, to her and Mike and Sadie and the dads who'd chased him off the canal, Ted was a threat. To the Averys, to Alex and Kevin, he was a problem that needed to be solved. But to Luke and Sam, he was dangerous; he wanted something from them. Mrs L hadn't protected them as she had the younger boys.

Whatever the Averys had planned for Ted would have to be final. Alex wouldn't have the guts or inclination to make an end to him, but they might. She put her faith in the Averys. If they were involved, they must have their reasons. Ted would finally get the message. They loved their dogs and treated them as if they were their children, but the stories about their cruelty were legend. If half the rumours about them were true there would have been repercussions, but the Averys seemed to be untouchable. 'I don't think they've ever killed anyone,' Gary said. 'But you never know.'

She was getting ready for bed when she remembered something Gary had told her about the Brothers. He was working upstairs, and she rang him.

'Did the Brothers…'

'Yeah, their dad abused them. Mike told me. Why?'

She rang Mike. He and Sadie were still up. Asked him; Did the Averys' dad…?'

'True. Why? What are you thinking?'

The Averys as avenging angels. She slept well for the first time in weeks.

Chapter 43

Angie hugged the box holding her new camera close to her chest. 'Thanks for this.'

Today was a celebration – the sale of Gary's project. They had taken a day off and spent the morning in Gary's favourite camera shop. They were on their way home, tired and looking forward to lunch.

'There's Amina,' Angie said. 'She looks fed up. Her dad is on her case all the time. Study, study, study. She used to love maths. I don't think she does anymore.'

Slender and fragile, Amina seemed lost in thought and started when she saw them.

'Have you got some time off?' Angie said. 'Come back with us.'

'I've got to get back; my tutor's coming round.' She was tearing at a tissue as she spoke. The fragments fell from her hands and the wind set them skittering down the street. 'Dad's counting on me getting into Oxford. He's bragging about it to his mates and my mum's phoning all my aunties. What if I don't get in?' She sighed. 'I've got to go.' Her sandals made a whispering sound as she walked away. She turned back.

'Have you seen Hayley? She told me they found a body in the canal; it was in the paper. I hope it wasn't someone we know.'

Gary and Jen stared at each other.

'What's up? Are you OK? Have you seen a ghost?' Angie linked her arm through theirs. 'I want to get home and study my camera. I'd like to learn how to take proper photos.'

'You go on, I'll catch you up. I want to get a paper.'

'Don't buy cigarettes,' Angie shouted after Gary. Nagging him about his smoking was her way of showing she cared.

Gary was subdued when he caught up with them at home. Angie was in her room, and he handed Jen the paper, folded to the relevant page.

The death of a man whose body was found in the Grand Union Canal is not thought to be suspicious. Paddington Police say they are unable to comment further about the circumstances and the cause of death is unexplained at this stage. Enquiries are ongoing.

Gary phoned Mike. 'It could be Ted,' Mike said. 'He was squatting on one of the boats.'

Jen phoned Sadie, and Sadie phoned Jaslene, who said she hadn't seen Ted or Emily and she wanted to forget them. 'I'm glad they're gone. I don't care who it is in the canal. Don't call again, Sadie.'

'It could be anyone,' Sadie said. 'Someone threw a cyclist and his bike in the other day.'

But Jen knew who it was, and so did Gary. They waited.

The man found dead in the canal has been identified as Ted Mason, a vagrant. Toxicology reports showed elevated levels of alcohol in his blood. Foul play is not suspected.

He'd been found wedged under an empty houseboat, face down in the water. No one knew how long he'd been lying there, or if he was alive when he got caught under the boat. Onlookers who'd watched the emergency services winch him out of the canal, the weirdos and ghouls who sensed disaster from miles away, said he must have been in the water for days, he was that swollen. 'Rolling like a dolphin', they said. 'It took them ages to get the hook into him. To get him out.'

'He must have been drunk and fell,' Sadie said. 'Good riddance.'

Jen played the film repeatedly in her head; saw his struggles, his desperate fight to free himself. What does drowning feel like? Did he fight for every breath? And when he stopped fighting, when he gave in, did he feel at peace? She'd heard the last phase of drowning was a gentle death. Floating face down and at peace under the wooden slats was more than he deserved. She wanted claw marks and broken nails, blood and piss. And then hated herself for wanting it. And then didn't.

A coroner's report stated that the death of the vagrant found drowned in the Grand Union Canal was due to a misadventure.

Jen folded the newspaper that recorded the final verdict and put it aside to recycle. He was gone. At last. No one would mourn him, no one would see him put into the ground, no one would care. The window was open and sounds from the street filtered into the kitchen: music, the shouts of the market traders, and kids on their way to school. Life in all its banality and she had hers back.

*

The day was bright, and the air cool. The walk to the market from home was too short; she wanted to sit by the Serpentine and watch the water birds dodge the swimmers. Working under artificial light was no way to spend a day like today.

Micky, the security man, stopped her on her way in. 'A woman was asking for you. I think she's waiting. I haven't seen her come out.'

'What does she look like?'

Micky shrugged. 'Tall, well dressed. I haven't seen her in here before.'

Mrs L was waiting by the stall, and Jen faltered; she wasn't ready for this. She thought she'd seen the last of her, but here she was again, trailing her darkness back into her life.

She'd changed her image: Her hair was cut into a sharp bob and darkened to look natural. Ankle-length trousers and a slouchy jacket replaced the sharp lines of her tailored suits. Laidback boho-chic had replaced the sharp glamour of the successful professional. It didn't sit well on her long bones and sharp features.

'Can we go somewhere to talk?'

Ignoring the lift, Jen led her to the stairs and watched her use the handrail to haul herself up. She collapsed into the nearest chair on the terrace and pushed aside the used dishes on the table. Her hand shook as she lit a cigarette. Her eyes were huge and sunken, and her skin stretched like latex over her cheekbones and jaw; she looked like a cartoon ghoul.

'I've got to open up,' Jen said. 'Ted's dead if that's what you want to know. Good riddance, I'd say, wouldn't you? He drowned, stuck under a boat on the canal. It must have taken him a long time to die. No one came forward to claim the body.'

Emily stared at her across the table, her mouth moving soundlessly.

Jen wanted to say, why did you have sex with that man? She wanted to say, I thought I could help you. Go in peace. Instead, she said, 'I'm sorry for you. He made you what you are. You're the victim.'

Emily stood and pushed aside the table and sent crockery crashing. Jen stood to face her.

Mo, the manager, was standing by the counter, talking to the cook. The cook looked as if he wanted to intervene, but Mo held him back.

'You stupid bitch. You know nothing. Nothing.' Emily said. 'You think you're better than me.' She was leaning in towards Jen. 'Your friends, your perfect daughter, that closet case you sleep with, they all know what you are, your violence. They can't save you. You'll never be safe from yourself.'

She was back. Emily the mean girl. Tough and vindictive, and up for a fight. But so was Jen.

'You disgust me,' she said. 'You're as bad as he is. You threw everything away, all you had, for your dirty secret.'

'He was my escape. Always. Every time. He served a purpose, but I'm glad he's dead.'

Jen watched her walk away. Mo was standing by the table, a dustpan and brush in her hands. 'You OK?' she asked Jen.

Jen nodded and left her to sweep up the broken crockery. She was shaking and close to tears. Her legs felt useless, so she took the lift down to her floor. She phoned Iris, told her she felt unwell and wouldn't be opening the stall, and went out into the street. Gary was at Mike and Sadie's. She called him and told them what had happened; she needed her friends.

'Are you OK? I'll come and get you,' Gary said.

Sadie took the phone. 'Come here, Jen. You don't want to be alone. Mike's cooking lunch and you need a drink.'

What Emily had said was true, but it wasn't all there was. She tried to know herself; so did Gary. They knew they were damaged, knew who they were, knew their failings, but knew there was more to them. More to come. They weren't complete, but they strove, failed, backed off, and tried again.

Emily would never be herself; there was no self, just a concept, a fantasy. Whoever Ted was to her, her father or her lover, or both, he had owned her. She had yielded to him a long time ago. He'd taught her, stamped her as his, and she had taken him back. Or he was as much her victim as she was his – 'he served a purpose.' But whatever he was to her, he was dead, and Emily would go on, take on a different persona, and live another life.

Chapter 44

Gary is studying the menu, and Angie has her face turned up to the sky, her eyes closed. They don't see Hayley walking past the restaurant with a group of friends. Hayley has found her tribe at last; her jeans and oversized sweater are identical to those of her new friends and of the boy whose hand she's holding. They're exuberant, unaware of others — stopping for selfies, calling out to each other. It's their world, their streets. She watches them, envying their youth, their confidence, and their innocence until they disappear down the steps to the canal.

Jen felt herself slipping back into the same paralysis that had dogged so much of her youth. If she'd tried to break through to Emily, could it have changed anything? But then she would remember how she'd reacted when Jen had spoken to her as an equal. 'Don't let him.' Woman to woman. Offering support. Saying what any woman would say to another about an abusive man, but their relationship had only worked if they kept to their roles.

'Where are you, Mum? You haven't touched your meal. What are you thinking about? Don't worry about your presentation. We can look at it together if you like.'

Angie was concerned for her; the child was becoming the parent. The restaurant was full, and they had a table outside. Gary reached out, the wine bottle hovering over her glass. 'Go on, then,' she said and smiled at him. He'd arranged this outing to allow them to catch up. The last few weeks had been intense for him – his project sold to a publisher, discussions with his agent, agreeing on terms, signing contracts, but it was done, and now they could be together.

She resisted the urge to take her hand mirror out of her bag and examine her face for signs of ageing – she'd become preoccupied with her appearance lately. Her jawline was softening and there were fine lines at the corners of her eyes, all signposts on the way to middle age. She didn't want to go there, but there was no choice. She would try to be like Sadie and laugh at age, or at Liz and Elsie who were making the most of what time was left to them – staying in posh hotels in Brighton, or fortnights somewhere warm. Elsie had made a lot of money during her days as a burlesque dancer and invested it. 'She's smarter than she lets on,' Liz had said, proud of her friend.

Sadie scoffed at Jen's fears. 'Don't be daft, you're still gorgeous. Don't believe anyone who tells you different. I'm older than you; hot flushes, night sweats, and mood swings are on the way soon. Mike escapes to the gym. I caught him making a muscle in front of the mirror. It's his mid-life crisis. We'll go through it together. You've got years yet. We'll be here for you when it's your turn.'

The sun swings over the street and in response, the hum of conversation and laughter around them gets louder. The waiters wind their way through the tables, pouring wine and taking orders. One of them puts a basket of bread on their table and a bowl of olive oil and balsamic. Suddenly she is hungry, famished. The bread is warm, and she dips a crusty piece into the oil and eats. And then another, and her mood lifts. It will be OK. 'Everything passes,' Gary would say, and he's right. She'll sit this time out, wait, accept Angie's offer to help her with her college work and make the most of their time together. The unease, guilt and regret will fade in time.

A couple walks past the restaurant, laden with bags from the market. The man is holding a huge fish wrapped in newspaper, its head lolling out of one end, its tail at the other. Angie grabs her camera off the table and chases after him. She wants to take his photo. The man unwraps his fish and stands on the kerb, cradling it in his arms and grinning, as proud as if he'd caught it himself.

She and Gary study the photo. Angie points something out to him and he nods. Satisfied, Angie puts away her camera but keeps it close.

This time next year she'll be getting ready to leave home for university. The world she will enter is mysterious. Why this university, and not that, she'd asked her daughter, why this degree and not that? Angie had tried to explain, and she'd pretended to understand. The meeting at the college for parents and carers had added to her confusion. She'd met her tutor – a brash and breezy young woman who had gushed about Angie, but whose eyes darted about the hall without once making eye contact. The other parents had looked her over and then turned away. She'd listened to everything the speaker said and asked what she thought were pertinent questions, but left feeling unseen and unheard. Angie would be supported by the school, but she had no idea what her role would be, or if there would be one for her at all.

She imagined how it would feel to come home to an empty flat when Angie left. To sit on her bed. To open the wardrobe and touch the outgrown jeans, the girly dress she'd hated. Open and shut the drawers, looking for traces of her daughter. How would she manage, so far from home? Would she make friends, would she be homesick? But she knew Angie would cope. She wouldn't squander her youth, wouldn't let herself be led as her mother had, and wouldn't fall into addiction like her father.

Angie was pinning all her hopes on getting into Durham University, miles away in the northeast. Cold and grey surely, so why there? 'It's the best choice for the degree I want to do, Mum,' she said, 'and look how beautiful the town is.' Together, they'd pored over the prospectuses and fallen in love with the images of old stone buildings, the arches and ancient mysteries, the stories, and the students strolling along the quads or sitting on the steps of the union buildings.

'And we could visit,' Gary said. 'It will do us all good to get out of London for a change.'

'It all depends on my grades, anyway. I might not get in. Lots of work yet.'

But she was confident and eager. Time would pass, the days, the weeks, the months and she would leave for university and start the life she yearned for, start her story.

Would Angie remember today? Jen wondered. Years from now, in a strange city, would she hear the hum of conversation and the clatter of cutlery from a pavement café, and wonder at the lurch of her heart. Would a burst of Arabic music from a passing car stop her in her tracks, to stand motionless on the pavement and remember the dirty, lively streets of home, remember old friends long scattered, and tell herself to get in touch with her and Gary; to arrange a video call or send a photo from Athens or the Atlas Mountains? And then forget. Because she's young, and there are too many places to see and too many new people in her life. I've been a good mother, flawed and failing at times, but proud and protective, a real mother. Of course, she'll think of me, I'm not going to lose her. The photo or the email or text will come eventually.

The traffic eases its way towards St John's Wood. It will be OK. She will thrive, learn, and progress, and she and Gary will come and go between their flats. They will circle each other, come together and part, knowing the other will always be nearby. What's a staircase between lovers? One day they may move in together, but not yet. For now, she prefers her tacky furniture, her bare walls, her shelves crammed with books jammed in anyhow, to his shabby-chic flat.

They are waiting for her; her lover and her daughter looking at her patiently. Jen picks up her bag and puts on her shades. 'A walk, then,' she says. Angie stops a couple and hands them the camera. 'A photo' she says and pushes her way between Jen and Gary and links their arms. Glad for this moment together, they cluster, leaning into each other, the sun in their eyes, their arms entwined. They stare into the camera. The shutter clicks, the man hands back the camera and they separate, but they stay close and start their walk, arguing over the direction: this way or that, the park, or the canal, and up to Primrose Hill.

Acknowledgements

Thank you to the tutors and fellow students at Mary Ward, Birkbeck University and City Lit for their constructive criticism and feedback. And many thanks to Ian Howe, my editor. Ian was easy to work with and gave valuable advice and suggestions. His work gave me a much sharper, cleaner manuscript. Finally, much love to my family for their patience and support.

About the Author

D.M. Pinto lives in London. 'The Dogs Do Bark' is her debut novel. The highlight of her writing life so far was reading her prize-winning short story 'Where Life Takes You' at the Small Wonder Literary Festival. Since then she has been long-listed for the Fish Short Story Prize. Although she enjoys writing short stories, she prefers the room to stretch allowed in the longer narrative. She can be found on her blog at dpinto.co.uk

>
> Reader.
> Writer.
> Urban Walker.

Printed in Great Britain
by Amazon

32994298R00158